RANDOM

PENN JILLETTE

BROOKLYN, NEW YORK

Published by Akashic Books
©2022 Penn Jillette

ISBN: 978-1-63614-071-1
Library of Congress Control Number: 2022931938

Akashic Books
Brooklyn, New York
Instagram, Twitter, Facebook: AkashicBooks
E-mail: info@akashicbooks.com
Website: www.akashicbooks.com

As always for:
Emily
Mox
Zolten

And in memory of:
The Great Tomsoni and Company
(This book is my world, and in my world
Johnny and Pam are still alive.)

PREFACE

In everyday life, you will find that your boss, your lover, or your government often try to manipulate you. They propose to you a "game" in the form of a choice in which one of the alternatives appears definitely preferable. Having chosen this alternative, you are faced with a new game, and very soon you find that your reasonable choices have brought you to something you never wanted: you are trapped. To avoid this, remember that acting a bit erratically may be the best strategy. What you lose by making some suboptimal choices, you make up for by keeping greater freedom.

—David Ruelle, *Chance and Chaos*

The Theory of Our Game:

1. **Making a decision promptly is often more important than making the best decision.**
2. **Committing to and acting with passion on a decision are often more important than which decision is made. Doubt is the weakness.**
3. **No one can outsmart Random.**
4. **Random is dangerous.**

ROCK/PAPER/SCISSORS—LOOK DEEP INTO YOUR OPPO-nent's eyes. She just threw this sequence: *rock/rock/paper/ rock/scissors/scissors/scissors/paper/rock/rock*. You have won five of these last ten throws, including the very last one with your *paper*. This next one is the tiebreaker, but just a temporary tiebreaker, there will be more ties. You've got another ninety throws to go with her; the wager is for the best of one hundred throws. If at the end of those hundred throws you have more wins than she, you get the deed to her house. If she has the most wins, you are going to be homeless. You do not have any nest egg. If you tie at fifty wins each, you both keep your respective houses and you've both had a hundred throws of heart-racing excitement. You have both been alive in the here and now for about seventeen minutes, more life than many people experience in a lifetime. The tempo is slow. There is no rush.

Look hard into her eyes. Smell her. Feel the vibe in the room. Psych her out. While looking deep into her eyes, say: "My next throw will be *paper*, really. Honest. Pinky promise." Does she believe you? Are you telling the truth? What is her optimum move? What's your optimum move?

Your best bet is to throw *random*. In the long run *random* always wins. Your opponent can't figure out your process if you have no process. But you can't naturally throw *random*. You can't generate *random*. No one can. Human minds generate patterns. It's what they do. It's what *we* do. Humans do patterns.

Some professional gamblers memorize starting at the hundredth decimal place, and use those numbers to make decisions that their opponents can't possibly predict. *Random* is power. Completely committing to *random* would be a superpower.

You throw *paper* and eventually . . . you win her house.

1

VEGAS HAS A BIG PYRAMID WITH A LIGHT COMING out of the top. Bobby Ingersoll was born and raised in Las Vegas, the son of a showgirl and a dissolute gambler. Before Bobby's twenty-first birthday he had never once rolled a twelve on the dice, a roll that would have made him get into full drag to give a professional lap dance. He had occasionally tucked his cock and balls between his legs, put on lipstick, and danced in front of the mirror. But that he'd done just for himself, without any dice telling him to. He had always done what he wanted to do the most, all things considered. He'd made the best decisions he could with the information he had.

Two weeks before his twenty-first birthday he found out his dad, Dave Ingersoll, was over two and half million dollars in debt to Fraser Ruphart, who was the worst of some very, very bad bad guys in Sin City. Ruphart had demanded his money on the first day of June, which was the date Bobby was born.

Happy birthday.

Very bad guys aren't fair. Very bad guys are not reasonable. Fraser Ruphart was unfair and unreasonable even by very-bad-guy standards. If Dave Ingersoll owed a good guy two and half million dollars and couldn't pay, what would happen? Would the good guy just walk away? Maybe a very stupid good guy. Fraser Ruphart was neither very stupid nor very good. He knew the chances that Dave Ingersoll would ever pay off two and a half million dollars, given his entire fucking lifetime, were pretty low. Only Dave Ingersoll would bet on loser odds like that. So Ruphart recognized that a live Dave was only slightly more likely to pay up the two and a half million than a dead Dave. It was like hoping to win the lottery without buying a ticket. Your chances go up an imperceptible amount if you buy a ticket, but they do go up. What made a dead Dave more valuable was the advertising to future customers that they should make sure to pay their debts. But for two and a half million dollars, just killing the deadbeat wouldn't be enough. For two and a half million bangs for the buck, Ruphart knew, you gotta kill his whole fucking family. That kind of advertising keeps you in first pay position with all your other customers.

Dave Ingersoll's $2,500,000 debt to Fraser Ruphart came due, in full, on June 1. And on June 2, his whole family—Dave, his wife Kym, his children Bobby and Carolina—would all die. Ruphart might not be that good at figuring out who to loan money to, but he was very good at making the whole families of guys who didn't pay him get dead. Would the family suffer? Yes. Would there be other very bad stuff happening to Kym and Carolina? Yes. Some of those very bad things would happen to Bobby as well. As the punch line to the old joke goes: "He has chosen death . . . but first *boomsha*, (or *chichi*, or *boobalooba*, or whatever the joke teller has chosen for his imaginary primitive tribe's nonsense word for horrible, unspeakable, anal gang rape. In this case, it would be all those words right before the final punch line of death).

Do what you want to me but leave my family alone is the message Dave sent to Ruphart. It seemed a fair request between reasonable men, but again, Ruphart was neither fair nor reasonable. And Dave had just sent the worst possible message. When the carny talker out in front on the bally stage says, while gathering the rube crowd—*the tip*—"Let me warn you, friends, there are pickpockets out there in the crowd, please keep a close watch on your valuables," the marks check their valuables with a quick reassuring pat. And the pickpockets, who really are in the crowd (and working with the talker), watch and see which pockets to razor to get the wallets. *Do what you want to me but leave my family alone* is a great way to signal to very bad guys that they should torture, *chi-chi, booba-looba,* and kill your whole family and do it in front of you. The smart move would have been for Dave to say, *How about you kill my whole family, I'll tell you where to find them, and leave me alone?* Dave was a card counter from MIT and blacklisted at every casino as a cheat. If MIT or hard knocks could teach that kind of smart, Dave would have it. He didn't.

Bobby didn't want his dad to be killed, he really didn't, but you can't always get what you want, and he would have adjusted fairly quickly to his father being dead. He wasn't ready himself to die on the day after his twenty-first birthday, but being dead is an easy gig once you get there. But even dead Bobby didn't want his mom and sister *boomshaed* and killed. To keep himself and the only people he loved alive, Bobby needed to get two and a half million dollars in a couple weeks to pay off his father's debt. You don't have to be an MIT mathematician to know that works out to somewhere over a million dollars a week.

2

BOBBY NEVER THOUGHT HIS DAD WOULD BE ANY HELP in motivating him, but Dave had finally come through. Bobby had been motivated to procure two and a half million dollars in a couple weeks. He wasn't going to earn it even though he had about the best job in Vegas. He drove a truck with a sign on the back advertising a service that would send a live nude dancing girl, or live nude dancing girls, to your private hotel room. He spent his whole shift driving this truck back and forth on the Strip. It's one of the few truck-driving jobs where being stuck in traffic is considered a good thing. It means people on the street have more time to think, *Wait just one single goddamn country minute . . . an attractive slutty woman or two like that coming to my room to do a sexy dance naked? . . . Hmmm . . . Maybe she or they would want to fuck me after she or they were done dancing* (the "they" in this case could be either plural or the chosen pronoun whether the rube knew or cared or not), and call the number to book an appointment without doing any other thinking.

The attractive women pictured on the sign didn't have to worry about dancing, or even going to rooms to pretend (for legal reasons) to dance. The women on the sign were just models. Bobby had nothing to do with the models or the actual "dancers" at all. He was just a truck driver. Bobby would pull any sign. Just the week before, he had pulled a Carrot Top comedy show advertisement and Carrot Top didn't claim to dance, get nude, or go to anyone's room—although there's always a price for everything and Carrot Top's fee is not unreasonable.

Bobby loved his job. He listened to audiobooks, called friends, illegally texted at lights, and spent time with his thoughts. The truck had Bluetooth for his phone, air-conditioning for the desert, and GPS so his bosses could make sure he was just driving back and forth and not getting anywhere—a pretty sweet deal. Even in the Mojave in the summer, Bobby sometimes turned off the air-conditioning, opened the windows, and enjoyed the heat. Vegas was so hot in the summer, you could roll down the windows and laugh. It was like the heat was kidding. Probably funnier than Carrot Top dancing in your room naked.

It was a great job but it wasn't paying him $31,250 an hour. Truck billboard advertising is not a cash business, so there was nothing there to rob. He went in anyway and conned a two-week advance out of his bosses. Good, now he was just under 1/2,000th of the way there. He was motivated to find other ways to get money. He, his mom, and his sister took out "payday" loans they could never pay back. The highest amount they could borrow together at rip-off interest was another $2,400—another 1/1,000th of the way to paying off his asshole dad's debt. Barely another snowflake on the way to a lifesaving avalanche.

Bobby weighed his other options. He could ask all his friends for loans that he couldn't pay back, but none of his friends had money. None of them even owned houses. His mom was renting. There was no equity in his circle. Many of his friends would know that his dad was in dutch to Ruphart. They might not know the amount, but they were aware that Ruphart didn't loan single Benjamins, so they would know their money was lost the moment they loaned it. Bobby's best bet was J.D., the one friend who might have some serious jingle. J.D. was a pro poker player who'd started playing online when he and Bobby were both in high school. He was good enough to have bought a stupid muscle car, and a 1961 three-tone sunburst Stratocaster with a Fender 1957 Custom Twin-Amp, for his own graduation presents. If the car and guitar were J.D.'s midlife crisis, he was on track to die at thirty-two. He'd turned twenty-one just last month so now he played live cash games in the casinos.

Bobby texted J.D. and rode his electric Vespa scooter over to the Orleans, a kind of locals' casino off the Strip with a hopping poker room. J.D. lived there, in a hotel room right in the same building with the casino. He'd commute by elevator to the poker room around four in the afternoon, grind for ten hours, then go back upstairs and play more online. The Orleans had an oyster bar and metal alligators for door handles. It was a New Orleans Mardi Gras–themed hotel. Themes in Vegas don't really mean jack shit. It's all just the same slot machines, the same table games with different printing in one place on the table felt, and the same empty desperate vibe. Themes come down to a sign out front, door handles, and one restaurant—the rest is all just generic Vegas.

Bobby got to the Orleans, parked his Vespa in the Mojave sun, and headed into the timeless dark chill of the casino. He had a plan. Even better, he had several plans. He was going to ask J.D. to borrow a lot of money. And if he could get J.D. to show him his PokerWinner.com account, and get him to leave the room to buy Doritos or something, Bobby could tap his own PokerWinner account on his phone and in one hand lose all of J.D.'s money to himself. It wouldn't work for long, but maybe long enough to put that toward paying off Ruphart. That would mean he'd get to deal with owing money to J.D. instead of a murderer. The final plan was to steal J.D.'s Strat and amp, and fence those. Whatever that meant. Bobby never considered himself the kind of person who stole things, but Bobby was in the situation where everyone becomes the kind of person who steals things. The Fundamental Attribution Error—we think what other people do is because of their character, but what we ourselves do is because of the situation we find ourselves in. Bobby was in a situation where his fundamental attribute was being a fucking thief. He was going to try to beg, steal, or borrow what he needed. He hadn't decided on which of those was best with J.D, so he figured he'd try all three at once.

He followed signs to the poker room and there was J.D. with dark sunglasses and an orange hoodie. J.D. had talked about how much he loved poker, so Bobby wanted to watch him playing for a while. It was hard to perceive any fun that J.D. might be having. He had his earbuds in, and Bobby thought he was probably watching the game play, but who could tell through the dark glasses? J.D. wasn't smiling, and wasn't talking to anyone. He seemed to be having all the fun of someone on a pork processing line night shift. He folded most hands, and then did robot-like digital manipulations with the chips, shuffling them, rolling them over his fingers, and restacking them while waiting for the next hand. Bobby walked up and touched his friend on the shoulder. J.D. didn't say goodbye to his fellow gamblers, just made eye contact with the dealer, nodded, picked up his chips, and walked away.

"Hey, dude, good to see you," said J.D.

"Yeah, you too." Bobby didn't know how to play it. He was being friendly but also scared and desperate. He wanted J.D. to feel sorry for him so he would give him money, but also confident in him so he would loan him money—and also relaxed with him, so Bobby could steal lots of his money. A complicated set of goals for this acting exercise.

"You wanted to talk to me? Your text was *très* mysterious."

"Yeah, can we go up to your room?"

"Sure. C'mon."

They walked through the casino to the elevator and headed up to J.D.'s room. There was a room service tray of fried chicken leftovers outside the door, still some good eating left. J.D. touched the key card to the door, and they were in. The blinds were drawn. The guitar was plugged into the amp, with wired headphones plugged into the back. The vintage amp didn't work with earbuds. On the desk was the fanciest MacBook Pro. Bobby sat down on the couch and J.D. sat in the easy chair.

J.D. wanted to get to it: "So, dude, what's up? What do you need to talk to me about?"

"Nice guitar."

"Yeah, you saw it when I bought it."

"Are you gigging?"

"Gigging?"

"Playing out."

"I know what it means, but we don't talk like that. We aren't musicians. I play poker and you drive an advertising truck. Hey, want me to order room service? I've been eating nothing but casino food for almost a year." He looked it. He was getting the casino paunch and pallor.

"No, I'm good. Maybe we can run down and get something later." Bobby was planting the seed that he might need J.D. to make a Doritos run while he emptied out the online poker account. "So, can you teach me to play online poker?"

"Sure, but that isn't why you came here."

"Right." Change plans. Now it was time to beg. "Hey, listen, J.D., I need some money."

"Bobby, if you want me to teach you to play online poker

to win more money than you can ask me for, you're not going to do it. You're just not. There isn't that much money there, and you suck at games. You have no sense of how to handle risk and chance and you can't commit. You're my friend—how can you expect me to do that when I know without a doubt that you'll lose money at it? Does a friend do that?"

"It's my own money that I don't have that I'll be losing. I know my chances. I'm not a fucking idiot. Be a friend. What a real friend would do is show me. Just give me what the fucking FAQ would have."

"Okay. But you won't win. Do you understand that you won't win?"

"Okay, then for a few minutes at least I'll have false hope. It'll help me unwind."

"Poker is not a game best played desperate."

"I know, but dude, can you just show me?"

"Yeah, later. But what's happening? Are you hitting me up for money? Is that why you're here?"

"I'm kinda in trouble. You know, like a lot of trouble."

"I'm not a fucking loan shark. Talk to your dad, doesn't he know those kinds of people?"

"Yeah, he does, that's who I need to pay off, those kinds of people."

"How much do you owe?"

"I don't owe any, but I have to pay my father's debt and he owes a lot."

"How much?"

"A lot."

"You came over here to ask me to pay off your dad's debt? How much money to you think I have?"

"I don't need to get it all from you."

"So, you need a few hundred bucks?"

"Um, a lot more."

"Like a couple thousand?"

"I need a lot more."

"What are we fucking playing, a guessing game? I can't give it to you, but how much do you want?"

Okay, well, Bobby would come back later to the begging and borrowing. Now, on to the stealing. "This is making me really uncomfortable."

"No shit, me too."

"Can we just take a break and you can teach me to play online poker?"

"Jesus, dude. Okay, I guess." J.D. flipped open the laptop, clicked once on the PokerWinner icon. "So, you know the rules of poker, right? This is Texas Hold'em, no limit, but they have pretty much every game. And you have your money here."

Looking over J.D.'s shoulder, Bobby saw that there was over ninety grand in his account. Great. Bobby needed to steal that right now. "Hey, dude, you got any snacks.? I could use some Doritos."

"Yeah, I think there are some on the table there."

"Cool Ranch?" Bobby already checked; they weren't Cool Ranch.

"I don't think so. Room service won't send up those kinds of snacks. Hey, I'll run down and get a bag and you can go into one of the free rooms on my computer and play a few hands. It's pretty intuitive. When I come back, you can ask me any questions you have. Start with getting a feel."

"Hey, thanks, man."

"Ain't no thing, I want some spicy sunflower seeds anyway."

And just like that J.D. left, with the computer open and the money right there. Bobby had a choice to make. He could get his phone and move all the money to his account. But he felt there was a chance J.D. would loan him the money and he wouldn't have to steal. And if he was going to steal, he should really steal the guitar too. If he pulled out his phone right now and moved the ninety grand across to his phone, he could then grab the guitar and amp and split before J.D. got back. That was a good plan. That would over a hundred grand. That would be a start.

Bobby pulled out his phone to set up a table so he could invite J.D.'s computer to play. At the first decent hand he'd have J.D.'s account go all in, the full ninety grand. Bobby would raise, and then have J.D. fold, and all the money would be paid into Bobby's account, to be moved to PayPal and then to cash. Maybe, he thought, he should pack up the guitar first so he'd be ready to scoot as soon as he had the money. He picked up the guitar, then realized he should find the gig bag and unplug the amp. Or he could just carry the guitar loose without a bag ... but how would he carry it on his scooter? He had saddle bags, and there was a storage place for the helmet that he would be wearing ... but no, the guitar wouldn't fit in that. He'd have to carry it while steering and using the throttle. On the other hand, now that he knew that J.D. had about a hundred grand, couldn't he just ask him for a loan? Standing in the middle of the room, holding the guitar by the neck with one hand and his phone in the other, Bobby rehearsed what he would say to J.D. to convince him to loan the money.

How long was Bobby frozen in that position? Exactly the amount of time it takes to ride the elevator down and back up, plus however long it takes to buy one bag of Cool Ranch Doritos and three bags of Frito-Lay Flamas Sunflower Seeds. J.D. walked in to find Bobby just standing there.

"What the fuck are you doing? I thought you were going

to play poker. Why are you holding my guitar? And don't hold it like that, support it. What the fuck are you doing?"

"I wanted to feel how heavy a Stratocaster was while I surfed porn on my phone."

"What? Put the guitar down. Did you play any poker?"

"Kinda."

"Any questions?"

"No. It was fun."

"So, you need to borrow some coin?"

"I guess. I'm sorry."

"Jesus, man. Are you okay?"

"I guess. I'm sorry."

"Listen, install the PokerWinner app on your phone. We'll both log in and get to the same table. I'll play both hands and lose ten grand to you. Then you can pull that into your PayPal and it's just cash. It don't mean shit to me. Just put down my fucking guitar."

J.D. did as he said. Bobby tried to hug him but didn't commit, so kind of just bumped into him and then went down to the casino and vomited up a bag of Cool Ranch Doritos and some sunflower seed chemical salt coating. He was 1/183rd of the way there. Bobby was fucked.

3

DAVE INGERSOLL HAD ONCE RECEIVED A HANDGUN IN one of the few poker games where he ever won anything. He was living with his family at the time, and left the gun at home where his children could find it and blow their brains out. He'd hidden it in Mom's underwear drawer. About seven years ago Bobby had been looking through his mom's underwear drawer (you know) and found the gun, but hadn't blown his brains out yet.

From the Orleans, Bobby went to his mom's house to tell her that he'd gotten another ten grand. While she was getting him some Cool Ranch Doritos and a Coke, he said he had to pee and walked right to the underwear drawer and took the gun. It was loaded—Dave Ingersoll, total asshole. Bobby was worried about blowing his balls off, so he tucked it into the back of his pants, preferring to blow his ass off. He ate the Doritos standing with his mom in the kitchen, and rode off on his Vespa with a gun tucked in the back of his pants.

At a Vegas bike and ski store, he bought a balaclava. A twenty-year-old man with a gun in his pants buying a balaclava kind of tells the whole next part of the story. He was trembling as he bought it, and he bought a Vans snowboard sticker too, like someone buying cigarettes when they buy condoms, so the clerk will figure they have to do S/M cigarette-burn play to get hard enough to fuck.

"I guess I'll put this sticker on my snowboard and keep my face warm with this mask."

"Okay."

He waited until midnight, vomited up another load of Cool Ranch Doritos, put black electrical tape over his scooter license plate, and rode over to the nearest "Stop 'n' Rob." The Vespa was completely silent. No one would hear him coming or going. He wasn't sure how that would help, but it might be important later. Most criminals get caught because they are high and stupid, and either of those two would be enough, but Bobby was neither . . . okay, well, at least he was sober. He waited until there were no other customers in the store, pulled the mask down over his face, grabbed the gun from his pants, and walked in. This was the way to do cardio. His heart rate shot straight up and stayed there. Bobby walked to the counter, showed the clerk the gun, and asked for all the money. The clerk was young, ESL, and pissing all over himself. Bobby, too, was pissing himself. It was a convenience store golden showers party. The gun in Bobby's hand shook like he had been dealt pocket aces at the World Series of Poker final table. He was most likely going to be dead in a couple days and he'd never felt more alive.

The clerk opened the register and took out just under two hundred dollars.

Bobby didn't count it, but he could tell it wasn't much. "This is all?"

"Yes."

"Is there other money somewhere?"

"In the safe, but I can't open that. And there isn't much in the safe either—you know, more and more people use credit cards and that stuff."

"This is like two hundred dollars. That's nothing."

"It's not nothing to me."

When Bobby first walked in and pulled the gun and his

heart rate shot up, he'd felt so alive. He'd felt great. Now he started to crash bad. He was getting depressed. His pants were wet, and his mouth was dry. He looked at the clerk. "Hey, my mouth is really dry, can I have some gum?"

"You're robbing me. You've got a gun. You take whatever you want, right?"

"Yeah, I guess." Bobby took a pack of gum and, both hands trembling, tried to open it without dropping the gun.

The clerk watched him fumble for a moment and then said, "You should open that later. You should run away now. I don't like the gun pointed at me. Please go away."

"Sorry." Bobby stuck the pack of gum in his pocket and took one of the singles from his stolen wad and put it down on the counter. "That's for the gum."

"Please run now."

Bobby's legs were like rubber and his heart was broken. He stuck the money into his front pocket right above the urine and got on his scooter. He was thinking that the urine wouldn't be too hard to clean off the vinyl seat. Then he realized he couldn't get the helmet over his ski mask, so he held the balaclava in his hand as he made his getaway, wondering why he didn't just wear the helmet into the 7-Eleven . . . too late for that now.

4

CRIME DID NOT PAY WELL. BOBBY WAS GOOD FOR FIVE figures, but the debt was seven figures, and he had just four days left. Being desperate with nothing to lose wasn't the superpower Bobby thought it would be. Morality allows us to self-righteously pretend the reason for all our shortcomings is our integrity and compassion. Morality becomes our excuse. *We could all grow up to be the president of the United States of America if we were just willing to be corrupted and lie. It's integrity that keeps us from successful leadership.* Most of us believe that. If we weren't walking the line, if we were willing to cheat on our spouses, we could fuck most anyone we wanted: *We made eye contact—she wants me, but I'm married.* If we were willing to play smooth jazz pop shit, write fart jokes for dumb situation comedies, and get breast implants, we could be Tom Cruise. Yet if we were willing to be unfaithful, we'd find out just how few opportunities to cheat are actually available to us. And far better to be morally superior to smooth jazz and fart jokes than to try to write either. Morality is ego's alibi.

It wasn't the presence of morality holding Bobby back, it was lack of ability. He didn't have the connections or the skills. He couldn't focus. He was weak. He was constantly full of doubt. J.D. had to help him steal the money. He had to be told by the 7-Eleven clerk to run away. His indecisiveness wasn't leftover morality, it was incompetence. He sucked, and he knew it—but he still needed money to save his family.

Could he be a mule and smuggle drugs from Mexico to Vegas? He could swallow condoms full of heroin and then pick them out of his shit as well as the guy in the next stall, but who would he buy the drugs from and who would he sell them to? Didn't they just make meth right here in Vegas now? Didn't the cartels or something smuggle fentanyl in giant drone planes? Getting around the nonexistent border wall with drugs didn't seem like a skill he could be paid for. He was willing to do anything. He was totally unencumbered by decency and still his entire family was going to be killed.

With his family's lives at stake, a risky crime was his safest bet. A nuttier plan with a bigger payday. The only people who had the amount of cash he needed were casinos and bad guys. Banks didn't even have that much cash on hand anymore. He had no idea how to rob a casino. He had no idea how to rob bad guys either, but that had to be easier than knocking over a casino. Way more dangerous, but easier. As for a bad guy to rob, the first name that came to mind was Fraser Ruphart. Fraser Ruphart, who his dad owed all the money to. Could Bobby rob Ruphart to get the money to pay Ruphart? It was a crazy idea, but it just might work.

5

NOPE, IT WAS A CRAZY, STUPID IDEA AND IT WOULDN'T work. He couldn't steal money from Ruphart and give it back to him. Stupid.

Another stupid idea occurred to him. This one concerned the LD50s, a young, violent street gang that sold drugs, pimped, mugged, robbed, stole, and ran protection rackets in North Las Vegas. They had all the skills that Bobby lacked. They also had money. They weren't people who did a lot of banking, so they'd have tons of cash around. Maybe Bobby could steal money from them.

Bobby rode up to LD50 territory on his Vespa. He was the right age to be a good customer for the LD50s. Just a guy desperately wandering into a bad neighborhood to buy drugs. He didn't need to pretend. He had to look desperate and he *was* desperate. He had to look scared and he *was* scared. There were no decisions to make so he was doing okay.

Here was the plan: He was going to find one of the gang drug dealers and say he wanted to buy a lot of fentanyl but had to try it first. Could they go someplace private? The dealer and his goons would make sure he wasn't a police officer. They would ask him, *Are you a police officer?* because they know that police officers aren't allowed to lie about being police officers if you ask them directly, and he would say no. (Police not being able to lie like that is not true, but Bobby thought he'd heard it somewhere.) Then, after making sure he wasn't wearing a wire (because maybe he was a police stooge, not an officer, and he thought you could lie about being a stooge), they'd take him back to their clubhouse to try out the fentanyl, which he would spit out when they weren't looking because he didn't want to be addicted to fentanyl and then die like a home-less junkie. He'd scope out where the money was kept, and then he would come back later with another plan to steal the money and save his family.

Insofar as this was a plan, it was a bad plan. A better plan would be to use the money he'd gotten so far to really buy fentanyl and use it for his whole family to die like Prince. That was the sensible plan. Maybe after casing the clubhouse, he would come back and suggest they just do that. But for now, Bobby put on his helmet, got on his scooter, and headed off into the night. The wind rushing around his helmet was loud, and his electric scooter was silent. It was like running at forty miles per hour.

Bobby didn't know it, but he hit the gang turf just as a big drug deal was going bad. In this neighborhood, there was often a drug deal going bad, but this was a very big drug deal going very bad. It was a Friday-night, fucked-up drug deal. Even when Bobby got a couple blocks away and heard shouting, even when he could just make out a bunch of tough guys from two different gangs holding guns on each other, he still kept moving toward the scene. A guy with Bobby's personality would never head toward that kind of trouble, but a guy in Bobby's *situation* would. Bobby was navigating his little scooter directly toward a drug war that he had nothing to do with. But he stuck to the plan. If he'd had a brain in his fucking head, he would have realized that this wasn't the time to case the gang's money stash. As stupid as Bobby's plan was from the beginning, it was getting stupider by the second.

Bobby was now a block away from the center of the altercation. Locals were scattering in anticipation of the inevitable crossfire, like they had just seen Godzilla coming over the top of the buildings. Dozens of people ran past Bobby as his Vespa moved smoothly toward the standoff. What was Bobby thinking? He wasn't. He was just sticking to his bad plan that was getting worse by the second. The bangers were waving their guns at each other, yelling and switching targets, only vaguely aware of bystanders running by and clearing out, but not one of them noticed a motor scooter running silent, running stupid toward them. He was an invisible asshole in a stupid motorcycle helmet swimming upstream.

Bobby was about a half a block from the bangers when the first shots were fired. It was so fucking loud. Bobby had been as scared as he could ever be riding into the neighborhood, but now he discovered a new level of terror. By the time he realized that he needed to turn around and get the fuck out of there, fleeing citizens were in the street all around him. The turning radius of his scooter was small, yet there were too many people running past him to turn around. His only hope of getting out of there was the street just ahead. If he climbed up the sidewalk and hugged the building, he'd be able to turn left into the street and get the fuck out of there. He might not even be hit by a stray bullet. Up ahead, bangers were firing wildly, running back and forth, ducking behind cars and into doorways, shouting incomprehensible insults and orders.

Bobby's only concern now was to stay on his scooter, not get knocked over by a running civilian, and make the left turn. Focused on avoiding people, hugging the wall, and wincing at every new gunshot, Bobby never saw one of the rival gangbangers grab a big fancy Gucci bag from the pavement and run right toward him. Bobby wasn't noticed either. The two of them were heading for the same street.

The guy with the bag got almost to his right turn before most of the LD50s started shooting at him. Most of them sported that movie sideways shoot, so what they gained in threatening sexy, they lost in accuracy. A lot of bullets were flying toward the Gucci bag, and coincidentally toward Bobby. Everyone with a gun was zeroed in on the man with the bag, trying to shoot him with their sideways handguns and missing badly. Apparently they all practiced holding their guns in front of the mirror and sneering, but never practiced actually shooting them. They certainly never received any instruction. They weren't exhaling gently and squeezing the triggers slowly. With Gucci man's fellow gang members in the way, they couldn't run after the bag, so they were just shooting like crazy. Their chances of hitting the guy with the Gucci were about the same as their chances of hitting a civilian, Bobby, or the side of a barn door if it was within two blocks.

The banger with the Gucci got to his right turn just before Bobby's scooter reached the same street to turn left. Gucci guy was running so fast, with the bag in his left hand, that he had to reach out with his right and grab the corner of the building to make the turn. And just as he did, a stray bullet caught him square in the back. It was a lethal hit. With his hand on the building he had just enough momentum and life to make it around the corner before falling. No one on earth was looking at Bobby on his scooter as he silently turned the same corner a few seconds later. Without a thought in his head, he steered his scooter toward the dying man. With the gangbangers still firing away at each other around the corner, Bobby found himself suddenly alone with the banger. Was he trying to help? We'll never know, because Bobby didn't know. Even if he'd wanted to help somehow, it was too late. There on the sidewalk was a dead fuck.

And there was the Gucci bag. Bobby had no idea what was in it, but it was right there for the taking, and Gucci guy had been willing to die for it, and Bobby had already decided to be a criminal. He didn't even completely stop, just reached down where the dead guy had dropped the bag, grabbed it by the handles, and slipped it over the handlebars. He started to cry, pissed himself again, and gunned the throttle silently. Electric scooters have good pickup, so Bobby was around the next corner with the bag before any of the gangbangers made it to the dead guy. What they found there was a mystery. No one had seen Bobby or the scooter—no engine sounds, nothing. The bag had just vanished. The LD50s, who had come out on top of the exchange, couldn't believe it. They looked up and down the street, under the dead guy, looked at each other. Finally, just to do something, they threw a few more rounds into the rival banger at their feet.

Bobby didn't know what was in the bag, but he knew a lot of people would be looking for it—and it was a very distinctive bag. He got about three miles away and pulled into the dark edge of a bank parking lot, behind a tree, before he opened it. Money. To be exact, a shit ton of money. Nothing but money. It looked like all the money he needed. Holy shit. Money! His family was saved!

Money doesn't know where it came from, but the bag was a problem. Everyone back on that bullet-riddled street knew what this bag looked like. He picked up money by the handful and stuffed it into the compartment under the seat of the Vespa, and into the saddle bags as well. It was a lot of money, millions, and it just fit. He had to get rid of the Gucci bag, it had his fingerprints on it. Do gangbangers have the equipment and expertise to do fingerprint evaluation? Bobby didn't know. He had to get rid of the bag, but first he needed to piss himself more, cry, vomit, and shit himself. He took care of all of that almost at once, and then set off to find a McDonald's dumpster where he could drop the bag. He tried to wipe his fingerprints with hands that were covered with many samples of his DNA. As the adrenaline poisoned him, he was too shaky to celebrate being saved.

He dumped the bag and drove around in circles. He was disgusting—no blood, but there was sweat and tears and a lot of piss, shit, and vomit. His scooter had thirty miles left on its battery and he drove around Vegas for twenty of those, making sure he wasn't followed. But no one had seen him. Who would be following him? He didn't know, though he wanted to be as careful as he could.

When he got back to his apartment, he had to figure out how to get all the money up to his room. He couldn't carry it all in his hands, and he didn't want to leave his motor scooter charging while it was full of money. No one was around, no one knew that this was the Fort Knox of personal electric vehicles, but he just couldn't leave it. He took his shirt off since it didn't have too much vomit on it. He tied the arms in knots, tied the neck, buttoned it up, and started stuffing money into it. He plugged in his scooter, made a mental note to clean the seat later, and waddled topless, hugging his zillion-dollar scarecrow, up the stairs to his apartment.

He took the rest of his clothes off right inside the door and walked carefully to the kitchen area to get two trash bags. He put all the money in one, and all his disgusting clothes in the other. He'd remember to throw away the right one. He walked to the bathroom and straight into the shower.

He could have cut himself and then jerked off in the shower just so every bodily fluid he was capable of producing would go down the drain at once. He sat on the floor with the hot water pounding on his head, sobbing and shaking almost to the point of convulsion. Was it over? Nope, but they were saved.

6

BOBBY SAT ON THE FLOOR OF THE SHOWER TREMBLING and crying until the water started running cold. Shivering and still crying, he got into bed and fell asleep for twelve hours. Deep, motionless, dreamless sleep. Safe sleep. He woke up not knowing what had happened, but there were two trash bags, one full of money and one full of shitty clothes. It took him another couple hours just to brush his teeth, get dressed, and walk down to the dumpster behind the apartment building to throw away all the clothes from the night before. Before doing so, he put a little soap and water on the previous night's shirt, and cleaned off the seat of his scooter. He kept running police shows through his mind. What if the police looked in the apartment building dumpster? For what? For a guy who shit his pants? There was no gun in there, no evidence. There was no money. He'd gotten the money from gangsters. They were looking for a Gucci bag and some other gangbanger or local resident who'd stolen it. They weren't looking for him. They didn't know he existed. He tried to run everything through his head. It seemed he was free and clear. His family was saved and no one was looking for him.

He went back upstairs, had an English muffin with peanut butter, set YouTube to play radio based on Kamasi Washington, and sat down to count the money. Maybe there would be more than he needed and he could pay off the loans and

J.D. Did he have to launder the money? What does *launder the money* mean? He had stolen the money from a bunch of criminals and was going to give it to another criminal. On both sides the money was someone else's problem. He'd just come out with his family alive. He had just gotten luckier than any lucky duck who ever lived.

It took him over an hour to count it all, and when he saw the grand total he froze. And counted it again.

Five hundred and fifty thousand dollars.

More money than he'd ever hoped to see in his life, and it wasn't enough. Over half a million dollars in cash in the trash bag and it wasn't enough. He might as well have used his luck to find a nickel on the street. More money than he had ever seen, and it was less than a quarter of what he needed to save his family. He'd used up all the dumb luck of his life and it hadn't saved him. He added in the money he'd already begged, borrowed, stolen, and robbed, and he had $574,532. He put the cash in a Home Depot paint bucket he had in the closet, then went to the bank and got bands to organize the money. He spent the afternoon blankly making it all neat and tidy. Bobby wondered if he could just take the half million, give it to Ruphart, and at least buy some time, but then realized the bad guys can't have people thinking they'll take deals. They didn't want half a million in cash as much as they wanted about two and a half million in scare advertising. It was an easy calculation.

It was May 31. To save his family, he needed to get as lucky as he'd gotten last night four more times before midnight. He'd need to ride unseen through four more gang shoot-outs, grab four more bags full of cash, and disappear four more times. Bobby was fucked. His whole family was fucked. But the luck from the night before had changed Bobby. He could now make decisions. He could now accept fate.

The Residents are an anonymous avant-garde musical ensemble from Frisco. They played Vegas once. A friend of theirs, a comedy magician who had once broken the news to Dave that Dave was not James Bond, a sometime collaborator who may even have been one of them, once asked a Resident (it doesn't matter which one, they're anonymous) if he or she gambled. "I've chosen to try to make my living and support my family with avant-garde music—that's real gambling. Casino games are for pussies." Bobby decided that he needed to really gamble. That night, one minute after midnight, when it became June 1, Bobby would turn twenty-one and could legally gamble in a casino in the State of Nevada. And he would make the only gamble he had even a slim chance of winning.

There is still one casino in Las Vegas that will take any bet, any time. It's the only casino that will take chances. The corporations won't do it. You try plopping a million dollars on one roulette number at the Mirage—they'll flag you, and someone will talk to you in a little unpleasant office with gold-flocked wallpaper. There will be questions to answer before that multibillion-dollar company will gamble a thirty-five-million-dollar payout on a single spin. And if you happen to win, they'll have a long talk with you right after. You won't just split with the cash. They will take high bets, but not a one-off, not often, and it won't be easy.

Shotgun Perry's is not a corporate casino. It is a casino owned by a nut. Perry Fresten made his money on stupid bets and continues to take them. Perry doesn't have an MBA. Perry likes stupid bets. You could walk into Shotgun Perry's on your twenty-first birthday, put $474,532 on a "Yo Eleven," and they would bat an eye or two, but then they would take your action.

$474,532 was not the full amount of money that Bobby would have on him at midnight. He would walk into the casino with a hundred grand more than that. He'd actually walk in with $574,532 on him in nicely banded hundreds thrown into a white Home Depot plastic paint bucket. He'd put a towel over the top of the bucket for modesty, and then thirty-two bucks in his pocket. The extra hundred grand would be set aside in ten stacks of banded hundreds. This was his family's getaway fund. The four hundred grand he was betting was a gamble. There was almost no chance of hitting that, but the hundred grand was worse than any gamble. It was a stupid, wasteful purchase of fake hope. People who owe money to bad guys and can't pay it always try to run. The bad guys are ready for that. Bobby might have had the slightest chance of getting away alone. He might have been able to make it to Chad or Syria or some other place that no one wanted to go. He could have bought a motorcycle and rode fast to an airport, maybe to Salt Lake City, and then the next flight to any big airport—New York, Chicago, Boston, Toronto, Miami—and then a flight to someplace so dangerous and unpleasant that even hit men didn't want to go there to kill someone.

But Bobby wouldn't be trying to get away alone. He'd be taking his mother and sister with him, and without passports. They all used to have passports. His mother had insisted the whole family have passports. She wanted her children to travel, and with Dave in the picture they never knew when they would have to split. So they all got passports and they were always up to date. But after the bad guys went to Dave Ingersoll's hovel to slap him around, they headed right over to the nicely kept little home that Kym shared with Carolina.

They came there to feel up Bobby's sister and mother. They tossed their place for fun, found the passports and driver's licenses, and took them all. They wanted the government to help them keep the Ingersolls from running. Who needs a passport in hell? Bobby wasn't home when they gave his apartment a toss, and he always carried his passport with him, it made him feel like a world citizen, even though it proved there was no such thing. They took his driver's license. So much for the job driving the hooker billboards.

It would be the three of them trying to escape on a hundred grand and one passport. This hundred grand was completely wasted, in fact it wasn't even giving him hope. Would they try to get to Mexico? Dye their hair in a gas station toilet and move to Phoenix? The Ingersolls didn't have a chance.

A hardened criminal has been interviewed by the police a few dozen times. The guy interviewing the criminal has done it a few hundred times. Practice and experience usually win. Police know how criminals lie. They know the game better than the shitbird. For the Ingersoll family it would be their first time running away. For the people from whom they were running, it would be just another in a series of people caught trying to run away. Where would the Ingersolls die? Mexico, Vancouver, Phoenix—they probably wouldn't even get that far. Most likely they'd die under a bridge in North Vegas. Maybe they should go back to the LD50s and buy that fentanyl. They were going to die together somewhere with most of the hundred grand still on them as a bonus for the goons. There was no hope in the hundred grand that Bobby was putting aside. None.

There's a lot of venomous critters in Australia. The folk advice if you're bitten by a black mamba (which is an African snake but maybe it was visiting Australia the same time you were) is to try to get comfortable before you die. Maybe that would have been a better use for the hundred grand.

It was three miles from Bobby's apartment to Shotgun Perry's and Bobby was going to walk it. He knew that on this last day Ruphart would have tails on him, his sister, his mother, and his father. If he drove to the casino on his scooter, his tail would get to drive. They'd burned up his driver's license—fuck the tail, make him walk. The bad guys didn't know Bobby had money, but they were ready for any move he would make. He didn't count the cash again before he left. He knew just what he had and had proven to himself that counting it a zillion times wouldn't make it quadruple.

He pulled out his phone and searched for *MMF threesome* on Pornhub, jacked off hard into a hand towel, wiped up what missed the towel with the towel, and threw that white cum towel over the money in the paint bucket. He grabbed the handle and headed out the door. He didn't live in the best neighborhood and Shotgun's was on Fremont Street, so it wasn't unlikely that he'd get mugged on his three-mile late-night walk. His mugging might create the world's luckiest junkie. He liked that.

If you're ever strolling with half a million dollars in cash in a paint bucket with a fresh cum rag over the top and a hit man following you on a hot Mojave spring night, you should sing some old Springsteen that your mom used to sing to you. *I've got a double oh seven watch and it's a one and only. It's got an* I Spy *beeper that tells me when you're lonely.* Bobby was a cool rockin' daddy in the USA. He was thirty-five minutes into his walk before he got the nerve to swing the money bucket in a full circle upside down over his head. Centrifugal force could still be counted on. His money and cum towel stayed in the bucket. Bobby was happy. Things were going well. He did it again. This was fun.

Fremont Street is stupid. All the big money moved to the Strip, leaving downtown with just a few little casinos, bail bonds, pawnshops, and people dressed up like Kiss (or maybe the real guys from Kiss, who cares?). They weren't really *dressed* up like Kiss, they were made up like Kiss, with huge boots like Kiss, and sheer, small banana-hammock thongs. They were Kiss with huge dicks exposed (so I guess not the real guys in Kiss). Hung Kiss was working with Spider-Man (with clothes) and a woman with really, really, really big tits with really, really small electrical tape over the nipples and areolae. Crazy-big breasts. Crazy-small tape. So big and so small she was easier to spot than a guy in platform shoes and clown makeup sticking his tongue out and throwing devil-horn fingers with the outline of his huge swinging cut dick plainly visible. Tourists took pictures with Kiss or big tits or another almost topless woman with an American flag painted on her ass, or another with a whip, or another dressed as a "naughty nurse," and then were badgered to give a bigger tip for the picture than they wanted to. There were magicians, jugglers, and those "living statues" whose skill set consists of standing still. There were guys doing caricatures, all in the same style, big heads like Marie Osmond, teeth like Donny Osmond, and a tennis racket, a gun, or a guitar in the three-fingered hand (one of the Osmonds must be missing fingers), with the tourist's name across the top, so the mark could tell it was a picture of them. There were other artists doing Day-Glo spray-paint pictures of Vegas and a piano player who brought his big stupid piano down to street-perform. It's easier to lug big tits and a little tape.

The Heart Attack Grill was handing out free burgers to anyone who weighed in at over three hundred and fifty pounds, but they dinged them on the drinks and souvenirs.

There were people going for that deal. Vegas isn't Marin. The Starbucks on Fremont Street at the Golden Nugget had an outdoor seating area where Bobby could watch the world go by for the last few minutes of being twenty, and probably the last several hours of being alive, with half a million dollars and his own cum in a bucket between his legs. Some idiot had gotten the idea to use taxpayers' money to build a canopy over Fremont Street and market it as the Fremont Street Experience. It was the largest and the ugliest LED low-resolution display screen. They added loud ugly old pop music to the environment and did the *experience* every hour. With people flying overhead like Superman, if Superman were drunk and on a dirty zip line. Nevada ingenuity built the Hoover Dam and found a way to make the Electric Light Orchestra worse. The people who walked by Bobby on Fremont Street were necessarily stoned to be this kind of *experienced*. They were different than the people on the Strip. They had less money, and consumers on the Strip seemed to like smaller breasts farther away for their entertainment dollar. Those were the only differences. People on the Strip had less money than Bobby had in his bucket right now and Bobby had less interest in the breasts because he had fresh cum on a towel in his bucket. He could smell pot and perfume and people. It was too bright, and the music was too loud, and the people were too everything. It was a good night.

Bobby went into the Starbucks and looked at the menu. They sell coffee, but there are still so many hard decisions. Bobby stood at the counter reading the menu over and over. He kind of wanted a Frappuccino, Starbucks's name for a milkshake, but there were so many flavors and sizes and did he want whip? Starbucks was a coffee place, maybe he should get coffee. If he got a really hot, really bitter Americano with extra shots, it would be so hot and taste so burnt and shitty, he'd have to drink it slow and it would last. If he had a really bitter drink, he could get a muffin, which was Starbucks's name for chocolate cake filled with chocolate candy, to go with it. But a Mocha Frappuccino was kind of the muffin and the coffee just blended together.

He'd been standing there awhile when the barista spoke up: "Can I help you, sir?"

"Sorry. Wow, there are just so many choices. Um, yeah, coffee and a muffin, I guess."

"What size coffee and what kind of muffin?"

"Jesus, whatever you think. Maybe a Frappuccino would be better."

"What kind of Frappuccino?"

"Fuck me. I don't know. Coffee. Yeah, coffee. Um. Medium Americano and a chocolate muffin."

"Room?"

"What? Um, no."

He sat down on the Starbucks patio which wasn't really outside, because of the stupid Experience roof over the street, and sipped his coffee while watching the people experience Fremont. How did they all decide to be there? Goddamn.

At 11:54 Bobby's phone quacked its alarm. He left a double chocolate muffin on his table, and his money bucket under the table, and bussed his empty coffee cup. He wasn't ever that far away from the muffin and the cash, but it still felt a little reckless. Oh boy. He picked up the muffin and dropped it on top of the towel and the cum and the money. He walked across the street to Shotgun's. He put his bucket down between his legs and stood staring at the giant fake-neon video cowboy with a shotgun on each hip. He stared at his phone and watched for it to turn to midnight. The LED canopy show started: stars, confetti, showgirls, an American eagle, and ELO. Celebration. Bobby methodically unwrapped the muffin. He sang, *"You say it's your birthday. Well, it's my birthday too, yeah,"* mixing with ELO like Charles Ives or the Residents.

He stuffed the entire chocolate muffin into his mouth and tried to keep singing the guitar part. Bobby Ingersoll was now twenty-one. Happy birthday.

He walked into the casino. Bobby looked older than twenty-one. He walked in easily. But before they would take the bet, they would check his ID. He had his passport and it was a good picture. As he walked in, the security guard asked to look in his bucket. Maybe it was a bomb. Maybe Bobby was a terrorist. It would be a good place to strike the American Satan except no one in real America gave a star-spangled fuck about the people in the Fremont Street Experience. No one would care even if it were the real Kiss, and their real dicks were that big. Bobby offered the bucket for inspection.

The African American guard, with a mustache like Neil deGrasse Tyson, didn't have blue gloves like at the airport, he just picked up the cum rag with his bare hands and revealed the money. "Holy shit. Holy shit. Fuck. What do you have all this money for?"

"I'm here for gaming."

"This is a lot of money."

"Yes."

The security guard thought it over. "Want me to call security?"

"You are security."

"Yeah, but you want me to get you guards or something?"

"I'm okay, I walked over from North Vegas, I'll be fine here. Can you put my towel back on top, please?"

The security guard dropped the cum rag back in the bucket and Bobby adjusted it just so. He headed for the one craps table with a *No Limit* sign. There were a few people playing dice. Bobby spoke to the dealer.

"Excuse me, I'd like to make a large bet."

"How large of a bet?"

"Four hundred and seventy-four thousand, five hundred and thirty-two dollars, please—on Yo Eleven." Bobby picked up the bucket, tilted it toward the dealer, and pulled off the cum rag. The dealer looked in skeptically and then wasn't skeptical. "I would like to make this all one bet on one roll of the dice, please."

The dealer called over the pit boss. They would both have good stories tonight.

"Would you like a more private gaming area, sir?"

"No thanks."

"Well, this is going to take a little while, so let's let these people continue to play at this table and we'll move you to another one." The pit boss used his radio to get more security and dealers.

Everyone at the table had heard the conversation and seen the bucket and they all followed to the new table. It was only a few tables over but by the time Bobby got there, there were already four security guards, two in uniform and two in plain clothes.

"Sir, if you would please, just put your money here on the table in plain view."

Bobby handed his towel, with his still slightly moist cum map of Hawaii, to one of the uniforms and carefully dumped his bucket of money onto the table. The pit boss was careful to make sure that the eye-in-the-sky camera could see the money. Fifty-seven banded stacks of one hundred hundreds in each stack and forty-five loose hundreds fell out onto the table. Bobby took a hundred grand, ten banded stacks of a hundred hundreds, and threw it back in the bucket and threw the cum towel on top of it and placed it on the floor between his legs. "I'm not betting that. I'm saving that." He reached into his pocket and pulled out a twenty, a ten, and two ones, and threw it loose on the pile. "I am also betting this. It's $474,532, but you should count it."

"We will."

Another couple security guards brought out a locked case of proprietary five-thousand-dollar chips with little micro trackers embedded in each one. Shotgun's five-grand chips were a very pretty magenta and gold. Security stood holding the case. Counting the money fast but carefully, you can do about nine grand a minute. Taking the paper off and stacking it and having another person checking the work, it took about an hour. Bobby was proud that he'd done it almost as fast as the pros.

While the pit bosses were doing all the counting, some night-duty manager took Bobby's passport to get it scanned in. He looked at the passport and then at his watch. "Hey, you just turned twenty-one twenty minutes ago."

"I know." No one knew how to treat him.

One of the other guards wished him happy birthday and then a bunch of others did the same. Word had gotten around the casino and most everyone there was gathered around Bobby's table. People were coming in from the Fremont Street Experience. ELO was over and they could see big tits and the hung fake-Kiss guys later.

Bobby thought he should check what he was feeling. He took a couple of deep breaths and closed his eyes for a few moments of mindfulness. He wanted to be right here, right now. He ran his attention from the top of his head down to his feet at an even pace. He checked his shoulders, stomach, and sphincter for tension. His arm was a little sore from carrying and swinging the bucket, but that was it. Bobby had changed. He was doing okay.

They opened the case and carefully took out the five-thousand-dollar chips. The pit boss counted out ten chips and spread them on the table for Bobby to see. He then stacked them in one pile of ten. He took another ten chips out of the box. This time he didn't spread them first, he stacked them next to the first stack of ten, so they matched. He continued to lay out stacks of ten until he had nine stacks, lined up nice and even. He took out four more magenta/gold chips and put them beside the nine piles. "That's four hundred and seventy thousand."

"Yup."

He reached into the tray on the table for normal play and pulled out four orange thousand-dollar "pumpkin" chips. He grabbed five black hundred-dollar chips, one green twenty-five-dollar "quarter" chip, one red five-dollar "nickel" chip, and then very carefully, for show, put two one-dollar blue chips on top. It was pretty. Gambling is showbiz and set design.

"That's $474,532 worth of chips. Do you agree, Mr. Ingersoll?"

"Yes."

The suit had some paperwork that he'd watch Bobby read. "Would you sign here, please?"

Bobby signed.

"Would you like to place a bet, sir?"

"Yes, I would." Bobby carefully slid the mountain of chips onto the eleven. They didn't quite fit.

"You have to fit them all within the box, Mr. Ingersoll."

Bobby stacked the piles of ten into piles of fifteen and threw the smaller chips on top. They all fit.

"Any other players?"

Three tourists threw on a couple of bets to make their stories better. The dealer gestured to Bobby to take the dice and throw them.

"Nah, let someone else throw them, please."

One of the people who had placed a bet said, "Me. I'll throw."

A guy with a greasy ponytail, a cheap suit, and gold sneakers yelled out, "C'mon, eleven!" Everyone else joined in. Even the people who had bet on different numbers were rooting for eleven. "C'mon, eleven. C'mon, eleven. C'mon, eleven." Everyone was wishing and hoping and praying except Bobby.

Bobby checked himself one more time. A couple breaths. Mindful. Focused. He wasn't feeling anything. He was done with hoping. He reached down to his bucket—the towel was completely dry. Bobby moved his fingers up to his lips, then brought a gob of spit to the front of his mouth. His mouth wasn't dry—how was that possible? He picked the spit up on his index and middle fingertips. He brought his hand back down between his legs to the towel and found a crusty spot. He wet the crust with the spit on his fingers and rubbed it around. His cum wasn't revitalized enough to impregnate, of course, it had been a long time, but he could feel it on his fingers. He brought his fingers up to his nose and smelled his cum.

"C'mon, eleven."

Yo Eleven is a stupid bet. If you aren't the house, all bets are stupid, but Yo Eleven is even stupider. "Yo Eleven" means you're betting on the next roll of the dice being eleven. It's that simple. One die needs to be either a five or a six and the other needs to also be either a five or a six. But they can't match. There's no "come" involved, there's no "line," there's no "craps." It's either eleven or it isn't. The "yo" is in there so "eleven" can't be misheard as "seven." The chances of rolling an eleven on one roll of fair dice is one in eighteen, so seventeen-to-one, but the casino pays fifteen-to-one on a Yo Eleven. That gives the house an edge of 11.11%. That's a big taste. So Yo Eleven is reserved for players who are on a roll and feel lucky. Players on a roll who feel lucky are stupid.

Bobby was not that stupid, but the house's 11% edge didn't matter to him at all. He wasn't playing the edges. He wasn't playing for a living. He was playing for his life. This was the only casino bet he would ever make. He would either lose all his $474,532, his life, and his family on the one roll, or he would be okay. His cum smelled good. He brought his fingers down to his mouth. "C'mon, eleven." He had a 5.5555555555555555555555% (the fives repeating forever—unlike anything real) chance of his family living. His cum tasted good. He felt nothing but that. He was dead.

Eleven.

It takes a long time to place a $474,532 bet plus the paperwork, vetting, and counting. It takes longer to collect $7,117,980 in winnings. When the eleven came, Bobby did another immediate mindful check: shoulders, stomach, sphincter—he still felt nothing, but motherfucker, it was a good kind of nothing. He reached down to the pail between his legs and pulled out the towel. He brought it up to his face and buried his nose in his dry cum. He inhaled the smell of life. He was reborn. He was alive again. He covered his face in the towel for a couple minutes. He tucked the towel into the top of his shirt and reached down and brought out a couple handfuls of the leftover hundred grand. He used this cash to tip the pit bosses and then gave a few hundred to each of the people who'd been saying, "C'mon, eleven." He gave five grand to the guy with the greasy ponytail who started it.

The casino was crazy for about an hour. It was loud. Word spread out onto Fremont Street and security brought Bobby into a back room. The pit bosses, security, and managers were happy he'd won. They'd be scrutinized, but they'd done everything right. Fuck bossman Perry.

They let Bobby use a computer to set up an account for the wire transfer. He told them they had to hurry. His family wasn't safe yet. The guy following him must have figured out what happened and told the bosses about it, but what did that mean? He called the number his father, the asshole, had given him and told the guy who answered that he had all the money his fucking father owed and would pay it back on time.

Criminals are not honorable. Not at all. They can't be trusted. Everyone is always running around Vegas saying that when the mob ran it, it was more compassionate, more honest. Bullshit. They are thugs. They have no joy, no grace, no truth, no integrity. But these criminals also had no move with Bobby. Word would travel all over that Bobby had won a shit ton of money and everyone would know he was going to pay his father's debt. So, the bad guys would take the money. They would take the two and a half million dollars and Bobby's family would live.

7

BOBBY DIED AT SHOTGUN PERRY'S CASINO AT 1:48 ON the morning of June 1, his twenty-first birthday. That Bobby Ingersoll was gone. His odds had been bad. He'd had a very slim chance of living. But Chance gave him another life. He was born again. The new Bobby Ingersoll saw through the illusion of cause and effect. The new Bobby had no agency of his own. This Bobby Ingersoll did not own his own life. The Dice now owned Bobby. He owed his life to Chance. He had a superpower under our yellow sun. Bobby knew and accepted that life was Random. Bobby was enlightened. Siddhartha was dead. Bobby was Buddha.

Bobby asked Shotgun Perry's if he could use a room with a computer and a phone. The security guards gave him one. Casinos will do anything to keep high rollers in the building. They need them to bet again and maybe lose some back. So Bobby had a room and dinner and any show he wanted. "Hey, you like hookers?" But Bobby was different from any other high roller, and everyone could feel it. It was not that he would never gamble again—from now on he would do nothing but gamble. But there would be no more *games* of chance for Bobby. Now it was nothing but Chance. It wasn't a fucking game. He called his mother and sister and told them they were safe. They cried. Then he told them again they were safe. They cried more. Then he told them for real they were safe. They cried. Then he told them why they were safe. They cried. Then he told them they really honestly were safe. They cried.

During all the weeping they each said, "Are you kidding?"

Bobby thought about that. He thought about if he had lost all the money and then called them and told them they were safe, but they weren't—he was just kidding. How great a joke would have that been?

You're kidding?

Yup, we're going to die tomorrow. But I had you going for a while there, didn't I?

Would that be the cruelest joke ever or is there a kindness in that joke? A kindness in letting them feel safe for just forty-five seconds. Your mom is dying of cancer. The doctors always lowball the number of months someone has to live. *We're afraid your mom has maybe six months to a year.* And then she lives eighteen months. *She beat the odds! She's a fighter.* They always do that. Why not?

If he had lost, would he have had the compassion to call his mom and sister and tell them they were safe and give them the gift of a few seconds of hope? That would be the truly Christian thing to do. The Christian kindness to give people hope when we all know in our hearts it's bullshit, but maybe for a minute the poor doomed asshole believes it. That's a nutty kind of kindness.

But Bobby wasn't lying. "You're kidding?" they both asked over and over.

"Nope." He had to pinky-promise his sister Doc. He called his sister Carolina "Doc" because she'd wanted to be a doctor since she was little. Bobby and Carolina, both Dave and Kym's children, were good-looking and smart. Not smart enough to pick a better father, but smart. Bobby had pissed his smarts away, but Carolina was straight A's and perfect SATs. She wanted to go to medical school. He'd call Mom and Doc back later, after they'd stopped crying, and tell his mom he would buy her house for her and he'd tell his sister she could go to any medical school she wanted on his dime. That would make them cry again. And maybe he *would* be kidding this time. It depended on what Chance told him to do. The new Bobby was going to kid about things that no one kids about. *Your cancer has gone into remission!*

You're kidding!

Yup.

He had to try that. He already knew that someday Chance would make him try that. Someday Chance would make him do everything he ever dreamed.

He hung up while they were sobbing. He didn't have time to wait for them to calm down. Next he called Fraser Ruphart. Ruphart's lackey answered.

"This is Bobby Ingersoll, Dave's son. I'd like to pay off my father's two-and-a-half-million-dollar debt. It's due today and I have the money. May I speak to Fraser, please?"

"He's called Mr. Ruphart."

"Of course he is. May I speak to Mr. Ruphart, please?"

"It's a *p* and then an *h*, it's not *ph* making an *f* sound."

"Right, no *f.*" Bobby waited as the phone was handed to the boss.

"Yeah?"

"Sir, this is Bobby Ingersoll. I have all the money that Dave Ingersoll owes you. How would you like it paid?"

"Cash."

"Of course. Would you like to come get it?"

"I'm not your fucking errand boy, I'm not running—"

"I wouldn't expect you to, sir. Just tell me where to come and I will deliver it to you with a smile. You want a pizza with that?"

Bobby asked the security guys at Shotgun's if they knew

a couple guys with guns that he could hire for ten grand to get him safely to Trump International. Yeah, Trump International. Of course Ruphart would live at a bankrupt Chinese apartment tower with the name *Trump* on it. And called *International*. An airport can be international. A corporation with offices around the world can be international. A bus station in Buffalo, New York, can be international. But a single hotel/time share cannot be international. It's in one nation. What an asshole. Ruphart was Trump people. There's an expression, *You can't bullshit a bullshitter*, that couldn't be further from the truth. The easiest people to rip off are liars. Ruphart believed that he was the bad guy. That he was the one ripping off people. So, when they put the name of a TV fake billionaire in big fake gold letters on a Chinese building in Vegas, Ruphart thought that was classy. He believed the "white-gloved twenty-four-hour security" bullshit. He thought he was buying a condo that would go up in value, not one that some incompetent TV personality and his shyster partners would take right into the dumper. He might as well have bought a time share, they do have them right in the same building.

There was a lot of typing and a bunch of forms to fill out, but after three hours Bobby got two and a half million in cash out of the casino cage. He threw it in the bucket, tossed his cum rag on top of it, and handed it to one of the large, serious men he had hired to go with him. It's like the fur-hat guys at Buckingham Palace—a big part of their job is simply not smiling. If this had been happening a few months later, when Bobby was more in the new groove, he would have bought them big fur hats and asked them to wear them, but he was brand new to the wonders of living by Chance.

The straight-faced guys came with their own limo and

Bobby got in the back with one of them. He left the money up front with the driver. Ruphart had said no to the pizza. Bobby stopped and got him a large Hawaiian pie. Fuck him. Just fuck him in the neck. The pizza said that. The kind of *fuck you* that pushes up your glasses with your middle finger passing an asshole in a revolving door. It's the pure *fuck you* of ham and pineapple.

The three of them walked into the penthouse of Trump International with a nice hot Hawaiian pie and two point five million in cash in a white Home Depot bucket with a schmatta dicka on top. Stephen Fry elaborates on Oscar Wilde's idea that needle-dick dictator wannabes have deplorable taste in interior decorating. Terrible taste—white and gold and pillars. Bobby gave two and half million dollars and a pizza to the fuck who sent lackies to finger and feel up his sister and his mom. The needle-dick fuck who had planned to enjoy killing Bobby's whole family.

Ruphart didn't take the money, one of his lackies did. It looked like Ruphart wouldn't touch anything. There was hand sanitizer all over his office. Ruphart gestured to his lackies to take the pizza out of the room. "Get this stinking pizza out of here."

Good, he understood. That made Bobby happy.

Ruphart clearly felt nothing as his lackies counted the money. Ruphart probably never felt anything. From now on Bobby would feel everything. Ruphart would be as happy with the money as he would have been to kill the Ingersolls. It was a wash. Bobby pitied Ruphart. Ruphart didn't know that everything was Random. Ruphart thought he was in control. Ruphart thought he had power. Ruphart thought he could cause an effect.

As Bobby gave Ruphart the money, he wept into his cum

rag for Ruphart. Ruphart would never roll the dice. "You can keep the pizza, but give me the towel and the bucket, please." The henchman who'd dumped the money on a table to be counted gave Bobby the bucket and the towel.

There was no receipt. It was simply over. Bobby called his father when he got to the lobby.

"You're not going to die this time, and neither are we."

"What?"

"You heard me."

"You're kidding."

He so so wished he were, and not entirely out of kindness. "I paid off your fucking debt. I just paid Mr. Ruphart two and a half million dollars in cash. Happy birthday to me."

"What?"

"You heard me, happy birthday to me."

"Son. I will repay you."

"No you won't, you dick. Get the fuck out of Vegas and never talk to me again. Happy birthday to me." He knew David Ingersoll would never leave Vegas, but he had to try to get him away.

"Son?"

"Fuck you. Happy birthday to me."

Half a million dollars should get Doc through Harvard Medical School. If she spent more than that, fuck her, let her get a job. A half million should get his mom a nice house in Vegas and a small nest egg. She could stop working. That was three and a half million gone, and after all his tips and pizza, he and Chance now had three and a half million in the bank and just under two hundred grand that he would take in cash.

He wasn't kidding.

8

GOOD MORNING. THE SUN WAS COMING UP ON BOBBY'S birthday and he had a couple hundred grand in cash in a bucket covered by his trusty, crusty love towel. It was payback time to everyone he'd borrowed and/or stolen money from. He had his limo with his bodyguards (sans big furry hats), it was Xmas time in the hot Mojave summer, and Chance had made Bobby Santa Claus. His temporary posse drove him around Vegas paying back all his friends and acquaintances with interest, good interest. He tripled their money. That seemed fair for a week's interest on money they had figured was lost. He paid back the family payday loans and gave notice at work.

The Stop 'n' Rob was a little harder to make square. He could never pay back that damage. He had really scared that clerk, and after the story got around, all the other clerks would be more scared too. He had taken away their feeling of safety and their trust of strangers. That couldn't be forgiven. *He* couldn't be forgiven. He couldn't go into the store himself. He couldn't risk being recognized. He sent his bodyguards in to give twenty grand in cash to whatever clerk was on duty and say, "You got lucky tonight, please share with all the other clerks." The clerk might pocket a little more than his share, but he figured some would get to the right guy. People are mostly good.

Over the next couple of days, he would do some research and find the owner of the 7-Eleven he'd knocked off and send them an envelope with a grand in it. He'd use gloves to handle the cash and the envelope, but they probably wouldn't show it to the police anyway. Who are they to blow against the wind? They may have already made insurance claims for the two hundred bucks and this was all tax free. He put fifty grand in his PokerWinner.com account and texted J.D. to tell him what room he was in. He went heads-up with J.D., waited until he got two/seven unsuited, and went all in. J.D. was taken care of.

He owed nothing to the gangbangers. That was just Chance. He owed everything to Chance. Chance had saved his life and now he would give his life to Chance. The limo took him back to the Fremont Street Experience where he thanked, tipped, and dismissed his temporary driver and bodyguards.

Ten in the morning is dawn in Vegas. Hung Kiss weren't even hanging in their banana hammocks yet. Mickey Mouse, Goofy, and Deadpool were offering people the chance to take a picture with them all together for five bucks. What the fuck are Mickey, Goofy, and Deadpool doing together? Maybe it's time to ask the CEOs that. When Disney bought Marvel, all bets were off. That might have been the moment where our world became Random enough to create Bobby Ingersoll. A very short and very Asian-even-through-the-mask Spider-Man joined the street corporate trio. Bobby would start paying back Chance by taking a Random picture. That was the plan. He would put together a picture that he himself could never predict. A picture he had no reason to take.

Bobby asked the Marvel/Disney copyright-infringement

brain trust to pose for a picture with him. He was rich and wanted to spread the wealth in Random ways. He gave each knockoff characters five hundred dollars and asked if they would wait for a moment. He walked a block away and gave a very busty woman wearing feathers on her head and tape over her areolae five hundred dollars to join this Disney/Marvel/Bobby photographic opportunity. He found a guy dressed as a cowboy, just a tourist—the cowboy didn't consider himself a character, even though he was dressed as a cowboy—to snap the picture. This was too important for a selfie. He needed a full body shot of them all. Twenty-five hundred dollars and there they were pictured left to right: Spider-Man, Mickey, Lisa (Bobby had asked the busty woman her name), Bobby, Goofy, and Deadpool. The picture symbolized Bobby's rebirth like a bunny, pastel eggs, and lurid plastic grass represent Easter.

Everyone was paid and dismissed, and Bobby stood on the drowsy morning carny street staring at the picture on his phone. Fuck. It wasn't Random enough. It was totally predictable. Knowing Fremont and knowing Bobby, this picture was pretty much inevitable. It didn't feel like Chance had any hand in it. He could not pay Chance back this way. He could not generate Random. He couldn't will himself to be Random any more than he could will himself to have diabetes. Well, he supposed he could will himself to have type 2, but it would take a few years and a more patriotic American diet than he enjoyed. He wanted to be reborn into Chance. He wanted to be truly Random, and he didn't just want the symptoms, he wanted the whole disease.

Wait, this was easy. He pocketed his phone and walked down the Fremont Street Experience toward the Golden Gate Casino. The ABC Gift Shop offered most of its junk for ninety-seven cents. There were some pricier items. The almost-flesh-colored-but-too-pink coffee mug shaped like a lactating breast with a hole in the nipple making it a ceramic dribble cup was more than three times that price. Bobby went to the back of the store. There were pairs of dice in little tubes: *These Dice Were Used in Actual Play in This Fabulous Casino,* the white sticker read in black typewriter font. There were a few different colors, but Bobby chose translucent red. Three dollars and ninety-seven cents, "Keep the change." It was a hundred-dollar bill.

The ace side read *Las Vegas* above the pip and *Nevada* right beneath it. The deuce had *Binions,* the casino name, between the two pips. The sice side had the serial number of the batch that each die came from. One die was *2451* and the other was *2455.* Thermoset plastic, polymethyl methacrylate, with corners hard and sharp. Right angles not found in nature and not like the friendly dice for home games. The corners of these dice cut into your palms a little; they didn't lay easy in your hand. These dice were fair and honest. These dice were cold and objective. These dice had no mercy. These dice had destroyed lives.

This pair of Dice was now God. They were Bobby's masters. They felt good in his pocket.

Religion is so easy. It's easy to believe in god like it's easy to eat fat and salt. We know it's not good for us, but we do it. We are compelled. Religion doesn't care where it lands. You're born in Wheeling, well thank you, Jesus. You're born in Tehran, inshallah. Whatever god sticks his cock through your personal proximate gloryhole—you suck it with relish.

Lenny Bruce talked about the goofiness of the cross around the neck. If the myth of Jesus had started just a couple thousand years later, sexy little Catholic school girls would have gold electric chairs dangling between their brand-new heavers.

Bobby had always been an atheist. But remaining atheist is like not killing, and not being racist. It takes a little tiny bit of work to keep it up. Kindness and sanity once in a while go against nature. Bobby needn't fight anything anymore. He gave himself up to the Dice. He was a cult of one, reborn in Chance.

He walked to the Starbucks outside the Golden Nugget. He looked at the menu while he was waiting in line and figured out his choices in his head for his very first roll:

Two (2.78%)—Iced Golden Ginger Drink
Three (5.56%)—Nitro Cold Brew with Salted Honey Cold Foam
Four (8.33%)—Smoked Butterscotch Crème
Five (11.11%)—Hot Chocolate
Six (13.89%)—Carmel Frappuccino
Seven (16.67%)—Decaf Americano, extra shot
Eight (13.89%)—White Chocolate Mocha Frappuccino
Nine (11.11%)—Hot Chocolate
Ten (8.33%)—Cinnamon Dolce Crème
Eleven (5.56%)—Starbucks Reserve Nitro Cold Brew
Twelve (2.78%)—Iced Pineapple Matcha Drink

He rolled the Dice quietly, just in his hand. He didn't roll them anywhere; he bounced them around and flattened his palm—Boxcars! When it was his turn in line, he ordered a Venti Iced Pineapple Matcha Drink without hesitation. He had no doubt. He sat down in the patio under the Fremont Street Experience with a drink he never would have ordered without the Dice, but that a small part of him, the part that would never have prevailed in any decision, wanted to try. It wasn't bad. His drink was more Random than that fucking picture. He squeezed the Dice in his hand. The corners cut into his flesh, not drawing blood, just hurting. Just letting him know they were now in charge.

Bobby pulled out his phone and checked the time. It was 10:49. Holy shit. This religion thing was already working out great. It was eleven to eleven. He would find a tattoo shop and walk in at 11:11 a.m. Two minutes after he had arbitrarily decided to give his life to the bones and already he had no doubts. Already he'd forgotten it was arbitrary. He could feel the seductive faith pulling his brain away. Two minutes and he was a true believer. He would walk into the tattoo parlor at 11:11 a.m. and it would be finished by 11:11 p.m. The tattoo would be all elevens: the word *ELEVEN*, in caps, the numeral *11*, the Roman numeral *XI*, a photo-realistic representation of two Dice, translucent red, a cinque on one and a sice (he'd probably have to explain that that meant *six* to the artist, or maybe just say "six") on the other—adding up to eleven. The piece would be on his left wrist almost up to his elbow and bleeding down to eleven pips, free floating, without the cubes around them. It would be lots of different colors and lots of detail. It would hurt like holy hell. He had twelve hours and twenty minutes for Chance to create for him the perfect tattoo.

Bobby pulled up the closest eleven tattoo parlors to his current location on his phone. He rolled the Dice . . . six: a cinque and an ace. He counted down six on the list of tattoo parlors and now he had nineteen minutes to get to SinCity Tat-Cat.

9

THE Dice knew what they were doing. SinCity Tat-Cat was perfect. It was upstairs above an "Indian" souvenir shop. Bobby stood outside looking at turquoise and leather fringe on prominently nippled mannequins in the window until it was time to walk up the stairs and into Tat-Cat at 11:11 a.m. He was aware that the most talented artists and most experienced employees don't work the opening shift at tattoo parlors.

"I'd like a tattoo, please."

"Sure, the book is over there, pick any design you want and I can do you, or Mindy can do you, your choice. I'm best at tribal and Japanese. She's better at new school and realism. Pick something out of the book and I can help you choose me or Mindy. I can just call Mindy if you want her. First tat, right?"

"Yeah, I don't want anything out of the book, I need something designed."

"That'll cost more."

"Yup."

"You're sober, right?"

"Yup."

"How much you looking to spend?"

"As much as I can."

"What?"

"Yeah, I have something very clear in my head and I want it on my body. So, I need someone to design it and do it, and I want it all done today. I need to be finished twelve hours from right now."

"That's plenty of time. I get a hundred bucks an hour for the tats and another fifty bucks for the design."

"Here's five hundred bucks up front for your consultation."

"Yeah, I can do a nice tattoo for that."

"Nope. Thanks. I bet you're great, but I want to pay you that as a consulting fee. I'm paying for your knowledge. That's for you to get me the best design artist in here ASAP to help me design this thing. We'll work three hours on that, and I'll pay five grand to whomever that is. Then I want the best actual tattooist you can find to put the design on me and be finished by 11:11 p.m., so he or she will have about nine hours depending on how long the design takes. I'll pay that artist twenty grand. Then at the end of all that, if I'm completely happy with my ink, I'll give you another two grand for treating me right. Here, let me show you the money. Deal?"

"Um, deal. Yeah, deal."

"Get on the phone and let's have some fun. If you have any choices to make, Chance will make them. I make them with my Dice. Okay?"

"Okay."

"Most important, everyone involved needs to have fun. I'm Bobby. What's your name?"

"Jonesy. It would be better to spread the tattoo over a few weeks."

"Nope, it's going to all be done by eleven tonight."

"It will hurt. You'll get tender."

"That's okay, Jonesy, now let's put a wiggle on, there's some ticktock here."

While Jonesy searched his phone and texted, Bobby studied the man's ink. He had dark sleeves with koi swimming all over. Nice color. His head was shaved, or he had gone bald, probably a little of each. He had ram horns tattooed on his scalp. He had a palmed card, a three of clubs, tattooed on his palm. He was wearing shorts and sneakers with no socks. He had Dr. Martens boots tattooed on his lower legs, all black except for the trompe l'oeil laces. He had his nose pierced, his tongue pierced, and really big plugs in his ears. Did they pay him exclusively in body mods?

Jonesy began talking quietly on the phone and started to wander into the other room. Bobby held up his hand and politely interrupted.

"Hey Jonesy, stay here in the room with me. I want to hear the conversations. I won't cramp your style. You can call me the crazy motherfucker that I am. But I want to listen, that's part of my fun."

It was the truth that he wanted the full experience, but he also didn't want Jonesy calling up some thugs to come over and roll him.

Bobby thumbed through the art books. It seemed like a design with a busty topless cartoon Jesus with an American flag and some kanji would pretty much cover everyone. He paged through and thought about how he was going to get as Random as possible. How he would really give his life to Chance.

The Dice would not make every decision for him. That would be like some Christian praying for their muffin to be good at Starbucks. You have to save that shit for when you need it. That wasn't the right spirit. The decisions he could make on his own, he *would* make on his own. If he was sure he just wanted a cup of coffee, he would get a cup of coffee just the way he wanted it. But whenever doubt crept in, he would give his life to Chance, whether that be what kind of coffee or whether to get married. He wasn't eliminating choice; he was eliminating doubt. All his uncertainty from the most trivial to the most profound would be given to Random. He would handle the sure and mundane himself. Random didn't need to be bothered with that. Random was there to destroy all doubt and allow him to express parts of himself that wouldn't be expressed without Random.

Now, what about the choices? The Dice couldn't talk. Bobby would come up with all the choices himself. He would come up with a choice for every number from two to twelve. All eleven had to be choices he was honestly considering. Whichever of his choices the Dice chose he would do immediately without any hesitation, doubt, or regret. He would lay out the choices, roll the Dice, and do what Random decided.

Democracy is stupid. Sports are stupid. Decisions are stupid. They all have winners. There is one winner. No matter the margin, the winner is the winner—a nose, a thousand votes in Florida, just the slightest lean for Indian food tonight, and that's the way it goes. All choices go to the winner. Yet in all decisions, the also-rans were and are a real part of who we are and what we want. But those also-rans are a part of us that never gets expressed. We all contain multitudes but winner takes all, and real desires are just ignored and eventually forgotten. Not so with Random. Random would give expressions to the multitudes of Bobby that were clearly there, clearly felt but just didn't win the decision. He would give Chance all his choices, all things he kinda wanted to do, and with the Dice, the losers would have a fighting chance. Random could shake things up a bit. He would let the sincere parts of him, sincere desires and actions, happen, even though they wouldn't otherwise cross the threshold to win. Random would make him completely himself.

Every time he had to make a decision that wasn't immediately clear, no matter how trivial or how important, he would offer that decision up to Chance. This would involve a lot of soul searching. *To live outside the law, you must be honest.* Non-Random people could lie to themselves and feel like they'd made the best decision, that that decision was part of who they were. But the things they wanted almost as much—that was still them. The losers were them too. When you decide to have Indian food instead of pizza, you make that decision because you want Indian food a little bit more. But the pizza desire is real and still there. Pizza is part of you too. Yeah, maybe you'd have pizza next time, but maybe not. That pizza choice didn't ever have a chance to be expressed in that moment. It was just the loser. That's an easy one, but this was true for every decision—what job to take, whether to get married, who to marry, whether to learn Dutch or study the oboe. When Bobby felt any indecision, he would look inside himself and decide exactly how much of him wanted to eat pizza as a Dutch-speaking oceanographer married to a hairdresser he met in his table tennis class. Those decisions wouldn't be all at once of course, but as they came up, they would all have a chance of being chosen and acted on. The Dice were perfect. There was no doubt. The Dice were perfect because they could also allow Bobby to weigh the likelihood of Random making each choice and then him acting on it. He didn't want to exercise as much as he wanted to watch Netflix and he didn't want to watch Netflix as much as he wanted to go to a strip club, but he would give them all the chance they deserved. This wasn't giving up his personality, this was letting more of his personality be expressed in Random ways.

Motherfucker, this was a good idea. This was truth. The whole brilliance of this was that there isn't an equal chance of

Random choosing seven and choosing two. Bobby could strip club at seven and do push-ups at two, that seemed about right, and the Dice would decide. Bobby could have his thumb on the scale just enough to be fair to his deepest desires.

He pulled up a Dice probability chart on his phone. There was a 2.78% chance of either a two or a twelve coming up on a single roll. Those were the long shots. Just a little crazy itch in the back of his mind. Some bugnutty thing he considered seriously but never *that* seriously. This was something he would really consider that, without Chance, would never really be chosen. Twelve was an Iced Pineapple Matcha Drink. Without Random these choices would never have a chance. With Random these things would have a 2.78% chance. Give a choice a two or a twelve and Random would have him do it about three times every hundred throws. Three and its twin, eleven, would come up 5.56% each because they could be made two ways, either a two and one, or a one and a two, or a five and a six, or a six and a five. Not likely, but way more likely than two or twelve. Four and ten, those could come up three ways, so they were 8.33% each. Five and nine were 11.11%— he was going to like five and nine. Not the most likely, but also not a long shot. If he kinda really wanted something, he'd give it five or nine. Six and eight were 13.89%. And then there was lucky number seven. Seven could be rolled six different ways, lots of choices. The chances of a seven were 16.67%. Six times more likely than a two or a twelve. He might need to incorporate a table into his tattoo design. Nah, these odds were his rosary. They'd become part of him. He didn't need to read them or memorize them. He would soon feel them like an iambic pentameter.

He didn't need to have eleven choices every time. If he felt equally about two choices he could do even or odd. But when would he ever feel equally about two choices? It could happen, like whether to have an English muffin with peanut butter now or a little later. "Odd" and "even" would give him his coin toss. Things would rarely be equal, so he'd more likely do "seven and up" vs. "six and down." Show Random his deepest honest desires and let Random decide.

He would decide on all the outcomes and let Random know how he was leaning, and Random would choose. Once the Dice were rolled there would be no turning back. Bobby could feel the power of his religion surging through his entire body. Yes, he had been born again. He was truly reborn as a Random person. He was holy.

This life was going to be fun. He could not wait to again not know what to do.

10

THE FIRST ROLL OF THE DICE GOT HIM BJ INSTEAD of "The Wolf." He'd been leaning toward BJ. BJ was a woman. Finally, a woman named "BJ." He'd known a few men called BJ but never a woman. He liked that name for a woman. And the more he thought about it, he liked that name for a man. Yeah. He gave the BJ choice five and up and rolled. That gave BJ an 83.34% chance of being his designer and she also had a reputation as a great tattooist. He rolled an Easy Six, five and a one, so BJ would etch his arm.

She got there pretty quickly. Bobby did not roll a two, so he didn't have to describe the tattoo he wanted to her in interpretive dance. Only a small part of him wanted to try that. He did not roll a twelve, so he did not have to draw the tattoo for his arm in one pass with his left hand and have her do exactly that. He did not roll a five, so it wouldn't be a tattoo of blood, just the needle cutting him with no ink. Ink is a lubricant and a coagulant, so it would have hurt more and bled more, and it would have ended up as just red scar lines. He'd have to get it redone every couple years. Did he want that? Yeah, kinda, a little, about 11.11% worth, he wanted a tattoo of blood, but he didn't get it. Any of the other numbers would mean he would just explain what he wanted to BJ. He wanted to do that most and that's what he got. He rolled a ten, Tennessee, so they chatted.

He really liked BJ. She instantly understood Random. He rolled a seven, Big Red, so the tattoo would be mostly pink. The eleven at just the right time put eleven purple peace signs circling around the design. He rolled a three to pick his animal mascot and that explains the hippopotamus. He didn't have any doubts about much else. The tattoo had a lot of elevens—Arabic, Roman, kanji, Sūzhōu mǎzi, crosshatches, dominos, pinyin, and, of course, the Dice. It was beautiful. BJ got the design done in a couple of hours, so there was a lot of time for the ink, and they needed it.

"Okay, Bobby, get comfortable, this is going to take awhile and it's going to hurt a bit around the bones. It doesn't really hurt more on the wrist, but you might not like the tapping on the wrist bone where it's close there. I guess you'll roll the Random for what music we hear, huh?"

"Already rolled, let's do some Tuvan throat singing for at least the first three hours."

"Wait, I saw those dice, you threw a seven."

"Yup, that's what I wanted most. If it's good enough for Richard Feynman, it's good enough for me."

"Jesus, what was twelve?"

"Tony Orlando . . . *without* Dawn."

"Your god is kind."

By the time a ten had them listening to classic Nirvana, the pink hippo and peace signs were in place. This was a pretty nice tattoo. BJ was respectful of the deadline. It was too short a time, and it should have been several sessions, weeks apart, but she had altered the design to accommodate it. It wasn't solid color, there was a lot of Bobby's flesh still showing. He needed that last bit of ink to go on at 11:11 p.m. and she sped up and slowed down, adjusting to make that work. Tattoo artists understand ritual. She flipped off her work lamp right when Bobby's alarm quacked.

It took almost an hour to get it all cleaned up, get the cellophane wrap on, and get all his lotion instructions. He was very happy and tipped everyone more than promised. He rolled a Railroad Nine and asked BJ on a date—supper and a helicopter ride over Vegas.

She didn't have to roll any dice. She said no.

11

HIS FAMILY WAS SAVED AND PROVIDED FOR. HIS DEBTS were paid. He had his tattoo. Now it was time to fuck. He had never paid for sex before and it was about fucking time. He had money. He had time. He had Random to take away all the fear and awkwardness. Random allowed him to admit that he might want different kinds of sex than he'd ever considered before. What did he really want and how much? He gave Random some nice choices. He'd start out with the number of paid sex partners for today. He let the Dice do just that. The most likely was seven but he rolled a five. Good. The next roll would tell him the breakdown. A six, seven, or eight would give him one of the sex workers being of transitioning gender. A two or a twelve would give him all cis guys to play with. He'd never had sex with a guy, but it crossed his mind, so why not? When he checked his heart for odds, he realized that his all-cis-women fantasy could be assigned a humble three. In pre-Random life cis women would have been the only choice, but with Random holding his hand and stroking his dick it turned out all cis women was only as desired as all cis men. Now he knew that. Random had woken his ass and served him blue oysters for breakfast. The other numbers would all be combos. He would open doors a crack and Random would have him run in and let that door slam shut behind him.

He didn't roll a nine or ten, so he didn't get fucked up the asshole this first night, but the four he rolled gave him a load of cum in his mouth, and the five gave him another load on his face while holding one huge breast in his right hand and a beautiful tiny one in his left. The passing daydreams of things he might do someday became things he would do right now. He hadn't ever before cum with the taste of cum and pussy in his mouth, but "someday" was always just a roll of the Dice away.

Elliot, Steven, Josie, Lexxi, and Sandy had never made more money than they made for twelve hours of sex work with Bobby. They had worked well together to satisfy him completely. It wasn't terrible for them. Bobby wasn't high or drunk. He was bad in neither attitude nor hygiene. None of them were afraid of being beaten or killed by him because they had safety in their numbers. Being a prostitute was never a great job, but the gig with Bobby was about as good as they could ever expect from a gig economy that was illegal. They had all been scared while doing their jobs. They had all heard boring coke rants, and had johns cry all night and declare real love. Bobby was better than all those tricks by a lot, but he was still a trick.

Bobby had cum enough for right now and they were still on the clock. Bobby rolled a nine, so they all had to sit naked as Bobby explained his Random life to them. In the nicest suite on Fremont Street, which isn't saying much, Bobby was standing in front of a picture window looking out at Mount Charleston. Using Josie's lipstick, the brightest red, Bobby outlined the mountain directly on the window. The mountain was a bell curve. Bobby wrote the seven on the window right at the peak of the mountain and the two and twelve on the opposite bottoms. He explained that the trick of Random was to look deep into yourself and really decide how much you wanted everything that crossed your mind right that second and assign a number to each desire.

Steven asked how often Bobby had to roll the Dice.

"It depends. It's only when I'm undecided. If I know what I want to do, I just do it. Like anyone. And like anyone, I can't do anything I want: I'm just not physically or emotionally able to do a lot of things, and some things are wrong, or I have to ask permission. Like right now I'm sure I want to cradle your balls again. I don't need to roll the Dice, but I do have to ask your permission."

"Go for it, Dice Boy," and Bobby did.

"When I have doubt about what I want to do next, I give the Dice choices that some part of me really wants and are all possible. I roll the Dice and all the doubt and indecision go away. I just have to lay out my options. Up to eleven choices is really easy, but if I ever have more, I can just add another roll of two Dice to get to twenty-four. I don't think that'll come up much. I'll often have fewer than eleven things, so I just break up the numbers differently. Even or Odd on the Dice is a coin toss, fifty/fifty."

Lexxi spoke up—"Nope, that isn't fifty/fifty because you can't get a one with two dice, and with two dice you *can* get a twelve, so there are six evens and only five odds."

"That's right, but the probability of the individual numbers is different, so it evens out. Our friends two and twelve are both even, but they are also the least likely. The odds start with better probability—the three is the same chances as two and twelve together, so it adds up to fifty/fifty. Think of it this way: whatever is on one die, the other die has three numbers that make that even and three that make it odd—fifty/fifty. But how often are you actually equally torn between two choices? Uneven distribution is going to be more useful."

Bobby wrote all the other numbers over the mountain with their probabilities. "I've already gotten a pretty good feel for the various combinations and I've been living Random life for less than twenty-four hours."

Steven again, "You roll and whatever it is—you do it?"

"Instantly without hesitation. I assign my choices. I roll. I act."

"What if you change your mind while it's rolling?"

"I don't know. I guess I'll see if that happens. I already know that while the Dice are rolling, I have the greatest feeling in the world. The Winnie-the-Pooh feeling. Pooh Bear felt that the best feeling in the world wasn't eating honey— that was the second-best feeling in the world. The best moment in the world was just before Pooh knew if he was going to get honey or not. Pooh didn't know what that better feeling was called. Well, Pooh, that mysterious feeling is the basis of all gambling. The wonderful moment right before winning or losing. Gambling takes the possibility of eating honey and drags it out while the Dice are rolling, the cards are being dealt, or the wheel is still in spin. You get to live both winning and losing fully in that delicious moment. You get to feel all of life's possibilities while the Dice tumble. But I don't need to play someone else's game. My life is my game. I always feel all the possibilities. Pooh didn't know what that was called. A. A. Milne didn't know what that was called. I do. It's called Random. Now, do I want to eat pussy or suck cock while I get sucked or fucked off?"

Bobby began scribbling the combinations in lipstick on the glass and they all watched in glorious Pooh Bear anticipation as he rolled the Dice.

12

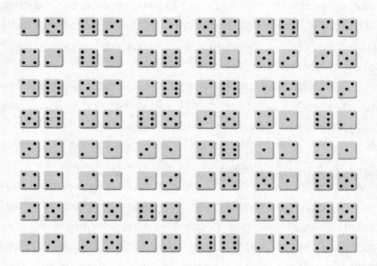

Put three and a half million dollars in the bank
at 4% interest and you can withdraw ten grand a month
forever. You can live like a regular guy in Vegas for about
fifty grand a year, so Bobby could live more than two times
as fancy as a regular guy on just the chump interest from the
money he had left over after saving everyone's life, paying his
debts, and banging a lot of prostitutes. But regular guys don't
live Random.

Even for regular guys the best way to invest money is at
Random. The stock market is bullshit. People who try to play
the stock market fairly with the same general knowledge that
everyone else has just make shit up to justify their successes
and failures. They see patterns where there aren't any and bet

on them. Sometimes they come out ahead in the short run and so they do it again with the same imagined scheme until that same non-Random nonexistent pattern bites them on their ass. Many people come out ahead, but many don't. Investing at Random is less volatile than considered investing. Random is more conservative than planning. What Random loses in one place, Random gains in another. Random doesn't make the same mistake once.

Bobby had the superpower of Random and he decided to see if he could get more money. He wasn't really greedy, exactly, it was more an experiment. How powerful was his god? Random did better than the Old Testament YHWH. During World War II, General Curtis LeMay found Random more useful than praying. The Germans were trying to figure out where Americans would bomb next based on where they had bombed before. LeMay decided to assign bombing lines at Random, and to do that, he would roll the Dice. If Random could help win a war maybe it could make Bobby even richer. Every week, Bobby rolled the Dice for his stock portfolio. It was kind of fun. Forty-four rolls of the Dice over a few months, and bingo, Bobby had ten times the money he'd need for the rest of his life—if his life were non-Random. For a Random life, no one knows. One roll on one night could have him happily giving all his assets to EffectiveAltruism.org. That would be the two or twelve option about once a month.

Random gave Bobby a shit ton of money. Random gave him money and focus, power, activities, and hobbies to use that money. He knew that eventually he'd use his powers for good. Like everyone, he'd always wanted to be a superhero. He wanted to be Batman. Wasn't Bruce Wayne just a wicked-rich guy who solved crimes? That's what Bobby wanted, he wanted to be Batman, but if he dressed in some sort of costume he'd just be another guy on Fremont Street posing for pictures. He needed some real-world way to help people that would be exciting. He needed to start his own DC, his own Detective Comics. Maybe he'd be more like the Equalizer. Maybe he needed to open a detective agency. Be a dick, a gumshoe.

He didn't want to do that yet. He'd help other people later—for the next couple months he'd let Random spend some of the money it made investing at Random. He took fencing lessons in Brazil, sucked a lot of dick on Capri, and bought *the* 1977 Cadillac Fleetwood Brougham with the chandeliers on the front from *Escape from New York*. He didn't have it long—three weeks later a Random six had him give the keys and pink slip to the guy in the Starbucks who looked a little like Snake Plissken from *Escape from New York*. In the movie the car belonged to the Duke, who was played by Isaac Hayes, but Bobby forgot that when he saw the Snake-looking guy. He told the skeptical but pleased accidental-half-assed-Snake-Plissken lookalike that it was an expensive car and "Snake" could flip it with just a little work. Bobby asked him to wear an eye patch when he sold it, but that was nonbinding. It was just a suggestion. Random bought Bobby the car and Random gave it away.

Terry Southern wrote a book called *The Magic Christian* about a very rich guy named "Guy" who uses his money for cynical pranks that make people aware that they'll do anything for money. It was made into a movie with Peter Sellers, Ringo Starr, Raquel Welch, and more than a hundred topless women rowing in the galley of a cruise ship five abreast to an oar. The book was comedy and satire, but Bobby read it as a road map to what he could become if he wasn't careful. He had given his life to Chance but he must be careful not to have fortune make him cruel. Was giving someone a goofy car

and asking him to wear an eye patch when he sold it whim-
sical or callous? Was there a condescension to it, some sort of
weird power trip? It was better to be Batman than just a rich
asshole. Bobby was thinking about that when his sister Carolina gave him a call. "The Doctor Is Calling" by Megadeth
played on Bobby's phone and he answered right away: "Hey,
Doc, how are you doing?"

Carolina screamed into the phone.

"You okay?"

Carolina answered quickly, "Very okay. Very," and went
right back to screaming.

"Good, I'll scream with you." Bobby began screaming into
the phone and after a while started talking again: "What are
we screaming about?"

"Harvard! AHHHHHH! Johns Hopkins! AHHH-
HHH! University of Pennsylvania! AHHHHHHH!"

"Which one did you get into?"

"Ask me which one I *didn't* get into."

"Which asshole school was stupid enough to not want my
Doc in their medical school?" Bobby screamed.

"None of them! Bobby, none! They all want Carolina Ingersoll in their premed schools. All of them! All of them! I
made it. You got that for me, bro, thanks, thanks, thanks!"

"Hey, I had nothing to do with you getting in, Doctor
Carolina Ingersoll, I'm not even paying for it. Chance is paying for it—I got lucky, you got skills. Now which one of these
institutes of higher learning gets even luckier and has you for
a student? Harvard, right?"

"Yeah? I don't think so."

"You've always said Harvard was the dream."

"It was the dream, but maybe Johns Hopkins will be the
reality."

"Whatever you want, Doc. Are you going to visit the campuses? Don't students do that?"

"Yeah, they do it, but what would I learn?"

"I don't know, but it's part of the ritual, right? Take Mom with you."

"Will you come with us, Bobby?"

"Sure. I can do that. Sure. I mean I'll try."

"Promise me, Bobby."

"I'm gonna try, but I can't promise."

"Why not?"

"I don't want to let you down. I live by Chance now, you know that. I don't know where I'll be, who I'll be, or what I'll be rolling then." Bobby didn't want to tell her that he might be Batman by then and wouldn't have time. "When is *then*?"

"Fall. Okay, no promises from Bobby. But when we're going, would you put me down for a seven?"

"I'll sure try, Doc, I'll sure try."

"Thanks. How are you doing, bro? You doing okay?"

"Yeah, I've been traveling around a lot. Doing weird shit. I'm doing a lot of weird shit that only a small part of me wants to do. Dice have been choosing some nutty parts of me. It's been great. How is Mom doing?"

"She's good, bro, we're both good. You saved our lives, Bobby, you should enjoy the lives you've saved. Give Mom a call."

"Yeah, I gotta do that."

"I love you, bro."

"Yeah, Doc, I love you too. Fuck Harvard! John Hopkins forever."

"Johns."

13

Fucking Hawaiian pizza. Smug cunt. Months had changed nothing. Ruphart still wanted Bobby dead. Wanted him deader than a hammer, except he wanted him to suffer. He wanted Bobby dead like a fully sentient hammer who didn't like being dead and could still feel pain. Ruphart killed people like it was going out of style, and according to Steven Pinker, it *is* going out of style. But everyone in town knew that Bobby had paid up his father's debt in full. Ingersoll was rich now and publicly eccentric. People knew about Bobby and would notice he was dead and know Ruphart killed him. Being known as a loan shark who killed people after they were flush would be bad for business. If Bobby got mugged or had a piano fall on him, or even committed suicide, it would smell of Ruphart. There had to be some way to get Bobby dead in a manner full of suffering that couldn't be traced back to Ruphart. He and Bobby would both still know in their hearts that Ruphart had made it happen, and as long as they both knew, that was enough. Oh, and he had to suffer a lot. Fucking Hawaiian pizza.

Ruphart had a fancy office. He killed people, scared people, sold drugs to people, gave people loans he knew wouldn't help them, and called himself a businessman. The office looked like that of an old-fashioned businessman. If this were a movie set for *Casino*, the only anachronism would be the hand sanitizer everywhere. Ruphart didn't like to touch other people or touch anything other people had touched. Ruphart had a beautiful, ornate wooden table with two chess sets side by side. Nothing else on the table, just two chess sets. One had the white pieces facing his favorite chair and one had the black pieces facing his chair. It wasn't just fear of germs on the chess pieces, although it was that too, it was that Ruphart liked to symbolically know what was his. He and his opponent would decide who went first in the traditional way with a pawn of unknown color in each hand and the other choosing, but both colors of pawn came from the same side of the table. If Ruphart ended up white, he would slide his chair to line up with the board that had white closest to him, and if the choice was black, he would move his chair the other way. His opponent would mirror him. When a piece was captured, it would be picked up by the person who had lost the piece and moved to the sidelines. In this way, Ruphart never touched a chess piece that someone else had touched. Hyperhygienic, but more importantly it allowed him to keep his disgust for the alien pieces pure.

Ruphart never wanted to win a game by taking advantage of an opponent's stupid move. He didn't want to win faster than he had planned. He wanted to win by cunning, not by opportunity. Ruphart would find a way to make it look like Bobby killed himself with stupid before Bobby really killed himself with stupid. Ticktock.

14

ASA EARL CARTER WAS A WHITE SUPREMACIST, MEMBER of the Klan, and speechwriter for George Wallace (the segregationist governor George Wallace, not the African American comedian George Wallace, who Bobby's truck had pulled the *I Be Thinkin'* advertising signs for). Asa wrote some nasty shit and led the KKK in their usual immoral nasty shit with perhaps some added atrocities under his direction. After years in the Alabama segregation movement, Asa Earl Carter moved to Abilene, Texas, changed his name to Forrest Carter, claimed to be Cherokee, and wrote *The Rebel Outlaw: Josey Wales,* which became a Clint Eastwood movie, and *The Education of Little Tree,* which he sold as his Cherokee autobiography. Asa and Forrest were the same piece of shit, no doubt about it. He couldn't change that, but surface changes were fast, *Plucked her eyebrows on the way, shaved her legs and then he was a she. She said, "Hey babe, take a walk on the wild side."* Whether Asa shaved his legs or not is not recorded, but he put on a cowboy hat (aren't cowboys the natural enemy of Native Americans?), grew a mustache, put on a bolo tie, and took a walk on his own make-believe wild Cherokee side.

When it was proven that Little Tree, the Native American, and Asa Earl, the racist, were the same guy, all hell broke loose. Oprah took his book off her bookshelf and the *New York Times* had a fit and fell in it. There were some outraged

Cherokees because he made up stupid shit about their culture. The general view of Asa was that he was a scumbag and that view is correct, but Random made Bobby see him a little differently.

Bobby decided to be someone else. He'd grown a little weary of the Dice telling him what to do. He didn't want more freedom, he wanted less. He didn't want to be told just what to do, he wanted the Dice to tell him who to be. Bobby contained multitudes and became fascinated by the idea that he could roll the Dice and be any one of them. He could be a different person. He didn't want to lie and claim an ancestry that wasn't his. He couldn't change the past, but he could change the present and the future, at least until the next roll of the Dice. He drew up his list. They all had to be parts of him he wanted to express. He wouldn't put "racist" as a choice, and he couldn't put "Cherokee." This was his first time trying something global, and he was a little sloppier. He didn't really know how long he'd go with the choice. He also wasn't sure if each of the new Bobbys would be living Random. He hadn't thought it out, but he rolled.

Two (2.78%)—Conservative American / Fox News
Three (5.56%)—Trans woman
Four (8.33%)—Hippie
Five (11.11%)—Metal Head
Six (13.89%)—Silent / one full month without speaking
    (whoever that would make me)
Seven (16.67%)—Buddhist
Eight (13.89%)—Stereotypical gay man
Nine (11.11%)—Beatnik
Ten (8.33%)—Liberal American / MSNBC
Eleven (5.56%)—Alcoholic

Twelve (2.78%)—Christian (real Christian, try hard to believe, and fake it until I make it)

Snake Eyes. Bobby saw the two pips and changed instantly. He just felt different. MAGA and shit. It felt good to finally have his guy in the White House. It felt good to not feel guilty for his luck and his privilege. This was easier than he thought. The Fremont Street Experience was two miles away, so he rented a big gas-guzzling pickup truck to drive there and had it delivered to his house. He watched Fox News while waiting. He let the Fox really speak to him and for him. He didn't bristle at what the hosts said. Not at all. He found a way to make everything they said true for him. Daniel Kahneman, the fancy-assed but still goofy Nobel laureate, had been quoted as saying, "When someone says something, don't ask yourself if it is true. Ask what it might be true of." That's a dangerous mind game and Bobby was playing it all the way with Fox. There were lots of ways to make this shit true, and after that last roll, he was using them all. You know, these Fox guys made a lot of sense.

He signed the paperwork on the truck, got in, tuned it to a country station, and turned up Luke Combs singing "Beautiful Crazy." Bobby drove through the nearest Dunkin' Donuts. He ordered a sausage, egg, and cheese sandwich on a croissant, double order of hash browns, a chocolate doughnut, a raspberry-glazed jelly doughnut, and a gigantic coffee served "regular," which meant half of it was cream and sugar. For the past couple of months the Dice had him eating strict WFPB, Whole Food Plant Based. All his intestinal guest critters who lived on animal grease and processed food had been dying away. Now the few carnivorous cooties starving in his guts were going to get a treat. As he washed the Dunks down with sweet, fat speed, the greasy belly bugs would multiply and start sending signals to his brain that a cheeseburger was required for supper. The Dunks breakfast made him feel groggy, sluggish, and like grease was oozing out of his pores. On the other side of the tug-of-war the twenty-four-ounce coffee, even with some of the room taken up with fat and sugar, still gave him 517 milligrams of caffeine, the equivalent of six and a half Red Bulls, to speed up his cheese-clogged sausage ass. Bobby was sluggish and speeding through *the republic for Richard Stands*. He got to the Fremont Street Experience and self-parked his truck. He walked down Fremont and bought a black T-shirt that read, *I stand for the flag and kneel for the cross*. He complemented his outfit with a trucker hat featuring an angry-looking eagle and American flag caught in midwave.

It's amazing what speed, grease, country, and Fox can do. Bobby really felt different. He was walking different. We are what we eat . . . or at the very least we are 517 milligrams of caffeine. He wanted to go somewhere patriotic. He wanted to feel more American, but you can't get more American than Vegas. Commie countries run Vegas B-roll for their anti-American propaganda. You gotta have that pan shot of desperate big bellies bellied up to slot machines sipping caffeine, alcohol, or both, and returning the quart-sized cup to the slot machine's built-in cup holder. Vegas was America. But Bobby wanted to see some cleaner America. Maybe a road trip across the country in his rented pickup listening to just two kinds of music, country and western. To DC to see the Washington Monument like a big cock. It seemed this American was still living Random. He rolled an Easy Four, and that meant Rushmore. He'd never seen it, and maybe they'd have a petition to add Trump's face to that big old rock that he could sign.

He drove back home and threw a few things into a bag and did some typing to find the next flight to Rapid City. He got to the airport and was able to buy a big-ass belt buckle after he got through TSA. He took his seat in first class, still speeding his brains out for the Dunks XL coffee. He laid a Coke on top of that, skipped the banana he was offered, and went for the Oreos.

The plane took off and Bobby began rolling Dice for stupid shit to kill time. Should he watch a movie on his iPhone? He was in the mood for *The Cannonball Run*. He could read some Bill O'Reilly, or maybe just gag himself with his fingers to try out the air sickness bag. Random was keeping things pretty normal—he was listening to country music and dunking his Oreos in his Coke.

Bobby had the aisle, and in the window seat sat Melvin Bern. Melvin was a stranger and Bobby hardly noticed him. Melvin looked like a rube, but the look was cultivated. No one could look that perfectly nothing without working on it. Melvin was a little tall, but normal tall, about six two. He was thin, but normal thin. He had a mustache, not a porn mustache or an ironic mustache, just a mustache. Melvin's sandy hair was worn in that weird floppy Beatles mop top that men over fifty who haven't lost their hair use to display their lack of testosterone. He was wearing a button-up shirt, slacks, and a sport coat that no one could remember on a bet. There were big bets on Melvin not being remembered. In Melvin's main job it was useful to be invisible. For years he was naturally forgettable, but that got a little fucked up by brain surgery. Even though Melvin hid it pretty well, the right side of his face drooped a bit. He was drinking hot airline tea through the metal straw that he carried with him. If Melvin tried to drink his tea like a non–brain damaged person, he'd drool it all over himself like a worse brain-damaged person.

Melvin was a frequent flier and when he sat next to people on a plane, the first thing he had to figure out was if he wanted to talk to them. Were they headed home or headed out? Monday fliers were headed out. Friday fliers were headed home. But leaving Vegas, if they were flying alone, they had been working in Vegas (or telling their spouse they were working in Vegas). Probably some sort of convention. First he'd ask what kind of work they had been doing in Vegas, and he'd ask them regardless of age. If they were retired, he might still want to know what they had done. They might be interesting; they might teach him something. The second question was always about their favorite place to eat in Vegas. Melvin already knew every restaurant in every city, but there's a lot of information in someone's response to that question. If someone is sitting in first class and eating at Denny's or Burger King, that's someone Melvin would want to talk to. With those two questions, Melvin knew if wanted to socialize or just sleep and read.

If anyone tried to be polite and ask him what he did for a living when he felt like sleeping, he'd say, "I am in the insurance business and am going out to take a look at some risk," which was true. It was true in the same way that telling your wife you weren't seeing another woman was true when you were blowing a different guy every night of the week. Not true at all.

Melvin wasn't following any of his rules of engagement with Bobby. He noticed the hat and T-shirt and belt buckle, of course, but Melvin also noticed they were all brand new. That wasn't right. Many things weren't right. This guy was faking. Melvin peripherally watched Bobby rolling the Dice on the tray table every few minutes. Melvin waited for a break in Bobby's focus, chose his words carefully but spoke them casually: "Mechanic? Tat? Agent? Sliding? Controlled shooting? What's your work?"

Bobby was the son of a Vegas asshole. He recognized all the dice-cheating terms. He didn't care about any of them except the last one. "Controlled shooting" referred to practicing rolling dice until you did it the same way every time, so in theory, and just barely often enough in practice, you could eliminate some of the chance and make a couple/two/three dollars.

Bobby was emphatic: "Oh no no no, sir, no controlled shooting ever. I would never do anything to eliminate Chance." Bobby was surprised to hear that he now had a slight Southern accent.

"Well, you're not riding in first class playing on the square."

Bobby looked Melvin in the eye and paused while he set his odds.

Two (2.78%)—Make beeping sounds like a robot or Martian.
Three (5.56%)—"Deep state, deep state!"
Four (8.33%)—QAnon.
Five (11.11%)—Talk about Sean Hannity.
Six (13.89%)—Tell the truth.
Seven (16.67%)—Talk about Laura Ingraham.
Eight (13.89%)—Tell the truth.
Nine (11.11%)—Talk about Tucker Carlson.
Ten (8.33%)—QAnon.
Eleven (5.56%)—"9/11 was an inside job, fell faster than gravity."
Twelve (2.78%)—Pretend to not speak English.

Sixie from Dixie. Bobby laid out his superhero origin story

in detail. He was Bobby again. His Fox guy had lasted under three hours. Clearly the Dice thought Melvin was worth it. The Dice, of course, were right.

Melvin wasn't living Random, but if he had been, he would not have had to roll the Dice on the next decision. There was no doubt what Melvin wanted to say and do next. Melvin wanted to show Bobby that he was worth knowing, so he went into the schtick he used on people he wanted to do business with, fuck, or get to know: "I have the strangest job in the world. In your entire life you have never met anyone that does what I do, as I am the only man in the world that does it. It will sound flippant, but I fly around the world and try to give money away. The smallest prize I have ever given away is forty-two cents and the largest is a billion dollars. That's billion with a B." He didn't want Bobby to think he was just in the insurance business. Melvin told his own origin story honestly too, in hopes that he and Bobby would become good friends.

Melvin was a lot of things. Melvin was a brain cancer survivor, but that was just the past five years, and who cares? Lots of people survive cancer. Melvin was ex-police. Melvin was one of the top-ranked bridge players in the world. Melvin was a working magician. Melvin was a motivational speaker (only since he could work the brain cancer angle). Melvin was an expert on all kinds of cheating. Melvin was a statistician. Melvin was crazier than a shithouse rat. All this added up to Melvin's very interesting job being about as far away from the boring insurance business as one could get.

Around thirty years earlier, he and his crazy crazy-rich friend had invented a business. A police-magician-statistician-card-player-cheat-normal-looking-guy business that you could do after cancer and while speaking motivationally.

Melvin and his partner underwrote promotional proposition bets. When a car dealer wanted to do a promotion and give away a brand-new car to someone who picked the right set of keys, Melvin's company would pay the wholesale price for the car, if the punter won. If a promoter wanted to give a lot of money to someone who made a free throw during halftime of a basketball game, but the promoter didn't want to risk that much money, for a price Melvin's company would underwrite it. Their business was just with things that might not be won. If the game were set up so that someone was definitely going to win, like a lottery, then that money had to really be there—it was spent, there was no gamble. But if the chances were heavy that no one was ever going to win, the promoter could go to Melvin and his rich guy to cover the unlikely but possible win. Melvin would figure out the odds of a punter winning the purse, and he'd decide how much it would cost to insure for that. Figure the odds as best he could and then add in their cut. Even casinos used the service. They sure had the money to cover the bet, but the bookkeeping was so hard: the guy pitching the idea would have to say, *It probably won't cost us anything, but it might cost us ten million.* No serious gambling business wants to do serious gambling. Melvin figured everything. If the win was really unlikely, you might could get ten-million insurance for ten grand. No gambling for the business, Melvin and his boss took all the heat. Win or lose, it cost the promoter ten grand. If no one won, Melvin's company kept the ten grand, and if a win did happen, Melvin and his company paid the ten million. It was a tough gig. The arithmetic was hard, it had to be right, and there were always some things Melvin couldn't know. Melvin had to figure prose and poetry. He had to really gamble.

On top of all that random chance going against him,

everyone was trying to cheat Melvin's company. Everybody. The punters wanted to win, and some would cheat to do that. The enterprise really wanted the huge press hit of giving away all that money with their name attached, so even if the businesses didn't actively cheat, they might at least look the other way. They had no reason to be careful. So, Melvin was there, invisible, to make sure it was all played straight. Melvin's company wanted to lose a few times a year—that's how people heard about them. That was their only advertising. But their big loses had to be rare. It was a high-pressure business and Melvin loved it.

By the time they landed in Rapid City, Melvin and Bobby were friends. Bobby didn't have to throw the Dice to decide to blow off Mount Rushmore and tag along on Melvin's gig, since Bobby wanted to see him work. They shared Melvin's nondescript rental car to the job.

Pretty Penny's Casino near Mount Rushmore wanted to get on the gambling map. They were giving five people a chance to win ten million dollars each. All they had to do was get cold dealt a royal flush in hearts from a single deck. Not much of a chance in hell of that happening. What would it cost them to insure that, a nickel?

Bobby's hat, T-shirt, and belt were perfect here. He could fit in as he watched Melvin work. Melvin quietly introduced himself to the VP in charge of the promotion. Bobby couldn't hear the conversation, but the guy was probably named Dave. Melvin explained to Dave that Melvin would unobtrusively watch things and maybe make a few little changes. There was a big rotating mesh drum containing all the names of the valued players (losers). There was a local deejay named Tommy building the excitement. There was a kinda pretty young woman with a sash that read *Miss South Dakota*. Tommy explained that Miss South Dakota was ready to reach in and pull out the five winners (losers) who would be given a seat at the table for a chance to be dealt a royal flush and win TEN MILLION DOLLARS!!!!!

Melvin ate a hot dog with mustard and kraut and chatted with Bobby while never taking his eyes off the drum full of names. There were a couple of cocktail servers in old-fashioned showgirl costumes behind Miss South Dakota. Melvin walked over and whispered to Dave. Dave shrugged to Melvin and called over DJ Tommy, who announced over the mic, "Just to mix things up a bit, we're going to have one of Pretty Penny's Pretties pull out our five contest winners at random." Miss South Dakota and the cocktail server were a little confused, but they kept smiling as they changed places. Melvin took a bite of his hot dog, making sure there was no mustard on the drooping side of his face, and continued explaining to Bobby how much he had to make up shit as he went along. Chaos made it harder to cheat. Good old chaos.

The five names were drawn out of the drum, and those five lucky losers threw their fists in the air and cheered and the whole crowd headed over to the table. Melvin finished his hot dog and whispered to Dave while Melvin reached into the drum and pulled out about twenty slips of paper with contestants' names on them. As Bobby and Melvin walked over to the card table, Melvin riffled through to check the slips for duplicate names. He didn't see any, so that was jake. He threw the slips in the trash. Those people would have just a slightly worse chance of winning the next contest.

Melvin had the VP switch the deck for a duplicate Pretty Penny's Casino deck that he'd brought with him. It was out of the box of stuff that they were contractually obligated to send him. Melvin had opened the deck and shuffled it himself. Melvin handed it to Dave and insisted that Dave check Melvin's dupe deck thoroughly to make sure it was a fair deck. He had to make sure the royal flush was in there. Melvin wasn't cheating and couldn't afford to have anyone think he was. The dealer looked over the cards and gave Melvin's deck a table wash and a few more shuffles. Good. With a deck that Melvin knew was legit and five "winners" who were really picked from a drum by chance—Melvin barely watched the play. He knew how likely they were to win. After the excitement and disappointment were over, Melvin went to the VP, shook hands, and said it was a pleasure doing business.

Melvin's attention was back on Bobby. "What do you want to do now?"

"What are my choices?" Bobby had his Dice ready.

"You can get a room and check in and we can meet at Founder's Steakhouse for surf and turf and then maybe go to the Granite Bar and check out the local talent."

"Yes. I don't need to roll for that. We'll just do that. I gotta hear more stories."

"Then tomorrow I have to get back to Texas to check out a lottery winner."

"You can't underwrite the lottery. That can't be in your business model."

"Right. But because I was on the job and police there like me, and they know what I do, they bring me in on really big wins for my nose. See if I can smell any scams. I do it just for shits and giggles. It's interesting to be near lives that are about to be changed that profoundly."

"Can I go? My last roll was just to fly to the airport near Mount Rushmore and roll again here. I don't actually have to go to Mount Rushmore. I'm free to go with you."

"This is real government and police shit. You're a nut. I can't bring a nut with me. It'll hurt my rep. I need to be invisible."

"I can be invisible with you."

"With that belt buckle and shirt? The hat is okay, and what if you roll a fucking two and start quacking or trying to blow a rookie? You do that, I'm fucked. I love you living Random, but I can't have it on my dime."

"Hey, listen, you know my disease, I only roll when I'm not sure. I will be sure of everything on this adventure with you. I will have no doubt. Can I go with you, please? I need to feel this. I really do. It's important."

"Here's the deal. I won't accept a promise from you, I'll only accept it from the Dice. You lay out your odds and roll. And one of the choices is you're my employee for the next forty-eight hours and you do what I say. I know if you roll it, I can trust you. Give the edge to going with me but have some other choices in there too. You need the Dice to tell you."

Bobby started thinking.

"And I need to see all your choices. I can't have one of the choices be, *Tell Melvin you're working for him, but . . .*"

Bobby picked up a keno slip and a crayon and wrote:

Two and twelve—go on a silent retreat for the next week. Three and ten—rent a car, go see Mount Rushmore since I'm here, and then drive the sixteen hours back to Vegas right after. All the other numbers, including lucky eleven—work for Melvin for the next couple of days.

Melvin looked at the paper and nodded. "Roll 'em where I can see 'em."

Five!

"But I'm still going to roll for surf and turf or steak Sinatra."

"Nope, I'll decide what you eat tonight. You're working for me; you don't roll for another forty-eight hours."

15

THEIR FLIGHT TO AUSTIN WAS TWO FIFTEEN IN THE afternoon, so Bobby had time to pick up some new clothes for Melvin's invisible dress code, with no words or logos printed on anything. Words are remembered. He shaved, got a haircut, and long sleeves covered his tats except for his palm, and who looked at palms? Tats are remembered. When Bobby met Melvin at the Uber pickup, he was getting close to invisible. The half of Melvin's face that worked gave Bobby such a huge grin that the drooping side of his face had to join in. Melvin had Bobby by the cubes. The Dice commanded Bobby to work for Melvin and this could be fun. It was a long flight to Texas, but they didn't care, they were dressed alike and babbling to each other like middle-school BFFs.

They landed and Bobby got settled into the Steve Austin Intercontinental. Melvin told Bobby to get some dress-up invisible clothes because that night they were going to Republic for supper.

"Wait, I read about that place. It's impossible to get into."

"Not for me. When I find a restaurant I love, I make sure I can always get in."

"Okay. What's the scam?"

"I used to work for tips doing close-up magic, so I tip well, but everyone does that. When any server does a good job, I take a moment and write a complimentary snail-mail letter about them to the owner. That server will never forget me."

"A server loving you doesn't get you a table."

"Nope. But bet your ass I get good service. Most restaurants have their daily meetings between three thirty and four every afternoon. Restaurant staffs all appreciate good food, so I show up every few months with a mess of ribs from the best barbecue joint around. They don't sell barbecue at Republic so it's a nice change for them. I make sure I tell Red at Red's BBQ why I'm buying so many of his ribs, so he loves me too—I get to cut the barbecue line. It doesn't take much time, money, or effort for me to fucking own every city I visit. Most people don't think and don't bother. I think and bother. Yeah, we're going to Republic and we'll be treated well."

They were treated very well. Melvin knew how to live. He dropped off a sated Bobby at the hotel with explicit directions for the next morning.

Bright and early, Bobby got Melvin his cheap black coffee (a taste from his police days) and a glazed, raspberry-filled jelly doughnut (which Melvin claimed, without evidence, was Elvis's favorite) and added a small hot chocolate and a cruller for himself. Bobby hadn't rolled the Dice since South Dakota, and that was like not checking one's phone at regular intervals, but he was keeping his word to the Dice. It was the first time a Random project had lasted a couple of days. It was good for him. The Dice had led him to Melvin and Melvin had control for the next couple days; he could bend over and let Melvin drive.

Melvin pulled up but had to roll down the window and call to Bobby. Melvin's car in the daytime was the same forgettable color as Melvin's sport coat, with no vanity plates. Melvin pulled out his silver metal straw and handed it to Bobby to put in the coffee as he unwrapped the doughnut.

"Next time let me get the doughnut myself, I taught the dishwasher a coin trick and he keeps his eye out for ones that are freshest and a bit more bloated with jelly."

They arrived at the downtown state police station pretty quickly and Melvin pulled into a prime spot labeled with someone else's name. They didn't wait in line for the metal detectors—Melvin had fixed that. How do you fix that? He called all the police by name and often asked a family question or threw in a joke. Melvin wasn't invisible to the police; he was a sibling. He introduced everyone there to "my associate Bobby, he's learning the ropes."

Melvin took Bobby aside. "Okay, this is your chance to blend. Here's your challenge: if anything interesting happens today with someone claiming to have won $352,420,332.41—if a story comes out of today for anyone in the room—I don't want that story to include you. You walk in the room and count all the people you see and that is the number of people who are part of anyone's story, do you understand? Under oath these peace officers who have all been trained in observation will not recall you being here. Disappear. Got it?"

"Yes sir."

"You need to throw another roll or something to feel good about this?"

"No sir, I'm in the forty-eight."

"Let's go."

They walked directly into the small viewing room behind the Mirropane E.P. Transparent Mirror. It's called a "two-way mirror," "one-way mirror," "one-way glass," and "two-way glass," and they all mean the same thing. They all mean something that looks like a mirror on one side and you can see through from the other. For it to work, the room on the mirror side has to be well lit and the room on the observing side has to be darker. It's a magic principle called the "half-silvered mirror." A half-silvered mirror is the one tool shared by police, magicians, and quantum physicists. The thing has a lot of names. TV and movies got good at realism on their set designs so there were no surprises for Bobby. It looked like a police show.

"They keep building these Mirropane rooms, even though these rooms all have video, good video. We could be watching on the other side of the building or even at home. The video looks better than live through the glass, but this is where they want us." Now Melvin's mustache looked like a police mustache and he was sounding like the police guy in the TV show who plays by his own rules.

All the people were introduced around. Officer Stowe was a young uniform in his late twenties, friendly and pleasant looking. Stowe was the only officer the claimant would ever see; he would be in the interrogation room and the rest would be behind the multinamed one- or two-way mirror glass. Peter was forensics, a chemistry-professor type. He'd be running all the tests on the ticket to see if it had been tampered with. Detectives Kenny Gorodetsky and Valerie Parks were the case officers. This claim was their responsibility. Everyone knew Melvin and that was the only reason he was there. He had no official capacity or power. They wanted him there because Melvin had watched a lot of people cheat. He had a nose. Melvin introduced Bobby in a way that no one would remember.

Melvin wanted to see where they were so far. "You got three hundred and fifty million and change exposed. Your live one, how does he smell?"

Kenny answered, "She. It's a she. And she smells like gym socks dipped in . . . you know, smelly cheese or something."

It seemed Valerie and Kenny hadn't talked much about this before, because she had a question too: "Did you do a face-to-face?"

"Nope, just a phone call. Guilty as sin. The poor woman."

Melvin spoke up again, "Well, thanks for inviting me, I eat this shit for breakfast."

The uniform got a text notification and glanced down quickly. "She's here."

Parks instructed Stowe to go to security and bring the claimant up to the interrogation room, and the rest of them caught up a bit. Melvin told a few jokes—not too funny, not too out there. Just clean, inoffensive humor, nothing worth anyone remembering.

Stowe ushered the winner, Joanne, into the interrogation room. In her midtwenties, very attractive and aware of it. It was easy to tell she wasn't wealthy but had gotten dressed up for this life-changing event. It was also clear she wasn't wealthy because she had a lottery ticket. Only poor people buy lottery tickets. It's a regressive tax. Joanne was all smiles and laughs, giggling, nervous. Her winning lottery ticket was in a baggie dangling in her hands.

"Woo hoo. Is this where I get my check? You give me the check in this dull little room? I thought there would be TV and the governor dude here to give it to me. Isn't it a big check? Like a *really* big check that I pose with."

"All that comes later. This is the paperwork part."

"Okay, and then the check part, right? I'm going to buy you some art to put on these walls. Real art. Real paintings." Oh, she was so guilty. This was going to be terrible.

"Yeah, it's a bit dull here. Now, this is very important. First you need to give permission to be recorded."

"No. You can't record me without my permission."

"Right. So now I'm asking your permission. If you want the money, we have to record you."

"Good, then knock yourself out. Where is the camera?"

"There are a bunch. See that one up there? Please look at that camera and say your name and that you give permission to be recorded for the entire time you're in the building."

"Sure. Um, I'm Joanne Haussmann and I give permission on this day to be recorded as I win a buttload of money."

"You understand that there are video cameras all over this room and you're also being recorded by all of them. Everything is being recorded and can and will be used against you if you make any false statements. Do you understand that? These recordings can be used in court. You are being recorded now and you will be recorded the entire time you are in the building. Do you understand that?" Stowe made sure one of the cameras could see his face and spoke clearly and pleasantly.

"Yeah, but this isn't the TV part, right? This is just regular cameras?"

"Well, they're police cameras. This is serious. What you say here is just like you're saying it in court. It can be played in court. And there are witnesses behind that mirror there. And there will be papers to sign. We're talking about a lot of money."

"Woo hoo, we sure are, it's over four hundred million dollars!"

"No, but it's close to that amount. It's a lot of money."

Bobby watched everyone on his side of the glass shaking their heads sadly.

Melvin looked heartbroken. "Oh man, even through the glass she stinks."

Bobby spoke quietly: "I don't understand. These are the kind of people who play the lottery, right? They all look like and act like her. So these are the kind of people who win the lottery. People like me. She's just excited."

Melvin fixed Bobby with a look that made him gasp. Bobby had asked a question that could make him part of someone's story. Probably best to shut the fuck up.

Gorodetsky heard Bobby and answered, "He's not talking about her style, class, and education. You can smell her in the eyes. She's dirty. So dirty."

Meanwhile, back on the well-lit side of the room, Officer Stowe pulled out a really thick contract and placed it in front of Joanne. "You're going to have to sign this before we can process your winnings."

"Is this the check?"

"No, it's the legal papers that swear that you bought the lottery ticket yourself, that it has been in your possession the whole time, and that you haven't tampered with it."

"I don't want to sign that."

A lot of nodding in agreement behind the glass.

"Okay. Then we're done."

"I just want the money."

"Well, you can't get the money without signing the papers."

"Okay, I'll sign."

On the other side of the glass, four heads were buried into eight hands.

"But you want to sign only if that's all true. And you need to read it all first."

"Let me just sign, get my money, and get the fuck out of here. I don't need to wait for the TV and the governor."

"You really need to read it and make sure it's all true. If you sign it and it's not true, I can almost guarantee you'll go to prison. I've warned you that there are cameras and witnesses. You want to think hard about this."

"I've thought hard about the four hundred million dollars."

"Yeah. I'm going to leave you here to read this and I'll be back in a few minutes. Take your time. Read it all."

Once Stowe left the room to join the others behind the glass, Joanne didn't even bother looking at the papers. She went to the mirror, where she had to have figured people were watching, and adjusted her hair and breasts before sitting back down. With nothing in the room to do but read the legal papers, she sat motionless, not reading. Clearly Joanne was not the kind of person who reads the cereal box at breakfast in the morning.

From the dark room, they all watched her. Lots of people doing nothing.

Gorodetsky decided: "Well, we'll give her another fifteen minutes so she's had the time to read it. That's all we can do. We all know she's dirty, even little Mr. Don't-all-lottery-winners-look-like-this?"

Bobby could feel Melvin's disgust. Bobby was part of someone's story.

Parks put in: "Listen, Stowe, give the kid a break. Go in and don't let her sign. Knock her off it. We don't want Joanne going to jail for being stupid."

Officer Stowe headed back into the room with a big smile. "Hey, Joanne, you seem like a really nice person—"

She cut him off: "You don't have to suck up to me, I'm going to give you some of the money anyway, just for being so cute and I like your tattoo." He was cute, but his tattoo wasn't that attractive. Some Celtic mandala thing peaking a little out of his sleeve.

"Thanks, but I'm not allowed to accept any gifts, of course."

"Okay, not money gifts, but I can give you a little kiss."

"I'm not sure you should, but first let's confirm that you

actually bought the lottery ticket yourself and it's been in your possession the whole time and you haven't tampered with it."

"Sure, and if I say all that I get the money, right?"

"You have to say all that *and* it has to be true. That's what those papers say. If it's not true, if any of it is even a little tiny-white-lie bit not true, you'll go to jail. Right now, you haven't broken any laws, but signing those papers, if it's not true, would break a lot of laws. You can walk out of here right now a free woman and kiss whomever you want, including me, or you can sign those papers and, if it's not true, limit your choices of who you get to kiss by a lot and for a long time. You'd be in jail, real prison, for maybe four years. And that's if you're lucky. You're not going to enjoy jail, I'm sure of that, so you shouldn't sign these papers."

"Is there a way to get the money without signing the papers?"

"No."

"Then I'm signing!"

"But if it's not true, you won't get the money and you will go to jail. Whereas if you don't sign, you don't get the money but you also don't go to jail."

"I'm signing."

Joanne grabbed the pen out of Stowe's hand and flipped to the last page, but Stowe pulled the pen right out of her hand and tried again: "Please don't sign. Listen, just walk away and think about this overnight. Talk to some friends. The money will still be here tomorrow. There's no rush, it's not a gym membership."

"Give me the fucking pen!"

Stowe held the pen out of reach for a second, but really had no choice. He gave it to her and watched her sign on every dotted line. Fuck.

"You have to date it too."

"What's the date?"

"December 8. And the year, 2019."

"Woo hoo! I'm rich."

"You can still back out. You haven't sworn yet."

"I sure as fuck have!"

"You haven't sworn in front of the State of Texas that all you've signed is true. Are you sure you want me to swear you in? Please think about this."

"Fuck yeah!"

Parks shook her head as Stowe signed the witness line. "Oh dear."

Gorodetsky held out some hope: "We have to see the ticket. There's a chance it's real."

Parks laughed in his face. "How old are you?"

Stowe came in carrying the baggie with the ticket in it for verification from forensics, and Bobby did his best to peek at it without becoming part of any story. First, Melvin glanced at the front of the ticket and grimly shook his head. Next, Parks took the bag, peered through the plastic, and sighed sadly. All the while, Gorodetsky kept amending an affidavit to keep the chain of evidence perfect, while Stowe shot video of the tickets moving from hand to hand. After Gorodetsky signed a tag on the extra police baggie, he handed everything to the forensic chemist, who looked at the ticket through the baggie and laughed. "Do I really have to test this in under a scope? I can see the forgery in this light through a dirty baggie."

"Run all the tests, Pete."

Gorodetsky had the others sign the chain-of-evidence affidavit and then he, Stowe, the video camera, and the baggie all followed the chemist to the tiny lab, which was just a microscope attachment to a computer and a few bottles of various solvents.

Neither Bobby nor Melvin signed anything. Bobby whispered to Melvin, "Is there any chance it's real?"

"Negatory."

They all waited patiently, watching Joanne fix her makeup and breasts again in the mirror, as the chemist ran the tests, filled out the necessary forms, took the required photographs, and finally shot a video swearing that the ticket has been tampered with.

Pete came back in, looked through the mirror at Joanne still grinning, then at the somber faces of the others. "The numbers were changed with a Sharpie. Five of them. Just written over with a Sharpie. How did this get so far? This was a waste of our time."

"Yeah, and a waste of years of her life. Years. Pretty much a waste of her whole life. She won't come out the same. Did she think she would get away with that forging?" It was Parks talking, but it was everyone's question. They were all perplexed. They watched as Stowe headed back to the interrogation room.

Then Melvin got it: "She didn't do any forging."

A moment later they heard Joanne screaming from the other room, "Fucking Terri, that fucking cunt! Arrest fucking Terri. Cunt. Bitch. I'm innocent. Arrest her. She changed the ticket. I didn't do anything. Nothing. Here's her number. Trace where she is and go arrest her. Fucking cunt!" Joanne pulled up the contact information for whoever Terri was on her phone, and threw it to Stowe.

Stowe silently copied the name and number into his notebook, and hung onto the phone. "I'm going to have to arrest you, Ms. Haussmann."

It took three more uniforms to get Joanne out of the room. Add assaulting a police officer to her charges.

Once Stowe had passed her into the other officers' hands, he came back into the darkened room. "Wow, she's really pissed at this Terri."

No one but Melvin understood what was going on. "May I give Terri a call? Just as a civilian. Just citizen Bern cold-calling?"

The police looked around the room and silently appointed Gorodetsky to shrug.

As Melvin took the number from Stowe, he gestured at the phone on the desk. "Hey, can I use the landline? I want the caller ID to show I'm at an Austin police station." Melvin knew the area code, recognized it as a Dallas number. He used speaker phone so everyone could hear and dialed the number.

Terri answered on three rings. "That fucking cunt. I knew Joey was a fucking cunt. Backstabbing bitch. She was going to fuck me out of my $350 million. Fucking bitch. I hope she goes to jail forever. Is she in jail yet?"

"Hello, Terri, my name is Melvin Bern. Joey is now being processed. She tried to collect on a forged lottery ticket."

"No shit."

"No shit. You forged the ticket?"

"Yes," Terri responded, and everyone in the room pantomimed their amazement at the simple confession.

Melvin glanced around, a big smile on his face.

Terri continued: "It was a test. She failed. Stupid backstabbing cunt. I'll be bringing in my real ticket next week to collect. Fucking bitch."

Now the room turned from exultation to confusion. They whispered incredulously among themselves. "Terri is going to try to pass off another bad forgery?"

Melvin shook his head, still smiling.

Terri laid it out: "So, a week ago, I win the lottery. I've got the winning ticket. I'm going to have 350 million and change. That's a big fucking deal. The biggest fucking deal. So, I sit down and have myself a fucking think."

"You sure did think."

"I wanted a plan."

"And you sure made a plan."

"I got a boyfriend in Houston, his name is Big Mike. And I got that cunt of a girlfriend you met. I keep them separated. I win the lottery and all my problems are over, right? Except which one I want to pick. I do not want both. One has to go. So, I buy a couple more lottery tickets, actually I buy about ten more until I get numbers that are kinda close, threes for eights and shit like that. The dates are wrong, but who cares, I fuck retards. I grab a Pentel and do a shitty job. I'm just trying to fool two idiot fuckbuddies. I give them each a phony-baloney winning ticket and tell each of them to hold onto it for me because I gotta get my head together and clean up some shit. I tell each of them to just hold onto the ticket for exactly two weeks and then we'll cash it in together. We'll get all that cash and we'll go together to Vegas and get married. We'll have picket fences for life. Picket fences covered in diamonds with stacks of cocaine on top. Wait, you aren't police, are you?"

"No, I'm not police."

"I was kidding about the cocaine."

"I know, and you don't really want a picket fence either."

"Fuck no."

"How is Big Mike doing?"

"I haven't heard a thing about him."

"I hope you'll be very happy together. When you're in Vegas, go see Mac King's magic show in the afternoon at Excalibur and eat at Lotus of Siam. Best Thai food in the country. I'm not kidding, write down Mac King and Lotus of Siam."

"Thanks, dude. Man, that fucking bitch!"

"Terri?"

"Yeah?"

"You are a genius. Bye bye."

"Thanks, bye. Joey, that fucking cunt."

Melvin hung up the phone.

Bobby couldn't manage to stay out of the story: "Aren't we going to arrest Terri?"

"We? We? Who made you *we*? *I'm* not even we. What are they going to arrest her for? Being crafty? You can write on your personal lottery ticket all you want. That's not a crime. It's your piece of paper, you bought it. She specifically told Joanne and Big Mike *not* to cash them in. There's no forgery, no fraud. You could try for conspiracy, but a good lawyer will take it on contingency and win. If she burns through the 350 million, she can write a relationship advice column. I like her. She's smart."

Bobby had to meet Terri.

16

IN THE CAR OUTSIDE THE POLICE STATION BOBBY WAS bursting. "Jesus fucking Christ! I mean amazing. People are crazy. How do people get that weird?"

"Pot/kettle. You live outside of the law a little yourself, Bobby, don't you think?"

"Yeah, but the Dice make me weird, I'm not really that weird on my own."

"Okay. Bobby, do you know how to read the newspaper?"

"What?"

"Every story you read, add the following: *and they were fucked up*. With that added to the story, very few mysteries remain. We have powerful drugs, Bobby, and they make people crazy. All those Florida-man stories are just because people drink and do drugs. Opioids, meth, even beer."

"They are Florida-man stories because Florida makes their police reports public, that's all."

"Yup, and everyone in the paper is fucked up on something or other."

"I started living Random totally sober. I'm always sober. I gave heroin a twelve a couple times. And mushrooms show up on two now and again, or acid, but it hasn't hit. I considered being an alcoholic once."

"Everyone else has the excuse of drugs, you have Random to drive you crazy. Look at the Terri lottery thing. Did you notice that Joanne was fucked up when she came in?"

"You said Terri was brilliant with her plan, she wasn't crazy, she wasn't high."

"No, I don't think she was high when she hatched the plan. But you bet your ass she was fucked up when she fucked Joanne, and does anyone fuck someone named Big Mike sober? Go to your UMC trauma center in Vegas. Talk to an ER doc there and ask them how many sober people they get in that unit? Barbecue fires, children with boiling water spilled all over their faces, broken necks from dives into shallow water, traffic accidents, gunfights, knife fights, fight fights—ask them how many patients come in sober, brought in by other sober people. Remember when Roy of Siegfried and Roy got his head bit off by a fucking tiger? That was the last time they had a sober guy in that ER. Roy wasn't high. Roy doesn't need high; Roy is *your* kind of crazy. That's the rare kind. Unless some food poisoning (probably started by a drunk guy) or a big nasty pandemic virus (probably spread faster by drunk and high people) comes along, the people they see in the ER are all fucked up. Unless they're children, in which case their parents are fucked up. If you assume drugs and alcohol, there are very few mysterious stories left—really, just you and Roy. Now, what crazy thing are you going to do next?"

"I got another few hours to go with you."

"Nope. I've got work to do."

"I can go with."

"Nope. I gotta do some reverse shoplifting. I gotta take a product that has a winning promotional item in it and sneak it on a shelf somewhere in America. I've got to do that at random."

"I can help you with Random."

"I don't need help with Random. Random is an old

friend of mine, and I have to be alone with Her for this."

"You go into a store and leave something on the shelf?"

"Yup, I can't trust stock boys with that much responsibility. I can't have you follow me. I want to see you roll the Dice and go, and then I'll go back to my job. Okay, Bobby, you roll and I'll drive you right now to where the Dice decide."

Melvin was lying his ass off. He wasn't doing the reverse shoplifting now—that wasn't for a couple of weeks. Even he didn't know exactly when. One day he'd go into the office and add a winning ticket all by himself under the label of his client's salsa. He'd put that jar of salsa in carry-on luggage and take it to the airport. (He could always get what he wanted through TSA—ex-police, magician.) He would use cash to buy a ticket on the next domestic flight he could catch. His phone card would have no SIM card in it. He would get on the plane and fly with his carry-on salsa.

He would land and rent the cheapest car he could. One without tracking. He would rent it with cash. He'd just drive. No map, no GPS, he'd just drive. He'd drive a couple hours. Driving for at least two hours—one time he drove over five. He would drive until he found a supermarket that felt right. No one in the world would know where Melvin was. He'd savor the high lonesome of the parking lot for a few minutes. He'd take camera photos of the store in case the client needed to know where it had been given out, upload it to his secure cloud account, and then delete it and delete the "recently deleted" on his phone. He'd find some homeless person and offer them twenty bucks to help him shop for a tailgate party. They would go into the supermarket together and throw lots of beer, chips, dips, and salsa into a cart. During all the filling of the cart, Melvin would use his magic skills, with his back to the store surveillance camera, to pull the hero salsa out of his jacket and put it on the shelf, bury it, and take a few pictures of it there to please the client.

They'd go to the checkout and pay cash for the party supplies and then when he and his homeless buddy got to the parking lot, Melvin would say, "Wait a minute. You know, my football buddies are pricks, fuck them. I'm not giving them another party. Here, you take this cart full of beer and snacks and do whatever you want. Oh, and here's another twenty bucks. Be well. Nice to meet you."

After all that, Melvin would get back in the car and try to figure out how to get to the nearest airport. He'd take the next flight to the next-nearest airport and from there grab a flight back to Dallas. What a stupid amount of work for a salsa jar. But it was a salsa jar worth multiple millions of Melvin's company's money if the right person found it, was aware they found it, and acted on it.

Part of keeping that money safe was leading Bobby to believe he was doing this today, so if Bobby had someone follow Melvin, they would learn nothing. The real reason Melvin was sending Bobby on his way was just that it was time. They weren't partners, they were friends. They were becoming good friends. They would see each other a lot in the future, but for right now, it was time for them to stop going steady. Melvin had to see other people.

Bobby rolled a seven and Melvin drove him to the airport. Bobby left his American hat, T-shirt, and belt in Melvin's backseat. "Hey, man, this was so great. What a pleasure to meet you. We'll be in touch, right?"

"I get to Vegas all the time, my friend, and we'll hang, and I'll let you roll a few for me."

"Hey, Melvin, can you get me in touch with Terri?"

"I'm going to call her to interview her for my book. I'll

give her your email and tell her you'd like to be in touch. If I were a betting man, I'd bet she writes you."

"And you are a betting man."

"Yes I am, Bobby, yes I am. I love you, be well."

Bobby bought his ticket back to Vegas. The flight was uneventful. He sat in his first-class seat and thought about Melvin, Joanne, and Terri. He didn't think about Big Mike at all.

17

WHEN BOBBY GOT BACK TO VEGAS HE WAS JUST
plain sick of fucking around. If he kept going like
this, soon he'd own the Batmobile and his own
private island. For a long time, Random had kept away the
depression, boredom, and ennui pretty well, but they were
creeping in. He was becoming a regular guy. He didn't like
that. Trying to have the Dice tell him who to be didn't change
him enough. He had a house. The Dice had bought him kind
of a McMansion. It was a nice house that a regular guy would
own. He had bought it rolling a three. The other choices were
nuttier—seven was buying that Vegas house that is totally underground—but three gave him just a house, and as Bobby
was walking back to it, he realized that what he liked most
about working with Melvin was helping Melvin. He liked
having a job. Even though Melvin's job was wicked stupid,
Bobby liked feeling like he was helping someone. Thinking
back on it, he hadn't been really doing anything to help Melvin, but he had been knocked out of his silly self-attention. It
wasn't Random's fault, he had been rolling for the wrong stuff.
If he hadn't met Melvin on that last trip, he would have just
been playing dress-up at a national monument. Life had to be
more than that, and he was sure the Dice could make it happen. Saint Francis of Assisi, Leo Tolstoy, Winston Churchill,
Goldie Hawn (who has spent a lot of time fucking Kurt Rus-

sell, who played Snake Plissken in *Escape from New York*), and just about everyone else has told the simple truth that if you want to be really happy, you've got to help others. According to W.H. Auden, "We are all here on earth to help others; what on earth the others are here for, I don't know."

He put his rental truck keys on the counter, pulled out his Dice, and standing at his fancy kitchen island with the built-in deep fryer that had never been used, Bobby thought about giving Random some important choices.

Two (2.78%)—Give every penny to EffectiveAltruism.org.

Three (5.56%)—Keep enough savings to live on the interest, give everything else to EffectiveAltruism.org.

Four (8.33%)—Go to Africa and use money and nonexistent skills to help there.

Five (11.11%)—Go to India and use money and nonexistent skills to help there.

Six (13.89%)—Open a detective agency for lost causes (kinda Batman, right?).

Seven (16.67%)—Open a detective agency for lost causes (kinda Batman, right?).

Eight (13.89%)—Open a detective agency for lost causes (kinda Batman, right?).

Nine (11.11%)—Really be Batman, be a rich guy who fights crime.

Ten (8.33%)—Really be Batman, be a rich guy who fights crime.

Eleven (5.56%)—Keep enough savings to live on the interest, give everything else to EffectiveAltruism.org.

Twelve (2.78%)—Give every penny to EffectiveAltruism.org.

Those choices made him happy. He knew he'd be no help in India or Africa, but his money might be, and he would enjoy learning how best to spend it. It would also get him the fuck out of Vegas. Those choices were part of him, but he gave the heavy odds—six, seven, and eight—for opening a detective agency for lost causes, a storefront for people who had no hope except for his Random roll of the Dice. The stupider choice had a 44.45% chance of being the choice. That's the way he rolled.

He rolled.

A nice Easy Eight. It was time to open Outside Chance Detective Agency. The OCD Agency.

Bobby had given Random a stupid pain-in-the-ass choice and Random had thrown it back at him. Because Bobby assumed he could open a Nevada private investigation company with money, a trench coat, and a hat. Broads with beautiful gams would show up jammed up in fixes that he could private-dick them out of. But Vegas is not the libertarian paradise it's cracked up to be. You had to drive to Pahrump for legal prostitutes, and you couldn't be a gumshoe without a license.

How to be a dick in Vegas? Five years of investigative experience—including the time it took you to get the required associate's or bachelor's degree in police science or criminal justice. It all had to add up to a Gladwell ten thousand hours. It took a long time to be hard-boiled and Bobby was a watched pot.

He realized he didn't want even a two and twelve chance of spending five years getting legally qualified. He didn't really want to go to police school. He and Random had decided to open a detective agency but there had to be a better way to do it. Couldn't that be accomplishable with money? Couldn't he

buy an agency and work as an unpaid intern? He could hire
a guy to be nominally in charge of the pro bono division for
Random lost causes, and Bobby would do all the work. Bobby
wouldn't be qualified, but fuck them, if his clients had any
other hope, they wouldn't be coming to him. He wouldn't be
making any important decisions anyway, those would all be
Random.

Several days later, Bobby rolled another Easy Eight and that
picked Fitzgerald Discreet Investigators out of the agencies
on the search results list, and he made an appointment. After
a bit of flak from the woman who answered the phone, he had
a meeting with the owner set for the next day.

He hung up with flak-giver and had started to make a
list of choices for the evening when his phone rang. It was
Terri—she was already in town to marry Big Mike. Bobby'd
been back in Vegas less than a week, but he and Terri had
already exchanged a bunch of emails and texts. He still hadn't
actually met her in person, yet they had developed some text
and email intimacy. He had told her to call when she and Big
Mike hit Vegas.

"Hey, Terri."

"Bobby, we're here. Viva! We're here in Sin City, baby!" It
was the first time Bobby had heard her voice since the police
speaker phone with Melvin. Deeper than he recalled, more
damaged. He remembered the Texas on the vowels, but it
wasn't the voice that read her texts in his head.

"When are you getting married?" She had sent Bobby a
PDF of the prenuptial that her heavy lawyer had drawn up
and Big Mike had signed. She'd done everything right, she
even got Big Mike a lawyer to advise him so he couldn't say
later that he didn't understand what he was signing. Big Mike

would live high off the hog while he was with Terri, but if they split he'd walk away with right around nothing. He would be motivated to be a very good husband.

"We're heading downtown now to get the license and then do some Elvis wedding thing after. Do people still get married by Elvis?"

"Well, the trajectory changed. The end of the last century, the number of Elvis impersonators was growing with an alarming contagion rate. It was estimated by scientists at the time that every man, woman, and child on the planet would be Elvis impersonators in Vegas by the end of 2019, but we were able to flatten the curve. People still get married by Elvis, though not as much as they used to."

"Yeah, we want Elvis to do us. Promise me you'll come to our wedding, Bobby, I want to meet your face."

"I can't promise, but I'll give it a good roll. So, Big Mike made it, huh? He didn't turn in the ticket ahead of time? He didn't fuck you? Good for Big Mike!"

"He was a good boy and sat on the ticket, so now he gets to really fuck me. I'll text you which chapel we pick. Hey, what was that restaurant and show your friend told us not to miss?"

"I think Melvin said Lotus of Siam for Thai food, they are really good, and Mac King for comedy magic. Mac has afternoon shows, so you can go over after you get your license. I think there's a three o'clock show."

"Wanna join us?"

"Nah, it's your honeymoon."

"We're seeing a fucking magician, it's not our honeymoon. I was considering inviting you to the honeymoon too, but I wanted to meet you first. Come to the wedding."

"Text me the info and I'll give it a roll."

"Nice talking with you, Bobby."

"Yeah. Congrats. And give every inch of my love to Big Mike. He's as lucky as me and you, maybe luckier."

Bobby hung up and headed out to the Fremont Street Experience to wander around for a couple hours. It was a great place for contemplation. Who would Bobby be if he weren't Bobby? Who would he be without the Dice? It wasn't that others weren't living Random, it was just that, as Stephen Hawking once said, "Not only does god definitely play dice . . . he sometimes confuses us by throwing them where they can't be seen." Other people didn't access the Random directly. They never saw the random firings in their minds that made their choices for them. Bobby had simply made his metaphorical Dice physical and rolled them where he could see them. He was going to open a detective agency, that had been decided, but he was still thinking about Terri. He needed to throw the Dice on what to do next.

Two (2.78%)—Heroin.

Three (5.56%)—Go to that solo bass player with fucked-up legs and the distorted amp, put five hundred bucks in his collection bucket, and dance in front of him until passing out.

Four (8.33%)—Ask the next five people who walk by (couples or groups count as one) if they want to have sex.

Five (11.11%)—Put on a fake foreign accent and ask people directions to "the place with the titties."

Six (13.89%)—Go to Terri and Big Mike's wedding.

Seven (16.67%)—Go to Terri and Big Mike's wedding.

Eight (13.89%)—Go to Terri and Big Mike's wedding.

Nine (11.11%)—High lonesome at Starbucks.

Ten (8.33%)—Buy a Bible and preach on the street.

Eleven (5.56%)—Run to Terri and beg her to leave Big
Mike and marry me instead.

Twelve (2.78%)—Put a hat down in front of me and
recite what I remember of Allen Ginsburg's "Howl"
at the top of my lungs, until the police stop me for not
having signed up to street-perform.

Railroad Nine, a five and a four. He walked through Fremont Street, got himself a cup of joe, and just sat watching the world go by. The phone rang, it was Terri.

"Hey."

"Viva Las Vegas Wedding Chapel, 1205 Las Vegas Boulevard. We're going for pizza before and then after the King does the service, we'll go to the strip club a few doors over and get a few lap dances to gear up for our honeymoon. Did you know none of the really fancy hotels have heart-shaped jacuzzies in the room? Their view of classy and mine differ. We found one in one of the more reasonably priced vintage motels."

"Hey, I won't be coming to the wedding."

"You promised!"

"I did not. I said I'd roll, and I did. The Dice made another choice."

"Your Dice made a big mistake. We were going to have you be our witness at the wedding, and if you were really good, you could be the witness at the honeymoon as well. Big mistake."

The Dice did not make mistakes. He never second-guessed. He sat all night and sipped his decaffeinated coffee.

The next morning brought Bobby back to Fremont for his meeting at Fitzgerald Discreet Investigators. It was a seedy agency downtown—exactly what was called for. Bobby rolled an eight, a Square Pair, four and four, so he was wearing a bright-yellow NASCAR jacket. There were three people working at desks in an open room and one office in the back. Bobby walked in and met Mr. Fitzgerald. Tony Fitzgerald was fat; triple-bypass fat. He had a nose that had been broken a few times and now sat in the middle of his face like a red potato. He was wearing a weird blue Las Vegas 51s baseball cap backward over his bald head with crazy hippie fringe hair sticking out the sides and back. It complemented his sunset-colored Hawaiian shirt worn open over a T-shirt with writing on it. Bobby couldn't concentrate on anything else until he'd worked out what the T-shirt said from the middle letters showing through the opening of the Hawaiian shirt. It took him longer than it should have. *Fuck Trump and Fuck You for Voting for Him.* A *Fuck the Republican President* T-shirt no longer guaranteed the wearer was Democrat or even liberal. In the age of Trump, registered lifelong Republicans could proudly wear that T-shirt. Tony was in his sixties, looked about eighty, and probably gave his last fuck back in the nineties. Bobby liked him.

"What's your problem?" Mr. Fitzgerald had a Chicago accent.

"Well, sir—"

"Call me Tone. If you want me to find out who your wife's fucking, you can call me Tone."

"I don't have a wife, and if I did, I wouldn't care who she fucked as long as I could watch. I want to buy your agency."

"Not for sale."

"I think I have the money to change that."

"Well, enough jingle, I'll sell the agency and lick your taint on New Year's Eve on the Strip."

"I have enough for all of that and that's what I want."

"Why do you want to invest in a detective agency? Don't you have a nice gold toilet to flush away your ill-gotten gains?"

"I want to be a private detective for people who have lost all hope. People who think they don't have a chance. I want to give them one last chance."

"You're smart. That *will* be faster than flushing cash down the shitter. Jesus Christ, why don't you open a jazz club on the Strip and play sax yourself? You might be able to lose a bit more a little faster."

Bobby explained his plan to Tone. All he wanted was to work around the licensing rules and help people. He needed a guy he could intern with so he could do his Random shit.

"Motherfucker, you are crazy."

"Yes I am. I'll write you a check right now, and you never have to work another day in your life. You can still own the agency and keep running it. Change the name to Outside Chance and take me on as an intern or whatever you call them in the dick biz. You assign someone to sign anything I need to do my cases and give me advice once in a while. When I'm done with this I go away, you sell the agency again and keep the cash, or close it up—I don't care. If you get sick of running it before I leave, you can promote one of your guys as my new boss and fly somewhere where that festive sunset shirt is appropriate and live out the rest of your life."

Tone stuck out the biggest hand that Bobby had ever shaken. "You've got a deal. And I'll be your guy. I'll come in once a week and answer questions for you and sign whatever paperwork you need. I want to see this. You're out of your fucking mind."

"Yes, Tone, I am. And thank you."

Bobby's hand still hurt from Tone's handshake. It felt kind of sexy.

18

FRASER RUPHART WAS THRILLED. HIS DEADLY ONE-SIDED chess game with Bobby had just gotten more interesting. Now Bobby was playing. He'd opened a detective agency. Bobby had sat down at the table. He'd joined the game. Bobby was sick of being a flamboyant bisexual playboy dipshit and now he wanted to be a white knight for people with problems? Great, Ruphart was more than happy to be the black knight. They could battle to the death.

Ruphart was the black knight in Bobby's life, but make no mistake, it was Bobby's fault. He had sent that fucking pizza, and now everything that happened, and a lot was going to happen, was Bobby's fault.

Ruphart was great at assigning blame. He could watch TV and tell you who was at fault in every scene and what Ruphart would do if he were there (usually kill the liar). Ruphart riding in his limo past a fender bender would look over at the people getting each other's insurance information and say to his driver, "That was the Audi's fault. He was taking the corner wrong. Fucking asshole." No-fault insurance made Ruphart crazy. As did the word "accident." There was always fault. Someone must always be to blame. There were no accidents, only assholes that needed to be fucked up for their fuckups, and Bobby was one of those fuckups.

He would rather be blamed himself than have everyone blameless. He needed blame. He was thrilled to take blame when he deserved it. It wasn't so he could be a big man, a stand-up guy. He was neither. He was just storing blame in his bank. He would have that in reserve when he wanted to blame someone else. *When I do something wrong, I'm the first to admit it, so now . . . fuck you.* Taking blame on himself allowed him to not forgive and to not forget, and that's what he felt he needed to be his best self. He took a little blame on the chin to buy him the right in his mind to rip someone else's chin off. What made him always right was that he knew he wasn't always right.

It was all Ruphart's inability to accept Random. Like nut-job conspiracy theories—it's better to believe there are evil forces plotting together against you than to believe things are Random. Evil is better than Random. Trouble is, there's no such thing as evil. Bobby Ingersoll had never seen evil. His dad was a fuckup and had fucked up his whole family, but evil? Nah. Just a fuckup who ruined everything. You don't need evil to explain bad things happening. Bobby had the reason for everything. The reason was Random. Plug stupidity and Random into the unknown X and Why, and the equation always solves.

Fraser Ruphart considered himself misunderstood, not evil. Well, sometimes he felt that he might be evil, and he was okay with that. In truth, he was worse than evil. Calling him evil just takes the blame off him. He hadn't succumbed to some spiritual and natural force, he had decided to do bad things to people for his own gain. He wasn't going to be a fucking snowflake. What's worse, Ruphart believed in justice. He believed in revenge. Lou Reed sang, *"An eye for an eye is elemental."* Ruphart believed if someone spit in his eye, he needed to blind them in both. Fuck them. He considered that part of running a grown-up business. And for revenge to really be effective, it had to come *before* the transgression.

You had to fuck them before they had a chance to fuck you. You knew they were going to steal from you, so steal from them first. Get your revenge first and make them stand in line for theirs. That was the smart way to do things, and he was willing to do what had to be done. That was just life. And these minor justifications for his own decisions—well, they were way worse than whatever evil might be.

Ruphart prided himself on being able to forgive and forget, provided someone apologized correctly. But it had to be the perfect apology. "Man, that was fucked, let's just forget about it and move on," that did NOT work. "I don't know what I was thinking," nope. "Listen, I was going through a rough time and I fucked over a lot of people, and I want to try to make things right," no fucking way. Ruphart had the correct apology in his head, and you had to say those magic words.

"Tell me why you lied to me!" That was his most common question.

You couldn't say, "Well, it didn't seem like a lie, it was just a different point of view, and I was wrong to hold that, but I didn't set out to lie to you."

"But you *did* lie to me." He knew that and he could prove it. "Now tell me precisely why you lied. Tell me now! Just answer the question, why did you lie to me?"

"Yeah, I guess you could have seen that as a lie, and I'm sorry."

"I didn't *see* it as a lie, it *was* a lie, and why did you tell it?" Very few people could apologize right to Ruphart.

If you didn't ask for forgiveness in the exact right way, Ruphart killed you. The people he couldn't justify killing, he just stopped communicating with, like he was a fucking eight-year-old. He didn't talk to any of his three siblings, he didn't talk to his mother, and he didn't talk to his grandmother. His grandmother was dead, but that wasn't the only reason he didn't talk to her. He didn't know his father, but if his father ever showed up, he wouldn't talk to him. Maybe he would kill that motherfucker. You don't need evil in a world with Fraser Ruphart. Like Bobby's father, Ruphart was just fucking stupid. But don't tell him that. Well, Bobby did kind of tell him that with the ham-and-pineapple pizza.

Ruphart still couldn't let Bobby know. No one could know. People had to believe that if you paid your debt to Ruphart he wouldn't make you dead, but Bobby had to know, in his dying moments, that if you bought Ruphart a Hawaiian pizza you were going to fucking die. And Bobby had to know he had been outsmarted. A detective agency was perfect. Bobby had the exact wrong personality for a detective agency. Bobby didn't have a drop of cynicism in him. It was what Ruphart hated most about him. But it also meant that Ruphart had to work fast. Someone taking on lost causes with a detective agency who always assumed people had the best motives was not going to last long. Bobby was looking for trouble, and there was no doubt Bobby would find it. Ruphart had to make sure he himself was the trouble Bobby would find.

It had to be perfect, cruel, clever, smart trouble. And Ruphart, as always, wouldn't get his hands dirty.

19

TONE TOLD THE GUYS AT THE AGENCY THAT HE'D SOLD out to a nut named Bobby. The name of the joint would be changed to Outside Chance, and Bobby would be working with him as an intern. Tone would be around a bit less, but nothing else would change. They were detectives so they googled *Bobby Ingersoll* and soon they understood everything. They shrugged and went back to sneaking pictures of sneaky people sneakily fucking.

Bobby had spread the word around that he was now a crime fighter. He let it be known he was taking on hopeless cases. He bought some time on an Interstate 15 digital billboard for an ad that read, *Hopeless? Give Chance a chance!* which directed to the website LastChance.com. Who would see that billboard and check out the website? Losers. And what was he looking to find? Losers. LastChance.com didn't link to Bobby or to Outside Chance so they wouldn't be inundated. He hired someone to sift through all the inquiries on the website and forward the craziest ones directly to him. Bobby was looking for crazy. Bobby was looking for a mission. While he waited, he was Tone's intern.

Tone made that clear: "You bought the fucking company, but you ain't my boss."

"I know."

"I work for myself."

"Right."

"And you are just my intern."

"Yup."

Bobby ran around getting iced Americanos and big bags of cinnamon gummy bears for Tone. He did web searches and delivered packages. Bobby wasn't using the Dice much at work because he wasn't making any decisions. Tone made all of Bobby decisions and Tone was plenty Random.

Bobby had liked working for Melvin and he liked working for Tone. He had been rich for long enough and accustomed to not making decisions for long enough that he liked being bossed around. It didn't bother him when his boss's motives were as opaque as Chance. If you need to hire an employee to do shit work, pick one who is worth almost a hundred million and lives Random. They don't need to exhibit attitude.

It took a few weeks, but Tone and Bobby had wound down most of Tone's cases and he was vetting to try to find Bobby's first real client. There were just two from the billboard that had been brought to his attention. The first was Carson.

Carson really didn't have a prayer. He didn't believe anyone had a prayer. He didn't believe in any of that shit. But Carson made his Uber driver get off at the exit after the billboard and get back on the freeway and drive in the opposite direction so he could look over his shoulder and across traffic to see the website on the billboard.

Carson should have been able to memorize the URL in one glance. He was a fucking quantum physicist, short-listed for the Nobel. He'd worked with Richard Feynman back at Caltech. He had written a couple of best sellers about science in the movies. He had been on *Rachel Maddow* to be screamed at by a smart-looking fashion model for being Islamophobic for thinking that maybe little girls shouldn't have their clits cut off. A priest on a Glenn Beck podcast accused him of being "racist" because he said that Catholics might police their priests better. He had one of the sharpest minds around, but he couldn't think straight now. Now he was in Vegas having to look again at a URL he saw on a billboard to go to a website for people without hope. Just a year ago, he could have memorized a whole page of URLs in one glance.

He thought the rape trial was the worst thing that could happen to him. He was sure of it. And when the "not guilty" came in, he was sure his problems were going to start going away. But juries do not have "innocent" on the menu. The best they can do is "not guilty." Social media and universities and publishers and agents and TV bookers . . . well, they still chose to believe the victim even if the "victim" wasn't the victim. The culture hadn't developed the skill of flipping vic and perp. It was easier to see the horribly corrupted and flawed judicial system as horribly corrupted and flawed. The horribly corrupted and flawed criminal justice system was unable to find him guilty but that certainly didn't mean he was innocent, because it was horribly corrupted and flawed. It didn't seem to cross the hive's mind that the horribly corrupted and flawed justice system might have fucked Carson. Carson wasn't in jail, but he also couldn't get work. He had no job and he had no friends.

That's not quite true. He had two real friends left, but one was from high school and one was carny trash and neither one of them had meaningful work for a quantum rapist. There were a few dozen social justice hobbyist guys who would be spending just a few minutes a day to make sure that Carson didn't work or date or have friends ever again. Those few minutes add up to some serious person-hours.

Carson was also an atheist and a skeptic. He'd spoken at

skeptic conferences with the Amazing Randi and Richard Dawkins. He told himself he would write to Bobby's website in part to investigate whatever scam lay behind LastChance.com. What scam could start with that billboard? Where was the tie to Nigerians, Romanians, or Long Island psychics? It would keep his mind occupied. But if he really told the truth to himself, and truth was all he had left, part of him really hoped this billboard could help him. A drowning man will grab a snake. The odds were against him. Niels Bohr had a horseshoe over his doorway. A visitor was confused that a Nobel laureate would put stock in a good-luck charm and asked him if he believed. "No," Bohr answered, "but I am told that they bring luck even to those who do not believe in them." Was the billboard a scam? Almost certainly. Almost. Almost. Almost. But maybe it would work even if Carson didn't believe. He typed the website into his phone and filled out a help request.

Are you in physical danger?
Is someone you know in physical danger?
Could the police help?
Have you gone to the police?
Can you think your way out?
Can anyone think your way out?
Have you tried everything you or anyone you know, or the web, can think of?
Are you willing to break the law?
Are you fucked?

No, no, no, no, no, no, yes, maybe, yes.

Tell us your sob story.

In the empty space provided, Carson typed with his thumbs that he was accused of rape in a #MeToo moment that got out of hand. He was an outspoken atheist, and worse, he and his wife were in a very happy polyamorous bisexual relationship. He'd been fired from his college position because a graduate student in a different department, who had nothing to do with Carson academically, had asked Carson's wife if they wanted to have a threesome sometime. Carson's wife said it sounded like fun and she would ask Carson. She hadn't gotten around to asking Carson. For the record, he would have said yes because he always said yes to everything. It was his most charming feature. *Want to go to the movies?* Yes. He didn't ask what movie. *Want to go to Antarctica?* Yes. He didn't ask when or why. *Want to blow my ex-boyfriend?* Yes. He didn't ask who. But Polly (yes, that was his wife's name, it was cute and funny until they got into court and then it seemed too late to fall back to "Dorothy") hadn't gotten around to asking him yet. Carson wasn't even in the loop, let alone the threesome, when an undergraduate cis male overheard the conversation in the quad and brought a complaint to the administration because of the power imbalance. Carson was a big shot, so considering sex with a graduate student was wrong, even though Carson hadn't even known about the request to consider it. The investigation went on and on and brought up all sorts of things. It was a pig pile on a pig. Any lawyer will tell you the pervert always loses, but add to that that the pervert was cis male, considered "white" (who knows for reals what that even means?), successful, a free-speech extremist, and an asshole, and Carson was belly-up dead in the water floating.

Then came the rape charge. There had been a drunken orgy years before, when Carson was an undergraduate. It really was drunken, and it really was an orgy, it really was rape, and Carson really was there. There was a picture of his ass that was presented in court and someone swore on the fucking Bible it was Carson's ass fucking, but who cares? He was there and had already admitted it. It might have been his ass. He had fucked at the party, all sober and all with consent, and he admitted it. He wasn't very drunk, and he remembered who he fucked, and it wasn't her. It wasn't even a woman. And the accuser didn't remember who she fucked, and she thought it might have been him. There was the trial and it was awful and there went all his and Polly's money to lawyers, paralegals, and investigators. There are really good, important laws that protect the victim by not allowing the defense attorney to bring up the fact that she was going out all the time during this same time period and drinking until she blacked out. During this time, she never remembered who she fucked. Who wants to fuck someone who's blacked out—that's easy, a rapist—but she couldn't remember them. His accuser confessed that to a lot of people and a lot of people knew that but weren't allowed to testify to that. The investigators had video of the victim giving clear, sober consent to someone else before and after the sex act, who she then accused of rape, and even that wasn't admissible. That's not bad. That's good, society needs to protect those people, and even with all those protections in place and not cheating in court at all, Carson had "won." The truth hadn't locked him up, but it sure hadn't set his pimpled ass free.

Carson wasn't in jail, but that was it. Polly left him. She stood by him for the whole trial. Polly was true like ice, like fire. She studied the case and became pretty much a legal aid. She spent her family trust money on lawyers for Carson. She stroked his troubled head. She made jokes—cruel dirty jokes that he loved. He would not have made it without her. She loved him completely. She trusted him completely. Polly was perfect. When he was found not guilty, she celebrated with him and was relieved with him and cried with him.

And then, two weeks later, she left him. She had decided their relationship was over before the trial started. Unrelated to the case. She knew he wasn't just not guilty; she knew he was innocent. She really knew. She'd been at the same orgy. Polly knew the accuser well. Polly had been so drunk at that party it was possible that Polly herself had fucked the vic, while they were both sober and with consent, of course, but fortunately that never came up. Polly had done the right thing and Carson had no complaints with her. None. The only complaint was that she was gone. She was still his friend. There were no hard feelings. But she'd been his friend so much and so well that he felt he was overdrawn on her friendship account. So, Carson was alone and unemployed and writing to a billboard in Vegas.

Carson's story was cut off after five hundred words, but it wasn't hard for Bobby to guess that Polly had left him. He had tried to attach all sorts of PDFs of the trial, but they all bounced.

Bobby thought that Random could really help Carson. In about ten rolls he would have another life and all his worries would be gone. Carson was perfect for Random. But Bobby didn't put up that billboard to proselytize. This project was not about winning other people over to Random, this was a chance to team up with Random to be a detective. That's where the fun was, that's where his service was. He wanted to be a crime fighter. He didn't see how he could help, but he rolled the Dice—seven, Big Red, a three and a four. It was what he wanted the most and Random gave it to him. He called Carson.

"Hey, Doctor, this is Bobby. You're way too smart to fill out a questionnaire you got from a billboard on a highway in Vegas."

"Who is this?"

"I'm Bobby, I'm the crime fighter who put up the billboard. I just read your story. Well, the first five hundred words of your story. I didn't see the end. Hey, did Polly leave you?"

"Yes, she left."

Bobby nodded to Tone and they high-fived.

"We figured, but we wanted to know for sure. Hey, I don't think my detective agency can help you at all. Everyone knows everything. There's nothing to detect. You need one of those places that fixes public images, but you're what, over sixty, right? Yeah, you're fucked, I would think."

"Thanks, asshole. You called to tell me you couldn't help?"

"Right. My detective agency can't help. But if you want a job you've got one. You want to work for me? I could use a quantum mechanic to work on my really little teeny itsy-bitsy cars . . . Just kidding. You want to move to Vegas and help me fight crime?"

"No. I came here to wallow in self-pity, not to live. I hate Vegas."

"Too bad. I bet we would have been buddies. Bye bye."

"That's it?"

"What more do you want? You want to get drunk and bang some passed-out broad with me?"

"Not funny."

"I don't know, Tone is killing himself laughing." He was.

"What's the scam? Are you grabbing my credit information or something? Really, what's the scam?"

"No scam, I'm just a nut who rolled a seven and wanted to offer you a job. You know the chances of rolling a seven with two dice?"

"Six in thirty-six or one in six or 16.67%."

"See? You would have been a great employee. If you change your mind, let me know." Bobby hung up and addressed Tone: "Bummer."

"Yeah, I knew the wife would leave him."

Bobby had to keep looking for his first client.

20

⚃ ⚃

Like Carson, Bill Wills had written to the website after seeing the billboard. Bill was from Texas and wanted everyone to know it. He did real American much better than Bobby had. Boots, tight jeans, big belt buckle under a belly, one of those vertical-striped shirts buttoned up, and a hat. Grown men dressing up like cowboys. Like men wearing basketball jerseys, basketball sneakers, and basketball shorts in public. Is that a gender thing? Do women often dress up like occupations? In the case of cowboys, like fictional occupations? Women do cosplay, of course, and thank god for that, but they don't go to the local coffee shop dressed as cheerleaders, fuck god for that.

After Bobby was inspired by his first meeting with Bill, he rolled a six, the Lumber Number (because "two by four"). That six meant the next day he came into work dressed as a fireman—the big metal hat, rubber coat, the boots, suspenders, everything. Tone didn't give a rat's ass. When Bobby rolled the Dice, Tone just rolled his eyes. Eight would have been NASCAR driver again with full Nomex and twelve would have been full Whitney Houston drag queen show, so . . . blackface. Fireman wasn't bad, considering.

Bill had been thrown out of a casino for winning too much and he was pissed about it and that was certainly a hopeless case. He had gotten hot on a craps table. Really hot and won a load of money. When he said his hopeless case involved dice, Bobby was dancing in his fireman boots. Bill's story was nutty. Bill was playing craps and on the greatest roll of his life. The casino representatives came to him, grabbed the dice, and said he had won too much already. Security examined the dice—they were shavers, they were gaffed. Shavers have their sides altered to change the odds. Shavers in the game had given Bill his luck and when he started winning a lot, he started betting more, like losers do on a roll. He was a high roller to begin with and when the streak started (when the crooked dice were rung in), he increased his bets to the max and won a lot, a real lot. It's a federal offense to cheat in Nevada. How is that for a scam? The casinos get the fucking government to enforce their racket. Casino security felt they were being nice to Bill about it: they took all his money and told him to walk the fuck away and not look back. They had his name and picture—he was going in the black book and his gambling career was over in Vegas. The only smart move for Bill was to walk away flat broke for the night, but not in jail.

Bill didn't make the smart move. Not Bill. Bill screamed, "Bullshit!" and started swinging at security. He was efficiently zip-cuffed and escorted to the back room. "Efficiently," in the case of a six-three, 250-pound, thirty-five-year-old, bar-fighting man dressed as a cowpoke, took about six security guards and a lot of screaming. In any other state a half-dozen private security guards Cobra-cuffing a citizen is a kidnapping beef unless the rent-a-pigs can prove in court they were attacked first. But Clark County, Nevada, is owned by the casinos. Casino private security (which are guys playing dress-up as police officers—are all men just trying to be in the Village People?) can detain you for hours on just their suspicion. They can put you in cuffs if the leather-sniffer's Spidey sense merely tingles a little. These *faux po* had more than just suspicion—they had shaved dice in their hot little hands. Bill's ass was detained.

What kind of crazy was Bill? Security couldn't figure it out. "Look at these fucking dice, buddy—you can see the shave on them. Look at the corners! Look!"

"Yeah, I can see it, but those aren't my dice. I didn't switch them. I did not switch them."

"No, you didn't switch them, your partner with the baseball cap shading his face from our eye-in-the-sky switched them. We have that on video. But when you show up tomorrow to give him his 50% of jack shit, he's going to be pissed that you bet like an idiot and got yourself flagged, cuffed, and black-booked. It was a righteous switch, he walked away clean. You could have grabbed a nice modest payday for both of you and skated. Your partner is a pro. You suck. Now give us his name for the book, we'll put you both in the ledger, and let you both walk. If you try it again, and you seem stupid enough to do that, we'll get Metro to lock your asses up. Deal?"

"Fuck you, I don't have a partner, and I wasn't cheating."

"Let me get this straight, some anonymous super-altruist with an amygdala the size of my dick dome committed this felony so an asshole stranger playing cowboy in Vegas could win a ton of jingle to buy, what?—a personal-pizza-sized turquoise belt buckle, all the Lone Star beer in the world, and a VIP meet and greet with Garth Brooks for him and an escort who looks like Dolly Parton?"

"Dolly Parton? Garth Brooks? Lone Star beer?"

"Okay, a Sara Evans hooker, VIP with Blake Shelton, and a vat of Jack Daniel's. What the fuck do I know, you're the one who's dressed like Woody from *Toy Story*."

"I did not cheat. And fuck you. I don't know who switched the dice. I had nothing to do with it. I won fair and square."

"How exactly do you win fair and square on shavers? Just give us a name for our big ol' black book and walk."

Bill left the casino twelve hours later, but he was in the black book and he couldn't walk on any casino property ever again and he didn't like that. He went to lawyers and they all said it was hopeless. They wouldn't take the case on contingency. There wasn't any appeal system for the black book—casinos just did what they wanted. John Locke didn't mention the inalienable right to lose money gambling against billion-dollar corporations. Wills saw the billboard for hopeless causes and wrote out his case.

Bobby was hoping for some sort of life-and-death thing. He was hoping for a damsel in distress, but this really was a crazy case and a case no one else would take. And it was dice. It was dice, for Christ's sake. The case wasn't perfect, but it was worth a roll.

*Two (2.78%)—Call Bill and tell him he is a cheater and
    he should go fuck himself in the neck.*
Three (5.56%)—Take Bill's case.
Four (8.33%)—Take Bill's case.
Five (11.11%)—Take Bill's case.
*Six (13.89%)—Keep Bill on the list of possibles and roll
    to choose one later.*
*Seven (16.67%)—Keep Bill on the list of possibles and
    roll to choose one later.*
*Eight (13.89%)—Keep Bill on the list of possibles and
    roll to choose one later.*
*Nine (11.11%)—Keep Bill on the list of possibles and roll
    to choose one later.*
Ten (8.33%)—Call Bill and politely tell him no.
Eleven (5.56%)—Call Bill and politely tell him no.

Twelve (2.78%)—Call Bill and tell him his name was cleared from the black book and he can gamble anywhere (but don't actually do anything, just lie).

21

JAYNE ALSTON DIDN'T GO THROUGH THE WEBSITE TO find Bobby. She hadn't seen the billboard. She just walked into Outside Chance and asked for Bobby by name. She'd heard that he had set up for lost causes and she had decided she was a lost cause. She had no hope. She was the reason a person would start any detective agency. She was in her early twenties, a tastefully tattooed damsel in distress. Her eyes were a blue million miles, long curly red hair, and a galaxy of freckles that were right in that sexy sweet spot between too cute and melanotic.

"I heard you're helping out people with hopeless cases." She uncrossed her legs.

"Yeah, people without any Chance left. It's what I want to do. I give them Chance back."

She began sobbing. It took forever for her to get her story out between breakdowns, trembling, and crying—she sure cried sexy—but it seemed her little sister owed some drug money to a local gang, the LD50s, a west side gang. Yeah, Bobby had sure heard of them. She explained the gang was a loose collection of young sociopaths, no rhyme or reason, just junior bad guys full of hate for everything, tempered by nothing. Yup, Bobby knew all that. Jayne's sister hadn't paid them the money she owed so they had brutally raped her, and they were coming back for more. Alfred Hitchcock said you always had to answer the question, *Why don't they go to the police?* The gang told her not to go to the police and they could enforce that. If she went to the police, her whole family was dead. So that was that. The bangers were going to keep terrorizing her sister and her and taking all their money. There was no hope. None. There was no logical way out.

Bobby asked if money would solve this. Bobby had money and remembered well where the seed money for his fortune had come from. It would sure be a funny use of some of his money. Could he just pay off the gangsters, then Jayne and her sister could pay Bobby back, in, oh, he didn't know, maybe . . . affection?

Nope. It wasn't money. The gang had money. They still had more money than boys playing gangster needed. They were young, stupid, and ignorant. They were stupid enough to have an invisible man on an invisible scooter disappear with drug money. They weren't businesspeople. They weren't sane. It was hopeless.

This was exactly the kind of case Bobby wanted. The kind of help he wanted to bring. It was so like his own story. His hopeless situation that Chance had bailed him out of, a chance to pay back someone for his luck. Bobby wasn't working for Tone now; he was working for Random. As Jayne sobbed and choked out the words, Bobby lined up his choices in his head. He dug into his heart and assigned his desires. It was time for Random and it wasn't a formality—he wanted to roll. The overwhelming odds were that he'd take her case, and the main choices were how he would take it. What questions would he ask next? How would he get things going? He had no answers. No one could think their way out of this. This would be Random's first real case. This would be our story.

You don't need to know every choice, but on the edges

of his bell curve—twelve was: he was going to kiss her and ask her to marry him right then. The perfect cute meet. He grabbed his Dice and rolled Snake Eyes, a two. He hadn't rolled a nut number since the Fox News thang. Random had thrown him a curve but it played fair. He had set the odds correctly. About 2.77% of him wanted this choice, that was the right number, and the moment the Dice settled on the two there was no hesitation, no doubt. Now 100% of him was going to act on what Random dictated. There were no second thoughts. He acted.

He looked up from the Dice, focused on the perfect blue eyes, moist and pleading among her freckles, and said, "Fuck off, asshole! Just fuck the fuck off, you fuck. Get out of my office, now. I ain't doing shit for you."

22

J AYNE WAS A WORLD-CLASS CRIER. AS SHE SAT IN FRASER Ruphart's office, her crying was real and indistinguishable from her theatrical crying in Bobby's detective agency. Even she couldn't tell the difference in the crying, but the panic sure was different. She was filled with panic. Her crying had won 97.23% of Bobby's heart and mind. Ruphart punched her in the fucking face. He didn't slap her, he punched her, and quickly handed her his perfect pocket square so she wouldn't bleed on his rug. He took out an antiseptic wipe and cleaned off his fist. Who knew what diseases this whore was carrying?

"Did you cry this well for that asshole?"

She kept sobbing.

"The crying was supposed to make Bobby help you and get himself dead. All your crying does for me is make me want to hit you again. I suggest you stop it. Now."

"I can't."

Ruphart raised his fist again. Hmm, she *was* able to stop. He hit her anyway, but not as hard. He took a fresh wipe to clean his fist. Yeesh.

"What did you do to tip it? Did you wink at him? This is your fault. What did you fucking do?" She had stopped crying, but he hit her again; this punch was involuntary and that pissed Ruphart off. He did not like involuntary. He opened the drawer and got another wipe. This was her fault.

Jayne wasn't crying at all anymore, just bleeding. She tried to explain, "He rolled dice. And then started yelling at me. I was sure I had him, but he rolled the dice and threw me out."

Wily Fraser Ruphart, supergenius, was no match for Random. Back to his Acme drawing board.

23

RANDOM HAD SENT A BEAUTIFUL REDHEAD OUT OF Bobby's life with a *fuck you*, and because it was Random it was no problem. There was no blame. Bobby had just enjoyed watching Jayne's ass sway as she walked out of his office.

Tone didn't understand. "You were right to walk away, brother. That woman was trouble. You don't want gang shit, man, especially amateur gang shit. Leave that fucking pussy on the street. You gotta know when to fold them."

"Did you just quote Kenny Rogers?"

"No, I just quoted Don Schlitz who wrote "The Gambler," Roaster Chicken Boy just sang it. *The best you can hope for is to die in your sleep.* I like the Johnny Cash version."

"Okay, man, let's gamble, shall we?"

"Do I want to know what you're rolling for?"

"Do you ever? I'll give you a hint: if it's twelve, I'm auditioning for the Legends of Country show over at Perry's to be Kenny Rogers."

"I'd go to see that."

Bobby rolled. "Six—I'm taking Bill's case. We're finally starting to do some Random private dick work."

"You go, junior gumshoe. I'll get my own gummy bears and Americano."

* * *

Bill Wills was surprised to get the email from Bobby. Bill had decided he needed to move on, though he hadn't made any meaningful steps in that direction. He hadn't even left Vegas. He was still obsessed with the injustice of not being able to lose his money to a giant corporation.

This wasn't the kind of case that Bobby had set up the agency for. It wasn't his dream. But he gave it a 16.7% chance and Random chose it. The seven he rolled next had Bobby meet Bill at the glitzy McDonald's on the Strip between Harrah's and Casino Royale. The incandescent Golden Arches flow out of the Strip sidewalk. It's what Vegas is—concentrated America with more wattage. Bobby didn't have to roll the Dice to know what he'd wear for this meeting. He wanted to be dressed like a cowboy too: a big ol' white Stetson, red vegan cowboy boots with silver toe tips, and a brand-new praying-Christian-cowboy belt buckle. He one-upped Bill, adding a red-checked gingham shirt and a yellow neckerchief. Two could play this game.

They sat at a red metal table outside, just two cowpokes in Vegas.

"A stranger rang in shavers so you would win a shit ton of money?"

"Yes."

"You do understand why this is hard for the rent-a-pigs to accept, right?"

"Well, I sure didn't switch them myself."

"The casino showed you the shavers, right?"

"Yes, but I didn't really know what I was looking at."

"You said they had video of the mechanic ringing them, right?"

"Yes."

"But he was a pro, not a glimpse of his face and with a ball cap and a shirt that were left in the street trash as soon as he was out of camera range."

"I don't know."

"I do." Bobby rolled another seven. He got up from the table and came back a few minutes later with two Double Big Macs without beef or cheese, two apple pies, and two Minute Maid Orangeade Slushies. He gestured to Bill to help himself. "The Double Big Macs are just Special Sauce, lettuce, pickles, and onions on a sesame seed bun. Still not vegan but closer. The pies and slushies are full-on vegan."

"I don't care, I'm not vegan."

"I'm not either, but I think that change might just be a couple rolls away. If the mechanic who switched the dice wasn't that good, they would have him black-booked along with you. It's insane. Was anyone else betting at your table?"

"Yeah, a bunch of people."

"Betting heavy?"

"I don't think so. We figured at first it was someone else who was making the bets, but they rounded everyone up and no one was winning big enough to matter. You don't have to roll to place bets."

"But they didn't bust anyone else, and they have everyone's winnings recorded by the eye-in-the-sky. Damn. No reason for us to cover the same ground that the pros have already covered with all their experience and expensive bells and whistles."

"What do we have that the pros don't have?"

"They don't know how to use the Dice like I do."

Two (2.78%)—Quit the case.
Three (5.56%)—Talk to a magician.
Four (8.33%)—Talk to a magician.

Five (11.11%)—Talk to a magician.

Six (13.89%)—Go to the casino, talk to the security people who busted Bill.

Seven (16.67%)—Go to the casino, talk to the security people who busted Bill.

Eight (13.89%)—Go to the casino, talk to the security people who busted Bill.

Nine (11.11%)—Order another McDonald's vegan hot apple pie.

Ten (8.33%)—Ask Fraser Ruphart for advice.

Eleven (5.56%)—Stand on a McDonald's table and strip naked while singing the Barbarella *theme.*

Twelve (2.78%)—Ask Dad for advice.

He rolled them. Five, Michael Jordan, a two and a three—the Dice had spoken. "We're going to see a magic dragon."

Bill had teamed up with a crazy person. He was walking down the Strip with a guy wearing a yellow neckerchief to see a magic dragon.

Bobby was texting: *Piff, this is Bobby. Birthday party last week.*

Party for the dick you didn't know?

Yup. Paid well. Tipped. You were great.

Ty.

Need to talk.

Gimme 10. @valet

Flamingo?

Yup, my theater. Call you from dressing room.

Walking on Strip now. In person?

K

About 15.

K, showroom.

Random chose talking to a magician and Piff the Magic Dragon was the only magician Bobby knew, because he'd hired him for a gig that the Dice chose. Two cowboys walking the Strip to the Flamingo. As they turned in, Bill stopped, worried that he was black-booked and couldn't trespass on casino grounds.

"Keep your head down and our stupid hats will protect us. We're just heading backstage. If you don't stop at a table, they won't flag you."

Bugsy Siegel's original luxury hotel was still there. They'd blown up most everything else and built new shit, but the Flamingo was still there. Bobby and Bill walked in the front door. Bill was nervous as fuck, but they moved quickly with heads down. On the elevator was an advertisement: a picture of a little guy and a little Chihuahua, both in dragon suits, and a showgirl in pink with breasts larger than two Chihuahuas. They were at the Piff the Magic Dragon showroom.

Bobby texted, *Here.*

K

They stood there for a few minutes keeping their heads down. The door to the showroom opened and a guy popped his head out. "You waiting for Piff?"

"Yeah."

"C'mon."

The guy punched a code into the inner door, and they were in the empty showroom of all red and gold. The theater sat about two hundred people. Ella Fitzgerald had played this very room in 1958. Duke Ellington in 1968. Fats Domino was here every year up to 1976. Rusty Warren did *Knockers Up!* all through the sixties and seventies. Now . . . they had a fucking magic dragon. Bugsy was rolling in his grave.

The guy led them down a narrow staircase into the basement and opened the first door at the bottom. Two Chihuahuas starting yapping like crazy.

"Mr. Piffles! Two-ey! Shut up. Shut the fuck up!"

"Piffles, Two-ey, shut the fuck up!"

There were two people yelling: the guy from the elevator picture with the dragon suit, now without the dragon suit, looking fairly normal in a *Legend of Zelda* T-shirt; and the showgirl with the tits, looking even more astonishing in a white T-shirt, stacked like Piffles and Two-ey wrestling under blankets . . . if the dogs were shaped like perfect breasts and made of plastic.

"Hey, John, thanks for—"

"Call me Piff. *John* is just what you write on the checks. This is Jade, my showgirl. The dogs are Mr. Piffles and his understudy, Two-ey, who is an asshole. The guy who showed you down is Zack. What do you want?"

"I'm Bobby and this here is Bill."

Jade was getting ready for the show, which was three hours away. Being showfolk is not an easy gig. The rug was covered with remnants of shit and piss from the Chihuahuas and pink feathers from Jade's boas, and real showfolk would still eat a doughnut off the floor. And there were doughnuts and every available large Walmart snack in big jars. There were mirrors, a couple chairs, a hot plate, a fridge, and a couch that had the same sheen as the carpet. The rest of the room was magic props. Everything was red, gold, and so much green—like Boy George's reptilian dreams. Piff's prop case was open and being loaded by Zack. He was putting in plastic thumbs, decks of cards, and dog food. The posters on the wall were all of Piff and Mr. Piffles. Their latest tour poster read, *Piff the Magic Dragon—EPIC HUNT!* (Say it out loud.) The only non-Piff poster was for a guy in a tux with medals and a red sash—it said, *The Great Tomsoni and Company*, and the "company" was a blond woman who was an earlier version of Jade. Magicians love tits, even the gay ones, which is all of them.

"Thanks, Piff, for seeing us."

"Grab a snack and a water if you want and sit down. We have those pretzels with peanut butter in them and everything is vegan."

Bobby winked at Bill. Piff had a fading London accent; he'd been in Vegas awhile. Bobby and Bill sat on the dog-marked, pink-feathered couch and begged off the water and snacks. The McDonald's lunch had been more healthful.

Bill hadn't had any contact with showbiz before. He had so many questions. "So, you dress up as a dragon?"

"A *magic* dragon. And I dress up to do a professional show. Why are you dressed like fucking cowboys?"

"I'm not dressed like a cowboy, I *am* a cowboy, I'm from Texas."

"Okay, and I frolic in the autumn mist in a land called Honahlee. What do you want?"

What the fuck was Bill doing? Was he really going to go one-on-one with a pro? Bobby jumped in: "We have a magic question for you, Piff."

"I got a human question for you: why the fuck did you pay me, and pay me well, to do a birthday party for someone you didn't know? What a weird fucking gig."

"I'm crazy," Bobby answered sincerely.

Jade laughed, and the standing wave moved under the T-shirt in such a pleasing way. Her breasts might have been bigger than Piff's head.

"Okay, I'll accept that. Now, what's your question?"

"Why would someone go to a casino and ring in shavers when they didn't have a plunger at the rack?"

"What the fuck are you talking about? I don't even know what those words mean."

"We're trying to figure what sort of scam would have someone switch in crooked dice for our cowpoke here."

"What the fuck do I know about scams?"

"Maybe misdirection?"

"Okay, now you're using words that you don't know what they mean. I have some gimmicked decks of cards. I have a fucking plastic thumb with a folded-up bill in it. I have a dog in a dragon suit and a three-thousand-dollar elastic band that goes up my sleeve to make it look like a borrowed ring has vanished. Mostly I have fucking jokes and enough attitude to kill everyone in Jersey and New Jersey put together. And my partner Jade is wicked funny, has big tits, kicks high, and does splits. We have an ugly dog with PTSD that doesn't move and that makes people laugh. I'm not Brad Pitt. Brad Pitt isn't Brad Pitt. We are in showbiz."

"I know you aren't a criminal, but you know about how people's minds work. I thought magicians knew, like, card cheats and stuff."

"I'm British. I'm not a criminal, I'm a dick in a dragon suit."

Jade didn't turn or stop gluing her eyelash. "John, they want Johnny."

This was promising. "Yeah, we want Johnny. Who's Johnny?"

"The great Tomsoni on that poster there," Piff said, pointing to the Wizard of Warsaw looking pompous on the wall. "Yeah, Johnny knows all that shit."

"Can you hook us up with Johnny?"

Jade spoke again: "You don't need us to hook you up, Johnny will talk to anyone. Piff, give them Johnny's number and get your cowboys out of here. I want to get dressed."

24

B OBBY MADE HIS COLD CALL.

"Hello?"

"Is this Johnny Thompson?"

"Yes."

"My name is Bobby Ingersoll. I got your number from Piff."

"I love Piff. Love him. Solid comedy. Solid magic. Solid guy. He's come a long way."

"Yeah. He said you might be able to help me. I have a question about a gambling scam."

"Sure, if I can help, I will. C'mon by the house. You coming by now? I got a few hours before I have to head over to Copperfield's."

"Um. Okay. We'll head over now. What's the address?"

"I'm in the book . . . but there's not a book anymore, right? I'm really old, I still think there are books. Look me up on the computer and head over. Can you grab Starbucks for Pam and me on your way? She's just black coffee, if they still serve that, but I'll have some swishy Frappuccino thing. Caramel. See you soon, bye." Johnny hung up.

Bobby got on his phone and did a search for Johnny and found some bio along with his home address. He'd played Vegas since a little before Vegas was Vegas. Opened for Sinatra. He was in the car with Shecky Greene when Shecky drove into the Caesars fountain and told the police to "hold the spray wax." Sideshow geek, pro wrestler, Harmonicat. He had consulted with every magician in the world. Johnny was showbiz.

Bill and Bobby's Uber brought them to a modest suburban house with doves cooing in a cage on the porch. They rang the bell and Johnny came to the door. He looked like a vampire. Lots of work, his face stretched tight, a black toupee, sparkling teeth, with eyes like a nineteen-year-old, full of joy and focus. He was wearing fashionable jeans and a nice pink sweater. Bobby offered the Bucky's drinks and Johnny beckoned them in. He didn't know them, and was thrilled to see them.

"How are you doing? I'm Johnny. Thanks for the drinks. Oh, Venti. Thanks." There were Chihuahuas barking and Pam was yelling at them to shut up. Stacked women yelling at Chihuahuas, that's magic in Vegas. "C'mon in."

The parlor was dark. The walls were covered with posters and pictures. Posters of the Great Tomsoni and Company from all over the world, since the beginning of time, always looking exactly the same. Maybe this was where the story would take a big twist, and Johnny and Pam really were vampires. In front of the couch was a big coffee table with a green fabric surface like a gaming table. There were decks of cards and coins ready for practice. Pam rounded up the dogs and disappeared. Maybe she actually disappeared, turned into a bat or something. Johnny sat on the couch and motioned for them to grab chairs.

"You guys doing a cowboy act? Piff tried wearing the dragon suit even when he wasn't working, but he stopped when he wanted to get pussy. Too expensive—not the pussy, wearing a costume all the time. I don't know a lot of the cowboy stuff. I learned some lariat work for one show, but I'm not good. The best guy in Vegas for that is Michael Goudeau. He's a coonass from Louisiana but does a little of the Western arts juggling shit: gun twirling, ropes, knife throwing, I think he does a tomahawk thing. There's a guy in Frisco who's really great. I can get you his number if you're serious. I worked with him at the Crazy Horse—Paris, not Vegas. I'm a lousy juggler. Francis Brunn tried to teach me but he gave up. It's like trying to teach Pam to sing in tune. So, what's the act? What can I do to help?"

"We're not in entertainment."

"So it *is* a cowboy act."

"I'm from Texas," Bill explained.

Johnny shrugged.

Bobby took back the reins. "You said you could help us with a gambling scam."

"In those outfits you're gonna be noticed."

"Someone rung in shavers on Bill here. He was playing craps and started winning. They caught him with shavers and the eye-in-the-sky covered a guy switching them in. But Bill doesn't know the guy. Now Bill is black-booked."

"A stranger risked getting busted so he could ring in dirty dice for a guy he didn't know to win? You are the luckiest man alive. Who are you, Joe Piscopo?"

"Who?"

Johnny shrugged again.

It didn't matter. Bobby went on, "We can't figure out what the scam would be. Why would someone do that? Were they going to have him win and rob him later?"

"Nah, but it could have been a distraction."

"I tried to tell Piff that it was misdirection and he said I didn't know what that word means."

"You don't. In 1968 there was a crew that hit five casinos here in town, a couple in Reno, one in Tahoe. They did their final score in Monte Carlo—Monaco, not Vegas. Then they all retired. They did what crooks always say they are going to do and never really do: they made their score and walked the fuck away. One of them taught school in the Midwest for the rest of her life. Another is still a working magician. They used an eyes-shut mark to do a distraction, keep security busy while they did the work." He peered at Bill. "You'd be perfect—big Texas guy who doesn't know the game, starts winning, and they catch him with bad dice. Did you fight?"

"Damn right. I was outraged, sons of bitches bust me just when I start winning. I don't take that shit."

Johnny started laughing. "Perfect. And while a bunch of security people are fighting with Roy Rogers here, the bad guys clean out another table. That's just what the '68 crew did. They had an inside person, a casino employee who is also on the crew. Everyone sitting at the baccarat table is in on it—including the dealer. There are no punters around. It's a show for the eye-in-the-sky. They bring in the best bones mechanic around and he isn't near the baccarat table. He's over at the craps table on the other side of the casino. Brilliant. The action starts rolling near shift change. Everyone but the dice guy, including the inside person, is in place at baccarat and the dirty dice are rung in way over at the craps table. Once the shavers are in, the mechanic splits. He's done. It doesn't take long for the guy who's winning there to be busted. The dice mechanic has chosen a table with a big guy—using a cowboy is fucking genius—and that eyes-shut asshole fights like a freak when they bust him, but the mechanic is already in a cab. During all the dice commotion, across the casino at baccarat, the table is cleaned out. The inside person ends the shift, changes clothes, and then changes their name. The ex-casino employee is on the next plane out of McCarran, on their way to Bali or some shit, before the casino has really even registered the loss completely. Never looks back. Inside guy just sips drinks on the beach and waits for the rest of his cut. Probably gets a partial payment before the scam to get everything set up. The logistics person gets the phony passports and the plane tickets. The crew hits all the casinos within ten days. Casinos do talk to each other, but it takes time. Probably faster now, but the '68 crew had a different employee set up inside at each casino. The way the crew looked on camera while doing the scam is not the way they'd ever look after all the jobs were done. Ten days and they shave, retire, and start teaching social studies in Boise with a nice cash nest egg to spend slowly for the rest of their lives. All the casinos have to go on is the old name of their crooked ex-employees and some eye-in-the-sky footage of a guy with a hat over his eyes switching dice for no reason. The crooked employees are out of the country and if they do ever get caught, they don't know anything anyway. They don't know anybody on the crew. They are almost as clueless as the craps winner. All the casino has is one unlucky asshole who thought he got lucky. Um, that's you."

"Yeah, I thought of that," said Bobby, trying to look with it.

"No you didn't," Johnny replied.

"Well, no I didn't. I mean, I thought it might be misdirection or distraction from something else happening in the casino. But the casino wasn't hit that day."

"How do you know that?"

"I checked the news."

"And you didn't find a feature, 'Casino Announces to Stockholders How They Lost Their Shirts to Criminals'? With a story on the facing page, 'Bullet Points on How to Rob a Casino and Walk Away Clean'? You didn't find those stories anywhere? That's weird. Seems they would have gotten that press release out right away."

"So, that crew might have hit the casino while Bill was fighting?"

"Not the '68 crew, they're all my age. I don't need money; I need my fucking dick to work again."

Bill spoke up: "So I was just a distraction? And now I can't gamble in a casino again?"

Johnny laughed. "The crew did you a favor. Just stop gambling. They saved you some money. Hey, want to see a card trick?"

What the fuck? They nodded.

Johnny picked up the deck of cards from the green felt on his coffee table. His hands were enormous. Just gigantic. They wrapped around a poker deck like Hendrix's hands on the neck of his Strat. When Hendrix touched a guitar, it looked like a uke. Johnny's hands made the poker deck look like a child's bridge deck. Maybe Pam was relieved that his dick didn't work like it used to. Johnny said, "I got a young student out of Korea, Ed Kwon, who came up with this thing. Very clever. Bobby, name a card."

"Me?"

"Yeah, just name a card at random."

"Random?" Bobby's face changed completely.

Johnny had no idea what was going on. "Yeah, just name any card. Free choice. I want to show you something."

Bobby pulled out his Dice to decide on a card.

Johnny's eyes lit up. "You have dice with you? Are these shavers or clean?"

"Clean."

"Let's use your dice." Johnny reached for the Dice, and Bobby lurched back like the guy was reaching to grab his small intestine.

Johnny pulled his hand back and rode right over it. "Okay, I'll show you something else. Just roll the dice."

"I have to roll the Dice to see if I want to roll the Dice for you."

Johnny had met crazy people before. "Okay."

Bobby set the odds in his head and rolled the Dice. It was an Easy Eight, a six and a two. He handed the Dice to Johnny with a big smile.

"Nope, you keep them. Give them a fair roll." Johnny was shuffling the cards in a way that looked to Bobby and Bill to be absentminded. It wasn't. "What you got?" Johnny was watching.

"I got a six, Lumber Number, two by four."

Johnny shuffled a little more, thought for a second, then put the cards in dealing position. "What was the number again?"

"Six."

"Okay, we'll do six hands of five-card stud." Johnny started dealing six hands onto the green felt of his coffee table. "Two by four. Bill, you want twos or fours?"

Bill didn't understand the question, but he answered, "Fours?"

Johnny kept dealing smooth, not the slightest glitch. When he finished, he motioned with his head at Bobby. "Turn over the dealer's hand, my hand." As Bobby reached across, Johnny said, "I dealt myself the hand you chose: full house—the three fours Bill wanted, full of deuces." Bobby turned over the hand and there it was. "Look at the other five hands, they're all okay, everyone has at least a pair so there's some action—but your dice hand wins."

Bill and Bobby were properly impressed. Bill picked up all the cards and started examining them.

Johnny gave a big warm smile. "What are you expecting to find? You couldn't find shavers in your own hands when you were beating the odds."

Bobby was setting his own odds in his head. He had a decision to make on this case. He rolled the Dice. Another eight. Okay, here we go. "That was great, Johnny. Amazing. Wow. Now, how do we find the crew that pulled their version of that scam a few weeks ago so we can get Bill out of the black book?"

"Why would you want to find them?"

"So we can prove that Bill had nothing to do with the shavers and he can game again."

"You will never catch them. You aren't playing with kids here. Just because you're dressed up like make-believe cowboys, don't expect them to be dressed up as silly make-believe Indians. Billion-dollar casinos that lost real money to these guys can't find them, so you sure can't."

"Okay, but where would we start?"

"I can't help you with that. I don't know criminals. I work the other side of the street or I stay off the road. I know people who dress up in dragon suits and tell jokes, I don't know dangerous scumbags. Not anymore. Why don't you talk to your old man?"

"Wait. Wait. What? How do you know my father?"

"Fucking Dave Ingersoll, man. Piff called me before you did. He knew your last name from the check from the gig. And I know Vegas. Fucking Dave Ingersoll. I was hoping you were working on a cowboy act." Johnny was still smiling, but it was forced. "Hey, thanks for the coffee. You came over here for advice, so I'll give you advice—stop playing cowboy or learn some rope tricks. Walk the fuck away." Still with a big smile, Johnny walked them to the door.

They thanked him and said goodbye. The doves cooed.

25

W HEN BILL ASKED THE UBER TO DROP HIM OFF AT the Strip before taking Bobby home, Bobby didn't wonder why. Bill said goodbye and hopped out. He trespassed into the casino he was banned from and, even before facial rec had made him, went to security and announced himself. They brought him into the same room he'd been in when he'd been falsely busted, and explained they were calling Vegas Metro to arrest him for real. Bill calmly, patiently explained how the scam had been run and how he was just an innocent dupe. He was a hapless pawn. He said that he knew there had been a baccarat scam going across the casino while they were fighting with him. He told them there was at least one inside person in each casino working the scam.

Nothing Bill told them was news to casino security. They'd known everything for some time. As a matter of fact, one of the inside people from the heist crew was in the room with Bill at that moment. Security told Bill he was still banned. Bill insisted that he would find out everything about the crew and bring that to the casino and to the police, and then he'd be able to gamble again. They took down his Vegas address and sent him on his way before Metro arrived. Bill left frustrated, angry, and doomed.

On the very next coffee break, one of the security guards went to his burner cell phone and texted his boss, a guy named Skiff, to curry favor. He wanted to show what a good mole he was. Texts from an ambitious dirty security guard to his crew boss are exaggerated and not nuanced. Skiff read the message with alarm. It looked like this cowboy dupe was actually onto him and all the details, and was going to hip the authorities to the whole thing. Was there a clever way for Skiff to handle this? No.

Bill sat in his room and stewed. He had gotten comfortable in his Vegas. He didn't really have much to go back to Texas for. He had some grown children and an ex-wife who were all cordial to him. He wasn't really a cowboy, of course, there is no such thing. He wasn't even from Texas. He was from Iowa. He was a software guy. He had gotten an idea for software that would help score rodeo events and track contestants. It was a variation on all the other sports software that was popping up. His company expanded enough that he was able to sell it and retire at forty. Following the windfall, his children grew up and his wife left him. He went to Vegas and lost money. He never touched his nest egg; he just lost part of the interest every month. His hobby was losing money, but now he was black-booked. His new hobby was trying to get the casinos to let him lose money again. He liked it. He liked meeting Bobby, Piff, and Johnny. He liked sniffing around even more than he liked losing money. He was in the black book and couldn't stay in any of the casino hotel suites, but he'd found a residential hotel that didn't have any gaming, so they didn't care about the black book. It wasn't a bad room. They had a bar. Fuck Texas, he was having the time of his life.

This wasn't going to last.

26

RUPHART WAS STILL TRYING TO COME UP WITH A NEW plan to make Bobby dead. Though Jayne had failed, he still felt the LD50s might be the key. Ruphart could never make any deal with them, so he hated them. Everyone in town, good guys and bad guys, knew that he had no connection with that gang. Ruphart hated all the money he was leaving on their streets. He wanted a taste of their business, but the gang weren't businessmen. They were children. Children full of drugs and anger with powerful hair-trigger ghost guns. They didn't even have a leader. They were an experiment in laissez-faire gang organization. For the most part, every member of the gang was an autonomous, high mental defective. They were not organized and Ruphart hated that the most. The closest they had to a leader was the oldest, craziest, and most violent, a guy named Jandro. This was a killing-positive group of young men; it shouldn't be that hard to get them to snuff Bobby.

Ruphart kept a guy in the gang as a kind of snitch. The mole was just information, there was no leverage at all. From his snitch, and from sources on the street, Ruphart knew that a drug deal the LD50s were making with an LA gang months ago had gone bad. Four gangbangers had died, but more important to everyone, a bag of money went missing. Word was that it was just under a million dollars in a Gucci bag. Ruphart needed to know what kind of Gucci bag, because he was going to simply frame Bobby for the theft. It wouldn't take much. It probably didn't have to even be an exact match for the stolen bag. These assholes wouldn't remember much more than "Gucci," and "full of money." He'd get someone to take some video of Bobby walking with a Gucci bag, have his snitch show Jandro, and let nature take its course. Someone could remind Jandro that Bobby had a shit ton of money that he claimed to have won at a casino. Even Jandro knew enough arithmetic to know how unlikely that was.

Bobby certainly didn't have the balls to rip off gang-bangers, but the idiot gangbangers didn't know that. They had done everything to get the money back. They had threatened the neighbors. They had scared everyone in the neighborhood that night shitless and still learned nothing. It had been months and they still talked about it every day. The prevailing theory was that some kind of silent ninja grabbed the bag of money and got out of the neighborhood with not one person seeing him. That Gucci bag filled with money had become a myth. There was no statute of limitations. They wanted that ninja motherfucker to die. Finding out it wasn't a ninja but just some stupid white kid would disappoint them but wouldn't make them less likely to kill Bobby. It wouldn't make Bobby less dead. They might even torture him first to find out where the money was, and of course Bobby wouldn't know, so the pain would last a long while. Bobby wouldn't know anything about the ninja. It was a good plan. Torture was a bonus. Maybe he'd ask the snitch to tell Jandro the picture was from Ruphart, so maybe Bobby would hear that and know who had really killed him. This was good.

It took awhile to get the snitch on the phone.

"Yo, Mr. RuPe-Hart, what do you want?"

"Listen, Jose—"

"It's Mateo."

"Good. About that money that was stolen back in May—"

"Yeah, a ninja took it. Like Spider-Man type shit, Mr. RuPe-Hart. He like swooped down from the sky or something, and then went right back up to nowhere. Nobody saw him. Some sort of ninja superhero that Jandro wants gone. I know nothing about it. Nothing."

"What kind of bag was the money in?"

"Oh, I know this—Gucci. It was a Gucci bag."

"What kind of Gucci bag?"

"Expensive."

"Right, they're all expensive, that's all they have going for them. That's the brand."

"Yeah, it was expensive because it was full of money."

"Yes. But what did the bag look like? If it was a million dollars, it doesn't fit in the briefcase-size Gucci but it fits in a carry-on. Was it a roll-aboard or a duffel?"

"What?"

"You saw the bag, right?"

"Yes, but I didn't steal it."

"I know you didn't, but you saw it."

"Yes."

"Was it on wheels or was it like a duffel bag?"

"There weren't wheels."

"And what color."

"Gucci?"

"Gucci isn't a color."

"Yes it is."

"No, Gucci isn't a color, it's a brand. Was it beige?"

"No, it was Gucci."

"Beige is a color. Was it light or dark? Was it tan? Was it like white but dirtier?"

"It was a brand-new Gucci-colored bag full of green money."

"Listen to me, you stupid motherfucker: was it a light color with a red and green stripe down the middle with two handles on the top and a zipper in between the two handles with no wheels?"

"Yes, it was a Gucci-colored bag with a stripe in the middle and you'll know it if you see it because it's full of money and it was stolen by a ninja Spider-Man."

Ruphart hung up.

27

ANOTHER YO ELEVEN—THE DICE TOLD HIM TO CALL his dad and told him how to act. Not his first choice, but it *was* one of his choices and Random picked it. Random had told him to be kind and forgiving to his dad for the whole day. The Dice were making it tough for him. His dad was a piece of shit, but Dave Ingersoll was good at math. Not good enough at math to understand that they didn't build casinos by losing, but good enough to count cards for reals. Card counting was one of the greatest things to ever happen to the Las Vegas casino industry. Almost everyone understood the basic concept and almost no one really did it right. The casinos are fine with people cheating as long as they continue to lose.

Dave really counted cards. He first arrived in Vegas as part of an MIT card-counting crew. He would have told you it was *the* MIT blackjack crew, but it was *an* MIT blackjack crew. Recruiting cheaters at MIT was just some sort of weird flattery; they could have recruited at Greenfield Community College and filled all the positions. The criminals didn't need mathematics, they just needed arithmetic. They needed people who could sit with a drink in front of them and play perfect blackjack at the lowest table stakes while keeping track of a plus or minus single-digit count. When that number was disadvantageous to the house, they would signal an old guy from Singapore whose job was to look like an old guy from Singapore—specifically, an old guy from Singapore who looked like he wouldn't know a nerd from Cambridge. In fact he was an old Singapore guy who really didn't know a nerd from Cambridge, but was working with one. The old Singapore guy would play the highest table stakes when the Cambridge Masshole alerted him that there was an advantage at that table. That advantage was one single red cunt hair over 50%, but that's enough. It's enough if you do this boring thing all day and all night. Later, the criminal team of nerds and guys who didn't look like they would know nerds would all meet back with the boss, who would pay everyone for their trouble. It's hard to make money without doing any good for anyone in the world whatsoever, but the MIT blackjack crews pounded out a tiny amount with their scam without any risk of helping anyone or causing any joy. They made a minimum weekend's worth of the dough-ray-me.

Who knows about the Asians—but the MIT guys could have made the same amount of money working the weekend as the eighties version of Apple Geniuses. And cheating at cards seemed sexy. What's sexier than flying 2,372 miles, sitting at a table under artificial lights for thirty hours, watching a guy from Singapore win some money, and having fatty prime rib with creamy horseradish in your comped hotel room alone? Of course, any pussy or cock would be sexier than that—but those never entered the picture.

Dave was hooked. Not on the math, or the fatty prime rib, or even the money. He loved cheating. He felt he was bringing down the man. This was his personal way to fuck with the 1%. He was Robin Hood, stealing from the rich and giving to himself, but mostly to some criminals who ate KFC buckets in an off-Strip hotel while the college kids and Asians were grinding at the tables. The crew bosses stayed in off-Strip hotels because they were all in the black book, banned from all the casinos. They were actually proud that they couldn't stay at casinos. They ate KFC because they were greasy fat fucks, and while they weren't exactly proud of that, they didn't care much about it either.

One of the fat bosses was great with a deck of cards. He didn't learn cards to do tricks, because that might make people happy. He wanted to be a card cheat because it was sexy ... except for no sex. The fat boss was good enough with his cardistry that he got to know a real Vegas Strip comedy magician, a headliner with his picture three hundred feet tall on the side of a building. One night the boss brought Dave to meet the magician at the Peppermill, a diner-type place on the Strip where nineteen-year-old women—too young to legally serve cocktails—sling patty melts to marks while dressed like the twenty-eight-year-old divorcées they worry they're going to turn into.

Dave assumed the magician would think their blackjack teams were just groovy as all fuck because they were doing it for real, man! If a magician fucks up, he just doesn't get as much applause, but if a card-counting crew fucks up, they go to fucking prison! Well, not really, they just get politely shown off the property with a stern verbal warning, but it's the same idea. Like it's the same idea to be sexy with no sex.

Dave asked the magician for tips on how to signal their Asian partners. The magician suggested waving their hands and singing Pink Floyd's "Money" in 7/8 time. The smart-ass magician asked Dave why he did it, instead of staying at MIT and studying. Dave said cheating made him feel like James Bond. The magician asked him if he had gotten laid last night, since James Bond got laid every last night, and twice after a kill. Magic Boy did some shtick about Dave not even managing to be a James Bond wannabe, just a Q wannabe. Comedy magicians—they aren't good enough magicians to be magicians and not good enough comedians to be comedians. Dave found out that comedy magicians are just dicks.

All the other MIT kids in the crew went back to MIT with a story, got degrees, began doing real science somewhere or starting companies that made money, helped people, or brought some joy. Dave moved to Vegas and raised the stakes. While he was still good-looking and had some life behind his eyes, he managed to get laid. He got laid by a showgirl. Maybe he finally was James Bond. Bobby's mom was a "showgirl"—she was beautiful, sexy, and fertile. She was also smart, very smart—but not smart enough to not fall in love with and get knocked up by an ex-MIT-blackjack-crew asshole.

"Bobby!"

"Hey, Dad."

"Listen, Bobby, I'm going to pay you back, I promise. I'm working it. I got it set up. I want to get all the money together and pay you in one lump sum, with a little interest, you know. That loan was the greatest thing anyone's ever done for me." Jesus, what an asshole.

"Sure, Dad. Take your time. Listen, I need your help." Random had told him to be kind, loving, forgiving . . . and let his father be delusional.

"Anything. I promise. Little cash-flow problem right now, but really, anything else." Lying sack of shit.

"I don't need money, Dad, I just need some info."

"Anything."

"Who did the big job in the casino three and a half weeks ago?"

"What are you talking about?"

"C'mon, Dad."

"Yeah, I guess I did hear a little something. It's a big crew. Real pros. They hit six different casinos in town. They scored a couple mil . . . each. I had nothing to do with it, Bobby, I'm playing it straight. I wasn't part of it. Promise. No more crime for me. I've learned my lesson." Bobby believed just one of those claims. If Dave Ingersoll had had anything to do with this casino scam, it wouldn't have worked, and his sister would be getting felt up by hit men again.

"Who was it?"

"I have no idea. None. I just read about it in the papers." Yeah, sure.

"Okay, Dad." Bobby stayed nice like eleven had commanded. This was starting to feel good.

"Hey, I'm glad we're in touch again, son, can we meet for coffee? Let me buy you a cup of joe."

Bobby rolled an Easy Four. "Sure, Bucky's at the Nugget. I'll be there by three."

Bobby had decided a few times in the past that he'd never see his father again, but here he was walking down Fremont Street to meet him. As he strolled, he was laying twenties on every street performer he saw. He didn't use any of the entertainments those tips bought him. He didn't sign the bill so it could appear in a lemon. He didn't take any pictures, staple any bills to performers' breasts, or kick any entrepreneurs hard in the balls for his twenty (yup, that's a real street act, check it out). Let the tourists do all that. He just dropped a bill, winked, and walked on by. They all knew him.

He arrived right on time to the Bucky's and Dad would surely be late. So much for Dad paying. He rolled for his order while he waited in line. Five—that meant decaf Americano for him, and he didn't need to roll for his dad—always a small black coffee. Bobby stopped at the condiment stand. He took a few hot sips of his coffee, all the bitter and none of the speed, and poured some of his dad's plain black into the extra space in his cup, spilling a little and burning his hand. "Fuck." He then filled the space in his dad's coffee with as much cream as he could and six sugars. He found a table on the patio and sat under the Experience watching Fremont roll by. Electric Daisy Carnival must be in town now, the street was maggoty with young abs and bunny ears. Maybe he'd go and hear some music. He'd find out the dates later and roll the Dice.

"Hey, son." His dad was not part of EDC. Dave Ingersoll was wearing a NASCAR jacket. He wasn't living Random, that was his only choice. Fucking embarrassing dick.

"Hey, Dad. I got you a drink. Coffee very light with six sugars."

"I taught you well. Did you pour some off into the space in your drink?"

"Just like you taught me." Dad never bought fancy coffee drinks. He got the cheapest coffee and then drank some or poured it off into a friend's cup (he never asked for "room," he wanted it full to start). Then he'd pour in six sugars and as much cream as he could fit, sometimes going back up to the stand when it was half gone to fill it up again with cream and a little more sugar. Like always, he was taking down the man. The expensive drinks were just paying for cream and sugar and the cream and sugar were right out there for free. Simple, Dave Ingersoll outsmarted Starbucks.

"Well, I didn't teach you well enough—are you drinking fancy black?"

"Yes, I am, Dad. I'm rich." It was true but they both laughed.

"Listen, son, I didn't want to talk over the phone, these are serious people."

Bobby was about to accuse his dad of being paranoid, but it was possible Dave's phone really was tapped. Who knows? "Just me listening now, Dad."

Dave looked all around and leaned in. "It's a crew put together by Skiff Norton. You know Skiff?" Bobby shook his head. "Really smart guy. He was out of Stanford, I think. Some fancy college. Chemistry or something. Then he raped some professor and had to split. He's been underground ever since. He planned all those casino jobs. The rest of the crew was one-and-done. They had an insider at every casino. It took him about three years to set it up. Skiff's a perfectionist. Really nice work."

"He raped a professor?"

"Not one of *his* professors, some visiting professor, I think. Something like that. They never caught him. It was long ago, he's a bad guy."

"What kind of name is Skiff?" Bobby was looking out onto Fremont. Some of the EDC people were just amazing. Bobby would give going to that event a five, six, seven, and eight. Goodness, that young woman was wearing nothing but daisy decals and an illegal smile. Fuck me!

"I guess the kind of name you choose after you've raped a professor."

"Do you know where I can find him?" The EDC woman had passed, so now he looked right in his dad's eyes.

"No. He doesn't ever want to be found by nobody, but right now he *wicked* doesn't want to be found by nobody. Probably banging some willing professor on a pile of money right about now."

"I need to find him."

"No you don't. You really do not need to find him. If you find him, they're going to figure who gave someone the idea to find him and that'll lead back to me and that'll lead back to you, and we'll both be in the shit."

"Where would I start to find him?"

"Start by giving up. Why do you need to know? Are you working for the man now?"

"I'm working for *a* man. Not even a man, I'm working for a cowboy. He was the chump they switched the dice on."

"The misdirection?"

"I think you're using that word wrong, but yes."

"So what? The guy wasn't busted, right? No one was busted, and he isn't entitled to a cut."

"No one is entitled, Dad, it was stealing."

"Stealing from thieves."

"Stealing from the rich and giving to Skiff."

"Sure, he outsmarted them, he won fair and square."

"Okay." Bobby was in this conversation because he had rolled the eleven; he'd do Random's will, he'd stay kind. "I need to find him so I can prove to the casino that my guy doesn't deserve to be black-booked."

"*I'm* black-booked."

"And you deserve it. My guy isn't a criminal."

"What's this guy got on you?"

"Nothing. He's got nothing. He really hasn't got a chance and I want to help him. It's what I do now."

Dave got up, went to the milk and sugar stand, and filled his half-empty cup with cream and more sugar. Bobby rolled the Dice while he was gone. Ace Caught a Deuce, three. Let's see how this plays.

Dave sat down with his cup of disgusting but free, dirty sweet cream.

"Dad, you've kinda known me since I was born."

"You're my son."

"Have you ever known me to bluff?"

"Nope, you got that from your mom."

"Listen carefully. I have Fraser Ruphart's phone number right here in my phone. You tell me everything you know about how to find Skiff or I drop a dime right now and tell Fraser you told me Skiff pulled the job."

"Son, they'll kill us both."

"Think I'm bluffing?"

"What's the difference? You go looking for Skiff, we're probably both dead anyway, right?"

"Maybe. Don't you like the odds of *probably* better than the odds of a fucking cap in your head by sundown?"

"Crazy asshole."

"I got *that* from you."

"Okay. Let me think."

"Don't think about how to lie, I'm not fucking around."

Dave Ingersoll started making phone calls to scumbags while Bobby looked out over Fremont Street. A cheap holiday in other people's misery, as Johnny Rotten said about Berlin, but also true here. How do people end up on Fremont Street? The Electric Daisy Carnival people ended up here because of fuck drugs with positive phototaxis as a side effect. Maybe alcohol, meth, and desperation did the same thing. It was the neon glow of the living dead and Bobby was sipping decaf and living it. His dad was sweating like a fucking pig. His dad *was* a fucking pig.

"Okay, son. Listen, I really think you should drop this. Really. Really drop it. No-kidding drop it, please. But if you've got someone else's gun to my head, Skiff seems to be holding up at Trump International now."

Of course. Skiff lived in the same stupid building with the same stupid name on it as the other stupid bad guy. Skiff lived a few floors below Ruphart. Skiff was that kind of Trump/Ruphart guy, except smarter than both of them put together, which is the same as saying smarter than Ruphart. If there was a god, the earth would swallow up Trump International and get a little closer to Paradise. (If you knew Vegas geography, you'd know that Trump International isn't located in Las Vegas, but rather in the adjoining town of Paradise, Nevada—not really a joke, just kind of silly wordplay.) So, Skiff was at Trump International. Wow, guessing where a scumbag was mostly likely to live would have accomplished the same thing as coffee with his dad. But maybe seeing his dad was okay. Maybe the Dice were right.

"Thanks, Dad."

"Please don't use this information, son. Please don't." His dad was mostly concerned about his own ass, but there was some honest concern for Bobby and Bobby liked that. His dad did care a little. Not enough to show any commitment to his family, but enough to worry a little. That was sweet. Not as sweet as his disgusting coffee, but a little sweet.

"I'll be careful, Dad. I will."

Bobby stood up and gave his dad a hug. He didn't have to roll the Dice; he would spend the next couple of hours on Fremont. He wanted to suck it up. Fremont was what happens when America really does fight for its right to party.

28

BOBBY HEADED OVER TO THE OFFICE. HE WANTED TO talk to Tone. Bobby knew that Skiff was behind the scam that fucked Bill out of his god-given right to lose money to OCP (Omni Consumer Products, which at some level must own all the casinos). He knew that Skiff was at Trump International. What was his next move? He didn't have any choices to give to the Dice. He had no idea. He was losing interest in this whole Bill case. Maybe he should just drop it.

When he walked into the office, Madilyn, the receptionist, called him over. "Hey, Bobby, someone sent a present for you."

"Wow. Great." He walked over to her desk and she handed him a Gucci men's Ophidia GG medium carry-on duffel bag.

She was impressed. "I don't think it's a knockoff, it's got a serial number, I checked."

Bobby froze. The last time he'd seen a bag like this, his pants were full of shit and piss and he was crying in a McDonald's parking lot. What were the chances that someone knew he'd stolen the money? The chances were zero, but someone knew. "Who is it from? Was there a card?"

"Just a typed card that said, *Bobby Ingersoll, thanks.*" Someone must know something. But why would they wait months to make their move? There was no demand for money on the card, there was no threat. But this couldn't be a coincidence.

Someone knew something. Bill and Skiff were suddenly the least of Bobby's troubles.

Bobby stood there holding the bag as Tone came in with his iced Americano and gummy bears. "Hey, nice bag. Is that real or a knockoff?"

Madilyn jumped in: "Someone dropped it off for Bobby. It's real, it has a serial number."

"All the knockoffs have serial numbers, you gotta go online and look up that number and you can see where and when it was sold. Also check the logo, the knockoffs have shittier metal logos. If that's real, that's a bag worth about two grand. You could flip that motherfucker for a few bucks. But what do you care? You throw your fucking money away."

Bobby was trying hard not to shit himself there in the office. Gucci still did that to him. He rolled the Dice. "Do you want the bag, Tone?"

"Nah, it doesn't go with my shoes. You want it, Madilyn?"

"It's a man's bag."

"You know plenty of men, and the men you are attracted to like Gucci, right? Lay it on one of them and get some head. Or flip it and buy yourself a bottle of something nice. Just take it."

Ruphart had someone set up, waiting to snap pictures through Bobby's window when he walked into his office with the bag. But Bobby didn't take the bag into his office. Nor did he come out of the office with it. There wouldn't be any pictures of Bobby with the bag to get to the LD50s.

Ruphart had unsuccessfully framed Madilyn's boyfriend for the crime that Bobby had committed, and Bobby now believed incorrectly that someone knew he was the ninja Spider-Man.

Bobby had moved closer to ninja in the past few months— now he was able to make it to the bathroom before he vomited.

29

BOBBY JUST SAT IN HIS OFFICE ALL DAY AND THOUGHT. He juggled the two Dice in one hand. He tried to figure what that bag had meant and what the next move was going to be. He was doing too much thinking, forgetting what Random had taught him. He was not going to be able to plan this. It was time to get outside and roll the Dice for choices he could make. Neither he nor the Dice knew the future. He had to get back to the present. He headed downstairs to take a walk on Fremont. He needed some chaos. It was getting late. He'd spent the whole day in the office worrying. The sun went down and the street got brighter. He rolled an Easy Eight and affected a limp. He watched a street magician do her show and his signed twenty showed up in a lemon. She could keep it. Electric Daisy Carnival must have started elsewhere in town, because the beautiful sexy people were gone, and he was back to the slow desperation of the night of the gambling dead. He dropped another twenty and posed with a couple of topless "showgirls." It was so fucking loud and so fucking bright that he couldn't pretend to think; he let the question just sit in the background: what did the Gucci bag mean? Did he want to add even more mortal risk to his life so a cowboy could gamble in casinos?

Bobby had been living on borrowed time since he first rolled the Yo Eleven at Perry's. Like all of us, he'd actually been living on borrowed time since birth—but unlike us, since his twenty-first birthday his superpower was that he knew it. Walking confused and alone in a crowd on Fremont was what citizens did. Bobby didn't need to do that; he had his cubed bracelets of submission. Anytime he wanted, the Dice would roll away all uncertainty. Anytime had come. Time to set the odds and get on with Random life.

When he really started laying out the numbers, he realized the Gucci bag didn't change anything because he didn't know anything. It was also clear that the part of Bobby that wanted to find Skiff and get Bill back to gambling was dwindling fast. Dealing with stupid criminals was Dave Ingersoll's thing and this apple had Randomly fallen so far from that tree that it was in a whole different orchard. There was still some small pull to finish the hopeless job he'd taken on, yet that would get only a twelve. Twelve would send him over to find Skiff and get Bill gambling again. A small 2.78% of him still wanted to do that. The rest didn't. If he rolled a two, he would try to find the gangbanged redhead and go get killed getting her sister out of her drug beef. The only big danger was two and twelve, and that's how much he still wanted that danger. Three and four were go home and have a fluffernutter and start fresh tomorrow in the office with Tone and find another case. He would just ghost Bill, fuck him. Five, six, seven, and eight, more than half of him, would call Bill while he was eating his fluffernutter and explain honestly that it was a dead end, it was just too dangerous to go further on this, and he'd start fresh tomorrow on something else. Nine, ten, and eleven were to meet Bill and tell him in person. He would stop on the way to meeting him and get a jar of Marshmallow Fluff, a jar of Skippy, and a loaf of Wonder Bread. He'd call Bill and tell him to bring milk. Right before he rolled, he added fluffernutter to two and twelve. He wasn't gambling on his fluffernutter. He knew what he wanted; he wanted a dense, sweet, sticky sandwich no matter what.

He rolled another Lumber Number, two by four—six. He walked toward the Nugget. His electric Vespa motor scooter now had an *Easy Rider* Captain America paint job—he had believed he no longer needed to be invisible. Maybe he was wrong. He'd parked at the Nugget valet this morning. He dropped a Jackson on the attendant, grabbed his helmet, and jumped on. The gas station stores didn't have Fluff. He hit the supermarket. Fluff, Skippy, Wonder, and milk—he was set.

He got home, made a big thick sandwich of goo, and called Bill with his mouth full of the paste. It would be easier to tell Bill the truth if Bill couldn't understand him.

Mark Twain would have written the way the words sounded through the Wonder/fluffy/Skippy gunky goodness, but let's just write what he was trying to say: "Hey, Bill. We're giving up. It's a dead end. You aren't going to be able to gamble in casinos. Go back to Texas and start fresh. Maybe start dressing like a fireman."

"Are you having a stroke?"

"Nope, a fluffernutter."

"What?"

"Fluffernutter."

"What?"

"Marshmallow Fluff and lots of peanut butter."

"What?"

"I quit!"

"Hold on, there's someone at the door." There was a short pause and then Bill gurgled into the phone.

Bobby laughed. "Don't make fun of the differently-fluffernutter-abled."

There was another voice on the line, a scary voice: "Who is this?"

Bobby swallowed the huge gooey ball and answered without thinking, "Bobby Ingersoll. Who is this? Put Bill back on."

"How do you know Bill?"

"I'm a detective helping him figure out how to get out of the black book." Fuck! Why did he say that? It was the fluffernutter talking, and he had swallowed, so he was understandable. All the peanut butter was now gone from his mouth along with all the saliva.

"Bill's just had his throat slit. He's dead, and you're next. Fuck you, Bobby Ingersoll."

30

A HOMELESS GUY SPARE-CHANGES A WELL-DRESSED man walking down Broadway in New York City. The man gives the beggar a quarter and scolds him, "*Neither a borrower nor a lender be*—William Shakespeare." The bum looks at the quarter, looks at his cheap benefactor, and says, "*Fuck you, you fucking piece of shit*—David Mamet."

Fucking David fucking Mamet writes really well about con artists, con games, and scams. Mamet explores the knowledge of humanity inherent in the scams. The scam that Skiff's gang had pulled was clever; using an innocent as distraction while the crew worked. Fucking Mamet's fictional criminals are immoral, but we can't help but respect their cunning. When a close-up magician does her three-card monte hunk, she underlines the smooth sleight of hand of the monte dealer and brings the audience inside by explaining that the dealer's sleights are not the real work, there are also the *sticks* (plants) among the monte crowd who are making the action happen and scamming the mark. It seems like a well-choreographed, -thought-out, and -acted presentation. But all this cleverness means nothing. Monte crews are usually about eight people, with lookouts and muscle all over. Let's say you can do sleight of hand as well as the dealer. Let's say you do a perfect switch when *finding the lady*. You still can't win fair and square, it's not fair and square. But let's say you are cleverer and more skilled than the monte operator. Do you walk away with the money? Do you stroll off while the operator and his partners are respectful and impressed to have been legitimately bettered? No. They pull you into the nearest alley, steal all your money, and beat the living shit out of you. These are not gentle game players running a skillful, insightful cheat that illuminates human nature. These are violent thugs.

Skiff was brilliant. He wasn't the smartest student the Stanford chemistry department had ever seen, but he sure wasn't the dumbest. Smart people know that intelligence is complicated and very hard to measure. Only stupid people feel they can rate smarts. In one season of *Celebrity Apprentice*, the president of the United States of America, hosting the show before he was the president of the United States of America, said to a Vegas magician on the show that he—the fucking idiot Vegas magician—was one of the three people that Trump had ever met who was smarter than Trump himself. Trump said exactly that: "You are one of the three people I've ever met who is smarter than me." Donald had met only three people smarter than him in his life and one of them was a Vegas magician. Who were the other two, a balloon twister and a ventriloquist? The magician was asked what he thought about that, and he replied, wisely, "Well, Trump must not have met many people." Smart people don't know how many people they've met smarter than them. There's no way of knowing how many people were smarter than Skiff, lots we guess, but he was smart.

The scam Skiff had run on the casinos was ingenious. The distraction was brilliant, the skillful, specially designed, false shuffles that fooled the eye-in-the-sky, the timing was clockwork . . . there was a lot of impressive work in the scam. But when something went wrong, Skiff spent just under an hour trying to think of a clever way out and then went directly to violence. That's what immoral people do. We don't know how smart Skiff is but we sure fucking know how immoral he is. Some Texas dipshit was sniffing around trying to find who was behind the baccarat scam? That was the problem. Fuck artful, slit the fucking cowboy's fucking throat.

Bobby didn't take Bill to talk to his dad about the scam. But Bobby did take Bill to meet Johnny and that was, for Bill, a fatal mistake. Bill thought the information that Johnny laid out for them was his get-out-of-jail-free card, or in this case his get-back-into-the-casino-and-lose-a-lot-of-money-free card. Bill figured he could just explain the scam to casino security, and they'd let him lose money again. That didn't work.

Fraser Ruphart hired men to threaten and kill people, but Skiff went and did it on his own. Skiff liked it, and he could trust himself to do it right. Ruphart liked the idea of people being scared of him. He liked thinking that people recognized his power before they died. Skiff didn't care what they thought. He was happy making people dead.

The residential hotels in Vegas don't really have security. Skiff had the address and the room number. He had nondescript clothing, gloves, and a hat covering his face. He didn't have to break in, he knocked on the door and Bill opened it with a smile while he was on the phone to Bobby. Who the fuck did Bill think Skiff was? We'll never know. Skiff didn't even ask if Bill's name was Bill. He just slit this throat. Skiff had a very sharp knife. There was no struggle. Skiff used enough force to almost cut his head off. Bill's neck was a fountain, all over the room and all over Skiff. Skiff didn't care, he would throw all the clothes away. He just dropped the knife on the floor. Just dropped it. There was nothing to get away with. Nothing. A fucking cowboy was dead in Vegas. Authorities might just pass it off as a very focused suicide with a lot of momentum.

The phone was covered with blood, but some asshole was still talking. Skiff disguised his voice in a cursory way and asked who it was.

The guy on the other end of the phone sounded like he was getting his throat cut too, or maybe he had a mouth full of dick—Skiff never guessed fluffernutter. "Bobby Ingersoll," the cocksucker answered like a fool, and then asked who it was and said he wanted Bill back on the line. Good, Skiff had killed the right asshole.

"How do you know Bill?"

"I'm a detective helping him figure out how to get out of the black book," the guy choked out. Jesus, what a fucking idiot.

"Bill's just had his throat slit. He's dead, and you're next. Fuck you, Bobby Ingersoll." Skiff had the name now and he looked at the phone for a number.

This shit was just way too easy.

31

OBBY WAS OKAY WITH HIS LAST MEAL BEING A FLUFF-ernutter, but not yet. Not fucking yet. Bill was dead and Bobby was next. He was thinking about a plan when "Get on the Good Foot" by James Brown started playing on his phone. It was Melvin Bern calling. Bobby was in a fight for his life, it wasn't really the time to talk to Melvin, but he rolled the Dice. If he rolled a two or a three, he would answer. Twelve and he'd block him until this whole thing was over. In the middle was letting it go to VM. Three, the Ace Caught a Deuce, and he would answer. Bobby was scared shitless and he was going to talk to his friend Melvin.

"Melvin, there is a guy on his way over here to kill me."

"I feel like I'm supposed to say calm down, but you seem maybe *too* calm. Should I suggest you panic?"

"I was helping a guy get out of the casino black book by exposing a gambling ring and they found him and slit his throat. Now the murderer is on his way to kill me."

"Who?"

"A guy named Skiff."

"Isn't he that rapist-math-card-worker guy?"

"Yeah, and now he's the murderer-rapist-math-card-worker guy on his way to kill me."

"Get out of town."

"I have stuff to do here."

"All you have to do in Vegas now is die. Get out of Dodge. Now. Drop everything and take a plane somewhere. Or drive. Don't tell anyone where. Can you decide the place at random?"

"Random I can do."

"Go! Destroy the phone and send me all your cloud passwords from the airport or the road. Use a burner. I know a guy who can make it a little harder for them to find your info."

Bobby took a moment to roll and got a five. Everything but two and twelve were to trust Melvin completely. "I use one of those store-all-your-passwords-in-one-place password-collector things."

"Because you're an idiot. But you've memorized the master password, right?"

"Yeah."

"Okay. Don't write anything down. Don't take your car or an Uber. Destroy your phone and computer. Completely. I suggest smashing them, flushing any memory that comes out down the toilet. Tell me your master password and what collector you use."

"Um, I use OnePassword and my password is 535234, lowercase a, capital S, lowercase a, n, a, the number 11, lowercase a, h, d, caret, e, s, h, and capital R."

"Not bad. I got it. I'll have my guy download everything and then transfer it to an air-gapped computer. If you live, you can get everything later, but you'll be gone from the cloud for now. Are all your banking and investments tied into your cloud and password accounts?"

"Yup. All of it."

"Idiot. I know another guy. We'll move all your money out of stocks and savings to Bitcoin, and I'll have that air-gapped on a different computer. You can get that whenever you want it. Now, burn it down and get the fuck out."

"Really? Is all this really necessary?"

"Probably not. I doubt it's necessary at all, but we don't know. Skiff has government people in his pocket who may be able to search all this. So just do it. Burn it down and get the fuck out."

Bobby hung up and thought for a moment. He rolled a seven, Big Red—Random wanted him to burn it down for real, with fire. His house had a lot of space around it. He wouldn't be seriously endangering too many other people. Firefighters and shit and, of course, it was a big drag. He took a hammer and smashed his phone. The SIM card went down the toilet and the rest of the phone went on the stove. He took his laptop, smashed it, and took the flash card and the hard drive and put them directly on another gas burner and turned it up high. He used a third gas burner for his iPad. They started smoking like bastards. He turned all the other burners on high and turned his oven on as well. He had a notebook or two and he put them on the last gas burner. He had almost twenty thousand in cash in the house because he was a nut. He threw the cash into a bag with his passport. He took nothing else but his Dice. He ran out the back door and kept running.

Being poor teaches you to want things; being rich makes you hate things. Some guys get divorced because they can't admit they just want to get rid of all the stupid things they've bought. Sure, they could sell the boat, the Les Paul, and the Beamer, and give all the money to charity, but isn't it easier to just fuck the au pair and have the wife get stuck with all that shit? And no au pair sex could compare to arson.

This was the greatest thing that had ever happened to Bobby. Fuck Marie Kondo and whatever piece of shit brings you joy—you want joy? Burn your fucking house down and

take nothing with you but cash and Dice. He felt really bad
about Bill. Really bad. It was kind of his fault, and he felt
sick about it, but he loved running for his life with cash, the
clothes on his back, and his Dice. A couple times Bobby
had assigned *Burn the house down and disappear* if he rolled a
twelve, but Random had never chosen it. This time it had been
a seven and Random grabbed it and Bobby lit it up and ran.
The house probably wouldn't burn all the way down, but the
kitchen sure was toast.

Bobby was running. Actually running. He wanted to get
far from his house before he caught transportation. It was
about two and a half miles to Fremont Street and he ran most
of it. He got to the Four Queens Hotel and picked up a shuttle bus to McCarran Airport. Bad guys around Fremont knew
him, but he didn't walk under the Experience, he went in the
back wearing a hat on that he never wore, and it was pulled
way down. Hunched over, he was just another loser trying to
get out of Vegas fast. It had been forty-five minutes since he'd
listened to Bill getting his throat slit and he'd made it to being
anonymous and panting on a shitty shuttle bus. He hoped
that Skiff would figure that Bobby would go to the police,
or hire some muscle, and try to stay in Vegas. Skiff probably wouldn't get someone to watch the airport until he got to
Bobby's house and saw the fire. If Bobby got the first flight
out of Dodge, he'd probably be okay for a while.

He didn't know it, but he didn't actually have to run. He
could have walked to the airport. He had plenty of time.
Bobby had figured everything wrong. Skiff knew that Bobby
wouldn't go to the police and Skiff didn't head directly over to
Bobby's. He figured that Bobby would be too scared to make
any move that would fuck things up. Bobby was wrong about
everything, but Melvin was still right about getting out. Bobby

would be in another world by the time Skiff really started to look for him. Bobby's image of the guy arriving to a burning house in the night didn't happen. The fire was reported by the neighbors and the fire department was there right away and stopped it from taking the whole house out, though the computers and phone were gone, daddy-o. We don't know if Skiff would ever have used those anyway, or knew anyone who could, but now they were gone, and Bobby was getting off a shuttle at the airport.

Bobby ran in and looked at the board. The next flight was to Salt Lake City. Who the fuck wants to flee to SLC? He wanted some Southeast Asian country that was maggoty with lady boys. But no international flights were leaving until the next morning. He had to get out now, yet he sure didn't want to be in the only place on earth with more Mormons than Vegas. He also didn't have time to buy the tickets and get through TSA to the SLC gate. There was a flight to Dallas a half hour later. He could make that easy. He had cash and a passport, so he put Dallas on everything but two and twelve, rolled his lucky eleven, and he was off.

"Did you ever see Dallas from a DC-9 at night? Well, Dallas is a jewel, oh yeah, Dallas is a beautiful sight." Joe Ely lying out his ass. Dallas is nothing. It's just a city with fewer Mormons than SLC. A city that no one in the world knew would soon contain Bobby Ingersoll. There is a special feeling you get when no one knows where you are. No one. It's got to be no one. It's not high lonesome. It's like the up version of high lonesome. Living Random, Bobby felt that all the time. He felt weekly what other people feel only during a major romantic breakup or a mental breakdown. The powerful feeling of being able to be whomever you want to be, regardless of who you are now. Bobby could roll the Dice in the morning and become anyone

right then, over coffee. Others had to wait for a life event to pull the rug out from under them and allow them to slip, slide, flip, splish, splash, and tumble slow motion into the air and come down as someone else. Bobby didn't think Skiff would go after his mom or sister. His sister was off to Johns Hopkins and who wants to harass someone in Baltimore? What would she know anyway? And his mom didn't know anything, and Skiff would realize Bobby was smart enough not to tell either of them anything. If they tortured his dad—well, that's a feature not a bug.

What about Tone? Tone would like the opportunity to tell a professor-rapist to fuck himself for a change. If Skiff went to Tone, Tone might go all Chow Yun-fat on Skiff's ass just for fun. Bobby was clean and green. He could enjoy watching that little bit of himself that wasn't quite pure Random unravel. He had been using the Dice about a dozen times a day, but mostly for little nothing decisions. Now Random could rebuild Bobby from the ground up.

When anyone lands in an airport, they rush for the local fresh air. They're eager to be where they're going. They have places to go and people to meet. That's why they flew wherever the fuck they flew. It was nutty to land in Dallas and not be in a hurry to be in Dallas. Who goes to a sit-down restaurant in an airport? Bobby. He headed over to Terminal A and went to Lorena Garcia Tapas y Cocina. He sat down and ordered ten small plates. Disappearing after arson made a fellow powerful hungry. Mexican food is all the same food in different shapes. He could have just gotten just chips and salsa and been thrilled.

What choices would he give Random? What were the choices for who he wanted to be? What were the choices for where he wanted to go? Would he ever go back to Vegas? He didn't know shit about Dallas. He knew that Terri used to live here. He hadn't gone to her wedding or her honeymoon, but he'd been invited. When she'd returned a couple weeks later for the divorce (annulment?), they'd gone to Lotus of Siam and seen the Mac King show together. They laughed about how good her prenup had been. Bobby and Terri had both been made rich by Random, so they had a little something to talk about that they didn't share with many others. Her email address was easy to remember, TerriTiger@gmail.com. He assigned seeing Terri to just a three, 5.56%, but Random grabbed it. Some airport restaurants have iPads at every seat. You can get to the web. Bobby set up a one-time email account on Gmail (11Eleven11Eleven11Eleven11@gmail.com) and dropped a note to Terri. It would probably just go to spam and she'd never see it, but maybe she checked her filter once in a while.

Hey Terri,

This is Bobby Ingersoll, writing from a different address. Some asshole in Vegas has decided to kill me, so I had to disappear. The Dice sent me to Dallas and another roll had me send this email. I see on the web there is a place called the Wild Detectives. It's a bookstore and coffee shop. It's open until midnight every night. I'll go there at 11:30 every night starting tomorrow, Saturday, the 9th. I'll read and drink coffee until they throw my ass out. If you want to stop by, I got some stories to tell. I'll be there every night until the Dice tell me to do something else. No one else in the world knows where I am. Let's keep it that way.

Every Inch of My Love,
Bobby

He hit send and deleted the account. Terri would get it, or she wouldn't. She'd show up or she wouldn't. He had beans, corn, and peppers to eat, and cheese to pick off. In many different shapes.

32

HERE WERE A BUNCH OF HOTELS IN THE ARTSY AREA
of Dallas near the Wild Detectives bookshop. Bobby
rolled Jessie James, a four and a five, so he would get
a cab to the Omni Hotel. Going through an airport with no
luggage and nothing in his pockets but a passport, money, and
Dice was like skinny-dipping. No wallet and his dick swinging free. From now on he would always give Random this
option when he traveled.

He got to the hotel after midnight and the desk clerk was
skeptical that Bobby's legal name was L. Harvey Oswald (his
lucky Yo Eleven, Six Five No Jive, chose it from a list with all
great options) but cash made everything okay. He put down
enough cash to empty the minibar, rent every PPV porn title,
invite Johnny Depp up to party, and a hundred-buck tip on
top of all that.

"Here's your Wi-Fi password, there's complementary
breakfast on the eleventh floor until ten a.m. Do you need
help with your luggage?"

"I don't have any luggage."

"Have a nice night, Mr. Oswald."

Bobby's underwear and socks were bamboo, so breathable,
and bamboo's natural antimicrobial and thermo-regulating
properties would help keep moisture and odor away, but he
still washed them out in the sink. It must be the best of all

possible worlds where your boxer briefs and your local Thai restaurant's *kaeng ho* could be made of the same substance. He'd get another day out of his shirt and he never changed his jeans unless the Dice told him to. He called down to L. Harvey's new buddy, Skippy, at the front desk and got generic toiletries sent up to him. His breath and pits would smell like a covered-up afternoon delight.

Bobby slept well. He slept almost eleven hours and didn't have nightmares of Bill getting his throat slit. Hitler probably slept like a baby. His underwear and socks were dry on the shower rod and his shirt had aired out spread over the TV.

L. Harvey Oswald was ready for some Dallas action.

His first decision wasn't Random. He had to get in touch with Melvin. He went to Walgreens and bought three burner phones. He could have just bought SIM cards, but he really wanted to do the movie scene of pulling out the card and the battery, ripping the phone in half, and throwing everything in different trash cans. Without any luggage or phone on the plane, he had one activity on the flight and that was memorizing Melvin's number that he'd written on the one notebook page he hadn't lit on fire when he left his apartment. He had memorized it and spent the rest of the flight ripping it into tiny pieces and putting them in an air sickness bag.

He called from the burner and Melvin didn't answer. When he got VM, he sang a few lines of the Talking Heads's "Burning Down the House" and hung up. He waited for Melvin to check the message and then called again, and this time Melvin answered.

"Don't tell me where you are."

"Fine, and how are you doing, my friend?"

"Burner?" Melvin asked.

"Yup, just like James Bond."

"No, not at all like James Bond, like an idiot."

"Do you have my money?"

"Yeah. Goddamn, you have a lot of money. A lot!"

"I'm a lucky son of a bitch, you know, for someone who has someone trying to kill him. We're grading on a curve."

"Have you got enough cash to get you through a few days?"

"Yeah, I think I can do a couple weeks living high off the hog."

"You won't have to," Melvin said, "I can do a fake account and set up a debit card for you. I'll put a hundred grand on it—we don't need to fuck around. You can use the debit most everywhere, and with a PIN they won't need ID. Some places won't take it, but you just go somewhere else. I'll get it to you in three days by general delivery. Oh, I guess you *are* going to have to tell me where you are."

"I certainly will. What's general delivery?"

"You can address a letter to *General Delivery* and the person can pick it up at the post office. But that person needs ID. I can work to get your money onto a debit card and get that done fast and then get it mailed, but you'll need your real ID to pick it up. How did you fly?"

"I have a passport."

"Yeah, I guess I can address it to your name—Skiff can't access the post office. But don't use that name for anything else. You got twenty-four hours to call and tell me the zip code of a post office you can get to that does general delivery and you can pick it up two days after that."

"I can do that. This is fun spy stuff. We're mostly playing, this isn't all really necessary, right?"

"I don't know. Skiff is a serious bad guy, and doesn't Ruphart hate you too?"

"He might."

"Then you're fucked. Probably still unnecessary, but let's do it right just in case. What name do you want on the card?"

"L. Harvey Oswald."

"You're an idiot. But give me a PIN. And not 1122."

"You're amazing. How did you know?" Bobby said.

"Jesus. Roll your dice and give me a number and never write it down."

"Six two, four two."

"You have a hundred grand riding on this, so don't forget it. L. Harvey Oswald. What an asshole."

"He was a patsy. Chosen at Random, don't you know."

"Get me the general delivery post office name and zip by tomorrow."

"Hey, how can I ever repay you for this?" Bobby asked.

"I took a hundred grand out of your Bitcoin to buy the computers, pay my guys, and for my time and shit. And you still owe me."

"Okay."

"Goodbye, Bobby. Make sure you destroy the phone."

"Call me Harvey, and destroying the phone is going to be the high point of my day. Goodbye, Melvin, and thanks."

Goddamn, ripping apart a plastic burner is hard. How many takes do they do in cheesy movies? Maybe the prop guys score them so the tough-looking Hollywood pussies don't hurt their hands. Jesus, it took Harvey about ten minutes to really destroy the burner and it wasn't fun at all.

33

ARVEY—NOPE, WE'RE NOT GOING TO CALL HIM THAT
. . . Bobby had to go shopping for clothes. He didn't
need to roll the Dice. He knew he needed dark pants
and white V-neck T-shirts. He was Harvey now. He got a
dark sweater to put over the T-shirt if it got chilly. All the
pictures of Oswald on the web were B&W or colorized, so
Bobby didn't know the exact color of the sweater and slacks,
but the T-shirt was white white white, like Bruce Willis's at
the beginning of *Die Hard*, and the pants and sweater were
dark. He rolled seven, a five and a two, and that meant he got
himself a liverwurst sandwich with mustard and raw onions
on rye bread (no vegan option on this roll) and a Coke, and
had himself a picnic lunch on the Dealey Plaza grassy knoll.
The plaza is so small. It's crazy small. How could something
world-changing like the Kennedy assassination happen in
such a tiny place? The reason for all the conspiracy nuts is
just storytelling. If you were writing the story of the end of
Kennedy's Camelot (called "Camelot" *only* because Jackie saw
a Broadway musical), you wouldn't have it end in itty-bitty
Dealey Plaza with a half-assed, stupid jive-Marxist with a
Mannlicher-Carcano rifle and a few lucky shots. But Bobby
understood. Bobby didn't live stories. Random had destroyed
the idea of narrative in real life. Random had prepared him to
understand assassinations and pandemics, but what it didn't

prepare him for was this large amount of mustard and this small number of tiny napkins the grocery store deli counter put into his picnic bag.

L. Harvey Oswald sat on the grassy knoll with a mustard stain on his new white T-shirt. The chances of Random turning Bobby into L. Harvey Oswald and putting him at Dealey Plaza that afternoon with mustard on a T-shirt were way lower than JFK being snuffed by a loser with a clean white T.

The day passed. At eleven thirty p.m. central time, Bobby rolled an Easy Eight, a five and a three, as he entered Wild Detectives, so he bought a copy of *Moby-Dick,* a Topo Chico, and a delicious *pan tumaca,* and sat down to read, drink, and eat them, respectively. He figured he'd be here every night for a few weeks, so he might as well get a groove—but right before midnight, Terri walked in the door. Wow.

He really looked at Terri for the first time. Terri wasn't the least bit fat, but everything on her was round. She was short and busty with a smile so big she needed a big round head to hold it. She had blond hair that was so blond it lacked all pigment and so fine it should have smelled like doughnuts, or like a newborn baby. She was wearing a thin washed-out Stones T-shirt with no bra and crazy-tight jeans. She was walking toward him and he could still tell her ass looked great. She was smiling, not because some asshole was trying to kill Bobby, she loved Bobby, but because life was so goofy. She walked over, tits bouncing, with a huge smile and a whisper on her lips.

"Bobby, what the fuckin' fuck?"

"Call me Harvey. My witness-protection name is Harvey—L. Harvey Oswald." Even saying it that way, it sounded nothing like *Bond—James Bond.*

"Crazy fucker."

"That's me."

"What are you doing in Dallas?"

"Random."

"Why is someone trying to kill you?"

"Random."

"Why am I here?"

"Random."

"Thanks."

"You know I give Random the choices, all my choices, but chosen at Random."

"What number was I?"

"Um, I forget."

"Not seven? You dick."

"Not two or twelve either, and if I'd seen you in that T-shirt I wouldn't have had to roll them at all."

Was he flirting with Terri? She shook her shoulders just a little when she giggled. Yup.

She reached across and touched his big mustard stain. "You're looking pretty classy yourself."

"Did I say *you* were classy?"

"Fuck you."

"What are you up to?"

"I spend my days fucking on piles of money," Terri replied. "How about you?"

"I don't know. I don't know what I do. I mean, I live Random, so I never know what I'm doing, but now I *really* don't know. I haven't done that fucking-on-a-pile-of-money thing for real in months."

"It's still fun."

"Good. Speaking of which, I need to pick up money at general delivery. I need money."

"I could use a chauffeur," Terri said. "But you gotta wear the hat."

"I still have a shit ton of money; I just need to go pick it up. I'm going to pick up a general delivery letter with a debit card in it. That's my only task for . . . maybe the rest of my life. Want to come with me?"

"What's general delivery?"

"It means someone sends you a letter to a post office, just the post office, with just your name, no address, and a person can pick it up with just an ID. I have a passport. Not many post offices do it, but I've found one in Dallas, not too far from here. It'll take a couple of days, but if we go there on Friday, they'll give me an envelope with my debit card. Then we can go together to a cash machine and fuck on a pile of money."

"Take a look from the back when I walk out. You think this primo ass could get fucked on the money an ATM spits out? What is that, five hundred bucks? Not this ass, nope, not even if they were ones."

"Noted. Hey . . . wait a minute." Bobby reached for his Dice and Terri grabbed his hand and held it a little too sensually.

She looked into his eyes. "Are you going to assign a number to fucking me back at your hotel?"

"No, I was going to assign a number to *inviting* you to fuck back at my hotel. I can't give the Dice any choice that I can't promise to deliver."

"Let me save you the roll and the breath. We're not going to fuck tonight. I mean, not you and me. I'm gonna fuck tonight and maybe you're gonna fuck tonight, if you use money or lose the mustard stain, but we're not going to fuck each other tonight."

"Who are you fucking?" Bobby asked.

"Nonya. Nonya Business."

"Can I watch?"

"I'll ask them, but I doubt it."

"Them? Gender fluid or multiple?"

"Yes, fucker."

"Oh baby. Ask them."

"Listen, how much trouble are you in? Really. How likely are you to get snuffed? And, more importantly, am I in danger sitting here with you?"

"I think you're as safe as you ever are. Me? I don't know. I started a detective agency for lost causes . . ."

"Jesus."

". . . and this guy came in who was in the casino black book for cheating he didn't do. He was a patsy . . ."

"Like Lee Harvey Oswald."

"Yes . . . and I found out who set him up. They didn't set him up specifically, he was picked at random . . ."

"Lot of that going around."

"Yeah, but not good Random, intrusive random without thought. So, he was just misdirection, a word I know I'm using wrong, but you get the idea. We found out what scam he was accidently part of, and the head of that scam thought we were going to bust them . . ."

"And you were."

"Yeah, I guess, but not because we cared, just to get my guy to be able to gamble again. The head of the gambling gang found out what we knew and slit the guy's fucking throat. He was a nice guy and I was talking to him on the phone and eating a fluffernutter while he got his throat slit, and that murderer talked to me on the phone and told me I was next."

"I love fluffernutters."

"You are trash . . . Melvin happened to call me right after that happened."

"Now that's Random."

"Kinda-sorta, and he told me to burn down my house and give my cloud identity and all my money to him for safekeeping."

"Smart," Terri said.

"Are you being sarcastic?"

"I don't know."

"Yeah, Melvin is smart and maybe honest, so I burned down my house and the Dice brought me to Dallas, then to you. And here we are."

"What are you going to do?"

"Give me some good choices and I'll roll for it. I don't know. I've got plenty of cash for a few days and I'll get my debit card with a lot more cash on Friday. I got money, but I don't have a life."

"You never had a life. You're a fucking Dice wackjob hot mess."

"I don't even know if any of this is necessary. Maybe Melvin made me a little bit paranoid. It sure feels that way now."

"A guy getting his throat slit over something that you did. And the slitter knows who you are? I'm with Melvin on this, Harvey. I think in Vegas you're a dead man walking. Stay in Dallas and live your Random life here."

"I love that you called me Harvey. We both know the Dice will send me back to Vegas eventually."

"We'll talk about this later, I gotta go get fucked . . ."

"Priorities."

"Right on. How will we get in touch with each other?" Terri asked.

"You mean I can watch you get fucked?"

"Well, I meant . . . I guess that too."

"I got a burner."

"Look at you, sexy—are you dealing hard drugs to school children?"

"Melvin told me to get a burner. I got three and I called him with one and then tore it apart. I have to call him with the zip code of the post office, so then I'll have one burner. Burners are really hard to rip apart, not like the movies at all."

"I've got a little time before I have to get fucked. Can I watch you call Melvin, all drug dealer like, and then rip the phone apart?"

"It's not sexy, it's really clumsy."

"The mustard stain is not sexy, but I still love you. Can I watch? And then you text me on the last burner and I'll text back if you can watch."

"Deal! Let me pay for the food and we'll go outside, and I'll make the call and then you can watch me rip it apart and throw it in a trash can. I'll go under a streetlight, kinda backlit. Should I get a pack of smokes?"

"I'll imagine the smokes."

Melvin thought hanging with Terri was a moderately stupid idea. Bobby gave him the zip code. The money would be on the way soon, or Melvin had already stolen it. Bobby hung up and Terri was grinning ear to ear.

"C'mon, bad boy, rip up the burner," she said.

"Stand over there." Bobby indicated a spot that seemed right for burner-breaking viewing. He was nervous and embarrassed. "You better let me watch you fuck."

As Terri walked over, Bobby realized it would have to be a huge pile of cash for that big sweet ass to be comfortable on. She turned and put all her weight on one hip, tilted her head, and watched with that smile. Nothing beat that smile.

Bobby ripped the phone to fucking shit, bit the SIM card in half with his teeth, and spat it in the trash like it was nothing and he didn't care. He glanced over and made eye contact with Terri.

She was impressed. "That was way hotter than I expected. Way. After that, I'm really going to ask my fuckbuddies for you. What's the burner number?"

Bobby gave it to her, and she texted him, *Hey Harvey,* as she was jumping in the black Uber SUV. He saw her making a call as she rode away. His hands were bleeding from ripping up the burner. He had never felt better in his life.

34

"CAN I JACK OFF?" BOBBY ASKED TERRI ON HIS BURNER.

"*He* and *they* say okay to watching, but *he* doesn't want you joining in. *He* doesn't want another dude involved."

"But if it's okay to watch, it's okay to jack off, right? Don't you think?"

"How do you know you're even going to want to. You don't know these people."

"That's the part that's making me want to jerk off right now. Are you really going to get fucked on a pile of money?"

"You are such an asshole. If you're polite about it, I bet it's okay for you to jack."

"I'll be nothing but *please, thank you, yes sir, no sir, yes ma'am, no ma'am, yes them, no them*."

"Don't be a dick. See you at one thirty. That gives us a half hour to get started. I'll text you the address and I'll leave the door unlocked. There's a big master bedroom upstairs. I'll leave a chair where I want you to sit. Sit down and shut up. And don't you dare stain my carpet, fucker."

"With mustard?" Bobby said.

"Jesus."

"See you at one thirty. Oh boy."

"You are cute. See you in forty-five minutes."

"Forty-three."

She hung up. Oh boy. Bobby so wanted to rip the burner

apart just for the turn-on. Just tear it the fuck apart. But he needed this burner for a while.

The cab pulled up at Terri's address. It wasn't a huge mansion; more of a McMansion like his, in a gated community. A little surprising, not really a tens-of-millions type crib. There were no cars outside. They all Ubered over. Bobby was envious of everyone's ability to Uber, then he realized he'd soon get to be envious of them fucking her. Oh boy.

Here's some advice for group sex: Never try to just fall into group sex, that's stupid and usually requires drugs or drink and acting like a fucking creepy predator. There should be no seduction. No one gets talked into anything. Do the setup cold, over email or text. Get complete consent and all limits laid out electronically, when erections and internal lubrication aren't going to confuse anyone. The limits are limits and can't be broken even by the person who set the limit, but anyone, of course, can end anything at any time without a reason. Limits stay in place; consent needs to be constantly renewed. Everyone knows all of that, but here's the important tip: start the sex the instant the first person arrives, don't wait for anyone else. Get your fucking mouth on something. When the other(s) arrive(s), they need to walk right into some sex scene. It's hard enough to segue into sex with two people; when there are more, and everyone is sober, you can end up killing prime fucking time trying to be witty talking about work and the drive over. Be witty on email, don't be witty when you could be fucking.

Bobby knew all these rules. For tonight he had been given the limit of just sitting in one chair, watching, and jacking off while being respectful of the carpet. He hadn't been rolling Random for decisions for a bit. There were no decisions because there was no indecision. He had his rules from Terri and her buddies. Random had taught him to follow rules perfectly. Random was still ruling his heart.

As smart as Terri was, she was from the class that bought lottery tickets. She was the class that considered What'shername, now in prison for turning in the fake lottery ticket, as a possible life partner. Bobby understood Terri because they were the same. Even Random couldn't take the fluffernutter out of their souls. Bobby and Terri weren't even *nouveau riche*; they were *immédiatement très très très le plus riche*; they hadn't even pretended to work for their fortunes. Terri bought a lottery ticket and Bobby rolled an eleven. They had no taste and no status. They hadn't had braces on their teeth in junior high, their teeth were a little crooked. They could listen to Celine Dion unironically. The Stones and Nirvana posters on Terri's wall probably weren't even real originals, but the Thomas Kinkades and Peter Liks were as real as they come, and no one knows, and fewer care, how real that is.

Bobby caught himself looking at her decorating and furniture for a few seconds before he remembered why he was there and rushed up the white-carpeted stairs. There was another staircase on the other side going to the same place. Even Terri's stairs had sex partners. Wait, running into the room was too goofy. He didn't have to be cool, but he also couldn't be an asshole. He stopped for a moment to gather himself. Who was he kidding? No one was going to notice him walking in. He was not the main attraction. He wasn't even an attraction. He opened the door and walked in quietly and sat down. Terri had moved the chair pretty close to the bed, about ten feet away, and kindly left the lights pretty bright. Oh boy.

He didn't know any names except Terri's and Terri was also peripheral to the action at this moment. *They* was sucking *his* cock. Just a normal gentle blowjob. *He* was lying across Terri's lap and reaching up and kneading her breasts. There was no pile of money. It was worth the price of admission just to see Terri's breasts. The Stones T-shirt gave up most of the information, but her body naked was even more attractive to Bobby than he had expected or hoped. Terri pulled *his* head closer, working on smothering *him* in breast-flesh while flashing that huge smile to Bobby. The smile was sexier than the breasts and that's saying a lot. Damn. They stayed locked in eye contact while she slid out from under *him* and moved down the bed. She gave Bobby a wink and, with a tap on *their* back like a tag-team wrestler, took over the cocksucking. *They* had been licking sweetly and sensuously. Knowing she had Bobby's full attention, Terri was going to show off. *His* cock was not small. It wasn't porn size, but it was pretty long and thick. Terri made it disappear like Siegfried and Roy and held it down her throat like a manticore. She wanted Bobby to know his *oh boy* was called for. Oh boy.

Bobby wanted to make it last, so he waited as long as he could before getting his cock out. That was another minute. Everyone was doing everything right. Terri and *they* took turns being the rubber roadie. They changed them after every hole change, and there was a nice little pile forming by the side of the bed. *He* was good. *He* didn't come until after everyone in the room, including Bobby, had cum a few times.

There are no sex tips for ending group sex. Goodbyes are easier and less awkward than with two people who have had sex. If everyone's sober, no one is considering falling asleep and they can walk each other to the car. Ending is pretty easy. Bobby really wanted to hang out and talk to Terri. He was crazy about her, though it seemed a little goofy to be falling in love with her tonight. His body would understand, but you wouldn't.

Bobby said as gently and politely as possible, "Hey, everyone, thanks so much for letting me kind of be part of this. I had a blast. Good night."

He walked out of the bedroom. Now he had to roll the Dice.

35

BOBBY HAD BEEN A SPECTATOR BUT NOT A PARTICIPANT in group sex. He'd set his house in Vegas on fire. He was cut off from his friends and family. He'd listened to his new friend being killed, and at least part of the blame for that murder was his. He had at least one bad person trying to kill him, and that bad person was competent at his job. He had no email or credit card to his name. He couldn't take an Uber. He had changed his name to L. Harvey Oswald. He was wearing a white T-shirt with a mustard stain now chilly and wet from his cum that didn't stain the carpet. He was in Dallas. He was hungry and . . . he was stone-solid in love. He'd never been happier.

He used the other staircase down and went to Terri's kitchen. She had a wine cellar or, since it was off the kitchen and not in the basement, a wine closet. It was lit real fancy and probably temperature controlled, but that was likely turned off. Terri didn't have any wine in there, instead there was nothing but a simple table with a 1980s three-foot-tall plastic sculpture of the Kool-Aid Man, with his big happy red pitcher belly. Terri had all these low-class Kincades and Liks and her own brilliant art installation in her wine closet. Genius? Seemed so, but Bobby was in love with her, he couldn't be trusted. He was walking around her place, not really snooping; he was just thinking about calling a cab on his burner phone and possibly getting a snack.

He figured that if he had full permission to watch her getting rimmed by an attractive redhead, he probably had permission to eat some of her peanut butter. At home he would just take a spoonful and eat it like that, but he'd burned his home down. If he did the spoon method here, that would leave a peanut butter spoon in the sink, and an obvious divot in the peanut butter. Too embarrassing. There was a pack of English muffins right there on the counter. He'd watched her being spit-roasted, so he could have one of her fork-split English muffins. Permission to watch the cum swap allowed him to use the toaster. Or did it? This consent stuff was very complicated. Time to go to the Dice.

This choice, unlike the redhead he enjoyed watching getting fucked, was binary. If he rolled an even, he'd sit quietly and wait for the cab. If he rolled an odd, he'd have a toasted English muffin with peanut butter. Ten, Puppy Paws—Random decided he would just call a cab and sit and wait. He'd have the cab drop him off at a Stop 'n' Rob and pick up a jar of the creamy and a plastic spoon and eat it as he walked a block or two back to the Omni. Better remember to get some orange juice so he wouldn't choke to death on the peanut butter. He still might drown in the orange juice that couldn't get around the peanut butter, but life is risky.

The dispatcher said the cab would be about twenty minutes. "Twenty minutes" is always a lie. That's the amount of time restaurant hosts and parents of whiny children say when they know it's going to be interminable. Bobby didn't care, there was a comfortable couch facing Mr. Kool-Aid and a Velvet Underground coffee-table book. He could smell sweat, mustard, and cum on his T-shirt. Even if this was a dad "twenty minutes," Bobby would be fine.

He hadn't heard anything from upstairs in a while. Had

the three of them really fallen asleep in the same bed like some stupid sixties "swinging" movie? Or maybe Terri had given them their own guest bedrooms. At any rate, there was no conversation or footsteps from upstairs. As he was musing, *Goodness, Lou Reed was young back with the VU*, to himself for the seventh time, he heard a set of light footsteps heading toward the stairs. He needed to warn her, *Don't be scared, it's just me. I'm down here in your living room, reading.*

"Don't let me scare you, I'm at my own fucking house. I thought you left."

"I left the bedroom," Bobby said, "but I had to wait for a cab back to the hotel. Where are your friends?"

"They're not my friends. They left through the garage so the Ubers can pick them up in the driveway."

"Some guys have all the luck."

Terri looked out the window. "Yeah, they're gone." She was glowing, gorgeous. She was wearing her same Stones T-shirt shirt and nothing else. It didn't cover anything below her waist. A T-shirt with her pussy showing, like Debbie Harry on stage in the seventies, even the same wispy, just-fucked blond hair. Terri reached down and scratched the top of her thigh. She either didn't think about how good she looked or thought about nothing else. It was the same either way. She smiled and flashed him her pale-blue eyes, "You want something to eat while you wait?"

And just when Bobby had thought his life couldn't get any better. "Well, I don't want to put you out."

"I'm not going to cook for you, stupid, I mean do you want a toasted English muffin with some peanut butter and a glass of orange juice?"

"I love you."

"That's a yes, I guess. Yeah, I was feeling the love thing too.

Full on. Why didn't we feel that in Vegas?" She walked into the kitchen, split two muffins, and put them in the toaster.

"Because you were there to get married."

"How about the second time? I was getting divorced. Wasn't that the perfect time?" He could hear the drawer opening for the knife and the cabinet closing.

"I didn't know you were interested."

"I guess I wasn't." He could smell the English muffins in the toaster, and hear the orange juice being poured. "Were you?"

"I don't know how I wasn't, but maybe I wasn't. Maybe it was a Dice thing, I don't remember."

"We sure had fun though."

"Yup." The conversation was happening slow motion, long beautiful pauses like an Annie Baker play.

"Hey, come over to the counter here in the kitchen, I don't want you getting crumbs all over my couch."

"You know, I was going to make this exact thing for myself before you came down, but I thought maybe that wasn't right."

"After you'd watched me getting fucked in the ass, you felt shy about peanut butter? You are such an idiot."

"You got fucked in the ass?"

"Not really, but kind of. You know, you were there."

He leaned over and grabbed a handful of her hair and kissed her deep and hard. She tasted of every kind of sex possible . . . and peanut butter—she had licked the knife. He smelled burnt toast. Maybe the English muffins were burning, or a few crumbs in the bottom. Maybe he was having a stroke. He didn't care which, he was very happy.

About thirty-six hours later they were gently arguing about

leaving the house. Terri didn't think they had to go out. "I've got more money than the Prince Rogers Nelson estate." (She did.) "We don't need to pick up your debit card."

"We don't want to leave a debit card worth a hundred grand at a post office general delivery. It'll be nice to take a ride over together. We can stop on the way back and lunch is on me."

"Tomorrow. Let's do it tomorrow." She took off her shirt again to make her point. "Is this the body of someone who runs errands?"

"Cheating. That's cheating. C'mon, let's go. Is your car in the garage?"

"I don't have a car, stupid. I'll call an Uber, just to do something you can't do. And I *can* pee standing up, so shut up."

They ignored the driver and made out in the back of the black SUV.

"Sir, could you put on a funk station, please?" Either one of them could have said it.

They got to the post office. General delivery works, and Melvin hadn't ripped them off.

They were rich, in love, and in a Dallas post office. So random.

36

AFTER TWO WEEKS OF HONEYMOON-TYPE SEX, IF THE honeymoons had multiple strangers involved, Terri started a serious conversation out of blue.

"Bobby?"

"It's Harvey."

"No, it's Bobby. Bobby, I have to ask you something."

When things got serious, Bobby went Random. He reached for his Dice, thought for just a few seconds, and threw them. Ace Caught a Deuce. "No, I won't quit living Random for you."

"I wasn't going to ask you to do that." She hesitated. "Wait, you can give the Dice a choice to stop using the Dice?"

"Of course. I can do whatever I want. I've given them that choice before." Bobby held a finger up to pause the conversation while he thought for almost a full minute and then threw the Dice again. Easy Eight. "I just decided to go back to Vegas and get this getting-killed thing out of the way."

"What were the other choices on *that* roll?"

"Seven was asking if you want to get married and move to Uruguay. Three, four, five, and six—same marriage proposal, different countries. Eight, nine, ten were going back to Vegas alone to clean this up. Eleven was quitting living Random . . . at least for a while. Two and twelve were asking you to marry me and go back to Vegas together to sort everything out."

"I want two or twelve. Roll again."

"You know that's not how it works."

"When are you leaving?" Terri didn't fight Random, that's why Bobby loved her, or maybe she didn't fight because she loved him. Probably the same thing.

Bobby was on a rolling roll. He rolled a Tennessee. "That's even, I'll leave the day after tomorrow." Bobby rolled an Easy Six. "Hmm. I've never done that since the first day, rolled for a number for a number. I'm leaving at six a.m., day after tomorrow."

"How will you get there?"

"I guess I'll fly, I don't have a driver's license—bad guys took that. And I don't want to take a bus or a train. Maybe I'll take a cab."

"Over a thousand miles? What's that, a twenty-hour cab ride? Nope. Tomorrow we'll buy a car. *I'll* buy a car; I can get insurance and shit. I'll drive you to Phoenix, that'll take us a full day. I'll let you drive some on the open stretches when we're not likely to be pulled over and you'll drive safely. I don't. An hour out of Phoenix we'll have a terrible fight. You start it. I'll drive us directly to the Phoenix airport in a huff, leave you, slam the car door, and fly somewhere, probably back here to Dallas, or maybe to Newfoundland. You take the car and take your chances driving without a license the rest of the way. It's not that far to Vegas from Phoenix, and it's a small gamble compared to the one you're taking by going to Vegas. You do your crazy Random thing. In days, weeks, or months you'll call me up and apologize, or you won't because you're dead or you've rolled a twelve or something."

Her insides were empty and scared but she went on: "How's that for a plan?" She started to cry. She never cried. Bobby was the one who cried. "Fuck, it better be a really serious fight getting into Phoenix. Start a good one. Don't call me *cunt*, that'll just turn me on. Call me a stupid fat pig and mean it. I should be able to hate you for that for a while. Maybe even wish you dead."

"I'll do my Random best to make sure that wish doesn't come true. All good thinking, cunt."

They fell into each other's arms and didn't stop touching until Tucson. They stayed in the bed the whole next day. They repeated the foreplay, play, postplay sequence again, and again, even in the car. They didn't pull over at all for the fore and post and sometimes not even for the play. While they were spending all this blissful time together, he was planning his Vegas trip. While he was rubbing Terri's feet, which were way less attractive than almost any other part of her, but he was in love, he called Melvin on one of the new burners he'd picked up. He left a message. Melvin called back a few minutes later.

"Well, you're still alive."

"Yup, and very happy. I'm here with Terri in Dallas."

"Don't tell me that shit."

"I'm going back to Vegas."

"I'm sorry, I have a bad connection, I thought you said you were going back to Vegas."

Bobby laughed. "Yup, I'm going back. I'm going to take my name back and figure this shit out."

"What's your plan?"

"I'll get my identity and money back from you and go to the police about the murder, and then take it from there."

"What about the arson? You know, the arson at your house, the arson where you were the arsonist?"

"I won't make an insurance claim."

"Who cares? You still burned your house down and that's a crime, a serious crime. Around police is the worst place for you to be right now. Going into the hospital sick, with a weak-ened immune system, is deadly—pathogens happily floating around looking for a warm, wet place to live. If you add those deaths to all the doctor and nurse fuckups, it can be argued that the third-largest cause of deaths in the USA is medi-cal care. With what's happening in China now, hospitals are more dangerous, but that's not my point. It's an analogy about police. With Skiff trying to kill you, you don't want to be any-where near a police station or a jail. Those places are crawling with bad guys and a lot of bad guys know Skiff and know Skiff is looking to make you dead and will pay for information."

"Oh yeah. What's happening in China?"

"Never mind, probably nothing. But don't go to Vegas."

"I already rolled; I'm going. Can you put a half million on my Oswald debit?"

"Yeah, I can do that, but Bobby—"

"Thanks for the advice. I won't be Bobby and I won't go to the police, but I'm going to Vegas. We can't live our lives like this."

Terri felt compelled to enter into this conversation—she yelled at Bobby and the phone: "You don't look like you're suffering to me! Let's go to some island and fuck ourselves to death. Have your Bitcoin put in my account or have Melvin keep it. We have mucho money, you fucking moron! We'll get our asses out of the country and everything will be over!"

Melvin could hear everything she said. "She's right. Is that Terri? A person you find attractive who also has a few hundred million dollars is asking you to run away to some paradise with her and you want to go to Vegas and get killed?"

At this point in most fiction, if the protagonist just did what the protagonist should do, everyone would be much better off—but the story would end. Authors go to a lot of trouble to justify the stupid shit their characters do. To answer the "plausibility" questions: *Why don't they go to the police? Why don't they leave for another country now? Why don't they stay together in the house until help gets there? Why doesn't she just leave him?* It takes a lot of plotting and writing to keep the story going. In this story, we can answer any of those questions and keep the story going with a simple roll of the Dice.

Bobby rolled again, then announced, "Seven," to Melvin and Terri, and then explained, "I'm going to Vegas as L. Harvey Oswald. I'll solve this whole thing and then call Terri and we'll live happily ever after."

Flabbergasted, Melvin and Terri asked in unison, "That was number seven?!"

"Yeah, it's what I want the most. I don't believe in revenge, but I also don't like the way Ruphart and Skiff treat people. Skiff slit Bill's throat. Ruphart pays people to slit throats. I don't want them slitting people's throats anymore."

"They're going to slit *your* throat." It didn't matter whether Melvin or Terri said this, they were of one mind.

"Maybe, but maybe I'll stop them. I have Random on my side. Now, how about the one who is here kisses me and the one who isn't here loads a half million bucks onto my debit card?"

Terri and Melvin did as they were asked. They really couldn't argue with Random.

Meanwhile, Skiff and Ruphart were still thinking about killing Bobby.

37

One afternoon, before Bobby burned his house down, he and Tone had been sitting around the office talking. Bobby mentioned that he'd never been in a fistfight. Tone took that as a problem to be solved. He said to Bobby, "What are you looking at?"

"*What?*"

"It's as easy as that. You just say that to someone at a bar and you'll be in a fight before you know it."

"No, I don't want to be in a fight. I like not being in fights."

"I *love* being in fights. That's why I quit boxing. I realized I was going into the ring to get hit. Not a good strategy for a boxer, but a lot of people go in the ring to be hit. People start fights to be hit. It's easy."

Bobby was thinking back on that conversation with Tone as he and Terri got about an hour outside of Tucson. Bobby was driving. It was time. He pulled over and rolled the Dice to see where he'd start. It was a six. He turned to Terri and said, "You're acting a little weird—you know, distant or something. You kind of stopped talking to me."

"Well, I had your dick in my mouth for some of that time. I couldn't really talk, but I hummed a little."

"I don't mean that. I mean since then. You've just been distant. We aren't really connecting like we used to."

"I was just looking out the window, enjoying the scenery. Thinking."

"That's what I mean. You used to talk to me about what you were thinking, now you just look out the window by yourself. Things just seem wrong. You feel it too."

"Well, I didn't feel it until you said that. I thought we were doing pretty well."

"Yeah, just pretty well."

She paused for a second. "I know what you're doing."

"Do you?"

"Yes, you're trying to start a fight just like you're supposed to. It's time."

"Sure, it's time, but thanks for making it easy by being cold and weird. I was supposed to start the fight now, but you've been weird since before Tucson. It was *before* Tucson when you made that crack about my sister."

"That was no *crack*, to use language from another century, I just said she got lucky her brother hit that Yo Eleven. You can't deny that was a lucky break for her."

"I think it takes more to get into Johns Hopkins than a lucky brother, like grades, smarts, hard work. I'm lucky, but she worked. She did a lot more than buy a lottery ticket. You *just* bought a lottery ticket. Because of my old man, I was forced to roll the Dice—it was a desperate move, but *you* bought a lottery ticket. Why? Just because you're bad at mathematics? I mean, that is such a fucking stupid white-trash thing to do. The fact that you won just makes it a little more confusing. When you strip it down, winning is just as stupid as losing. Just as fucking stupid. It's like a drunk bragging that he drove home safely while drunk. He was still stupid enough to drive drunk, right? You had dumb luck when you shouldn't have needed it."

"It was just a whim and I happened to win. I didn't spend my child's food money."

"Only because you didn't have a child. You *never* had a child. You never even got married until you were rich enough to sweeten the deal."

"Sweeten *what* deal?"

"The Terri Abrams deal. Wiggling your fat ass and offering it up to any loser who wanted it got you laid, but it sure didn't get a lot of marriage proposals, did it? Were sexy successful bachelors lining up for you before you had more money than god? Were they lining up for your stupid fat ass? I mean, they were lining up to gangbang you for an evening of fun, but no one wanted to marry a stupid fat cow, did they? My sister, on the other hand, she got into Johns Hopkins, pretty much with her own smarts, and still has time to keep herself in shape and watch what she eats."

Terri was dead quiet. She was crying a little. "This is so fucking hard. So hard. This is wrong. Bobby, what you're doing to yourself, to me, to us, is wrong wrong wrong."

"Stupid fat cow."

"There's the exit. Get off and leave me at departures. I'll find a ticket to somewhere. Keep the fucking car. I don't know if I'll get over this. This is so much worse than I expected."

She wasn't crying anymore. Bobby was.

They drove in silence. The car pulled up at departures at Phoenix Sky Harbor Airport. Terri didn't even wait for it to come to a full stop. "Keep my fucking suitcase, but the clothes won't fit the smart skinny women you'll be banging in Nevada. I'll buy new shit for myself in the airport. Take the car and fuck yourself all the way to Vegas." She slammed the door.

Bobby watched her walk away. She was so smart. She

didn't have an ounce of extra fat on her. And she wasn't a cow, she was the best person he had ever met.

He hoped he would see her again. He swung to the highway and saw the sign for Vegas. He brought the Dice to his lips and kissed them. Random was his only hope.

38

RIVING WITHOUT A LICENSE WAS NO PROBLEM.
Cruise control kept Bobby's speed legal. The casino
billboards started four hours out of Vegas on US-93.
He saw *Unlimited Shrimp!* and *$2 Craps!!!* and something
about Tiësto deejaying at a topless swimming pool dayclub.
And then time went away. High-lonesome fugue-state driving. Cuddling his cold, hard, plastic Dice against his lips like
those poor baby monkeys clutching those little scraps of cloth
stapled onto their wire synthetic mothers in Harry Harlow's
maternal-depravation studies. The fifties primate vivisection
that put a quantifiable value on a warm mother's love. Bobby's
mom loved him, but he couldn't see her without getting her
killed. Terri loved him, but he'd left that stupid fat cow at PHX.
Time flies when you Randomly become L. Harvey Oswald.

He was soon back home in Vegas.

Vegas don't give a fuck. He checked into the Golden
Nugget, a corner suite, why not, he still had more than half a
million on his debit card. All the Fremont Experience street
workers would make him soon, and word would get to Skiff
that Bobby was back in town. He had lost fifteen pounds to
be more like Lee Harvey. Terri had cut his hair exactly like
Oswald's mug shot. He was unshaven for a couple days. Not

Brooklyn-ironic unshaven—he had the old-fashioned five o'clock shadow of Oswald and Nixon. He did look a lot like Lee Harvey Oswald. The Experience would recognize him as Bobby, but Skiff would be going up against L. Harvey Oswald. Oswald who didn't give a fuck, was living Random, and was still a very lucky shot. Skiff better hold on to his pink pillbox hat. *Good luck, motherfucker.*

Bobby had been just driving, riding, or fucking for the past twenty-one hours. It was three a.m., and he was broken and exhausted. He wanted to lie down and look up at the ceiling, all Oswald noir and shit, but he didn't get to wallow for long. He was deep asleep in a couple minutes. Asleep in a hotel room in his hometown. Sound asleep in Lee Harvey Oswald's clothes. Asleep with Skiff trying to kill him. Asleep with the love of his life gone. No one has any idea what the next day will bring, but Random allowed Bobby to understand that he didn't know.

Twelve hours later, Bobby woke up dangerously refreshed. He pissed, romantically brushed his teeth with Terri's toothbrush, used her shampoo, and got ready to throw the Dice. Ace Caught a Deuce, and we're off. He didn't even wait to pick up the Dice, he left them on the bed, picked up his last burner, and rang his dad with a message: "This is Bobby, call me back on this number."

Two minutes.

"Bobby, Bobby, Bobby, Skiff says you're dead. As soon as he finds you, you're dead. You'd be safer in China, even now. Wherever you are in the world, keep hiding there. Don't pop your head up even for an instant. He's been gone for a while, out of the country. I thought he might be looking for you, he got back to Vegas yesterday."

"Where's Skiff now? I'm looking to find him. This is going to be over soon."

"No. What? No. He's looking to find *you*! You need to keep hiding."

"I threw a three, I'm calling you to find out where I can find Skiff, and not at Trump International."

"He's going to kill your ass, Bobby. Dead. You haven't got a chance."

"I do have Chance. He doesn't. Where the fuck is he? Dad, you owe me. Find out and call me back."

"Bobby, I don't owe you helping get yourself killed. I will never tell Skiff where you are."

Bobby yelled into the phone, "I'm not asking you to tell Skiff where I am! I'm demanding you tell me where I can find Skiff!"

"Everyone knows that Skiff has supper at Andiamo at the D Hotel every Thursday night."

"Thanks." There was a long pause. "Dad?"

"Yes, son."

"Dad. Can I ask you one more thing?"

"What?"

"Dad . . . what day is it?"

"Thursday. But don't go there, Bobby. Bobby . . ."

Bobby hung up.

The burner rang right back. Then it rang again a few seconds later. It probably rang lots after that too, but Bobby would never know. He was gone, daddy, gone.

Hang a lantern on it. That's the phrase some writers use to exculpate something implausible in a story by underlining it. It's the moment in *Die Hard 2* when Bruce Willis says something like, "How can the same thing happen to the same guy again?"

He asks that rhetorically to himself right about the time the audience is about to ask the movie the same question. And somehow that makes it okay. Like the technique liars use, the bullshit technique, where they tell you when they were lying in the past to make themselves look more honest now: "Listen, I was full of shit when I told you I loved you . . . but now I really love you." Shit works in fiction. It does not work in real life.

Bobby hung a lantern off the head of his dick, like Milton Berle hanging a hotel *Do Not Disturb* sign on his dick head and screaming, "Is this funny?" Bobby's life had ended and begun on his twenty-first birthday when he rolled a Yo Eleven at Perry's, and now he expected the Dice to save him again, against even greater odds. We're being unfair to Bobby. We're pretending he thought he was going to win. He thought no such thing. He didn't even think he'd be okay. His life belonged to Chance and he didn't need hope or even any thinking beyond that. His time with Terri he'd been making more decisions for himself. Desires seemed clearer with her, but now she was gone, and he was Random minus zero, no limit.

What was Bobby thinking, looking to find Skiff? Let's show his work on this one. If rolling a three was *Find Skiff,* what were his other choices? What the fuck were two and twelve? Were there crazier choices than looking for his murderer? Two was *Walk into the middle of the Fremont Street Experience, strip butt-ass naked, get hard, and scream, "Here I am, Skiff, come and get me," over and over.* Where would that have taken our story? To the police most likely. To arson charges and a shiv in the stomach? We'll never know. He didn't roll two. Twelve was *Leave Vegas, find Terri, and go back to life with her.* Most of him wanted the Vegas stuff finally ended, but 2.78% of him still wanted to leave Vegas where it was and run back to Terri. Three and eleven were *Call Dad, find where Skiff is, and confront him.* How would he confront him? He didn't know, that was a few more rolls down the line. Four and ten were *Call Tone and have Tone give me the next few choices to roll on.* That choice was a little meta, but it wasn't chosen. Five and nine were simply *Get a gun.* He might not do well with the background check, but that didn't slow down getting a gun in Las Vegas, Nevada, USA. He knew people. Everyone knew people. Once he talked to those people about getting a gun, Skiff would know how to find him, but . . . he'd have a gun. A gun that he wouldn't have the skill, nerve, or lack of morality to use. Six and eight were *Go to Fraser Ruphart and fuck with him.* Just stir the shit up. That was an exciting choice, it would make a good story, but it wasn't chosen. Seven was not the most likely in this layout because the other choices were doubled up, though it was still a good solid 16.67%. Seven was *Find the best lawyer in Vegas, go to the police, and make a deal.* Maybe he could bargain down the arson, swing some sort of witness protection, find Terri, and roll the Dice for the name of their first born. All of those choices were swirling in his head as the Dice were shaking in his hands. When the Dice landed three on that Golden Nugget honeymoon suite bedspread (a bedspread that no one but Bobby would want to see under ultraviolet light), his head emptied of everything but the white light/white heat of finding Skiff.

What time was it now? Bobby didn't know how old Skiff was, but even if he qualified Skiff probably didn't go for the early bird special at Andiamo. Bobby called the restaurant to see if they had a dress code. Nope. Good. It sure would be embarrassing to show up ready for the big confrontation and be turned away because of his plain white Oswald T-shirt. It was time to lay out his choices. What did he want to do to

Skiff? Bobby did not believe in revenge. He'd lived Random too long for that Judeo-Christian cause-and-effect bullshit. He was not going to avenge the killing of Bill by going all *Kill Bill*. He was okay with Skiff never being punished in any way for that murder. He just wanted Skiff to not murder anyone else, especially Bobby. Old Testament thinking tries to stop killing with more killing. *Vengeance is mine*, saith the lord, and that's where all the idiot hate starts; no one, not even an imaginary insecure megalomaniac, should have vengeance ever. *Vengeance is stupid*, saith the Dice. Lee Harvey for example: Oswald being killed accomplished nothing. Motherfucker was not going to kill another president anyway. If Lee Harvey had lived, we might at least shut up some of the conspiracy nuts (or proven them right). Jack Ruby snuffed Oswald and then the government sentenced Ruby to death. Were we afraid Jack was going to kill another person who killed a president? Jesus Christ. (Another argument against capital punishment—turning nuts into martyrs for over two thousand years. The Christ should have faded away doing close-up magic for the money changers.)

Bobby wouldn't allow the Dice the choice of killing Skiff. What Bobby really wanted was the equivalent of putting a bird-warning bell around your bird-killing house cat's neck. (Bells don't actually work to stop your cat from killing, you just get a sneakier, slightly deafer, more nervous cat.) Everyone else on Skiff's crew had run the casino scam a few times with him, made a shit ton of money, and disappeared, but the mastermind, Skiff, wanted more than all the fucking money in the world. He wanted to stay a bad guy. He wanted that fake fucking "respect" that people who will never deserve real respect talk about. Real respect never comes from fear. But Skiff liked being a bad guy. Threats wouldn't work against him. Threats don't work against anybody. Parents don't know this, and governments don't know this, but everyone else knows this. Threatened with Hell for eternity, Catholic girls still fuck. Never threaten, never bribe—just do what you have to do. Bobby couldn't threaten Skiff with *Stop killing or I will kill you*, because Skiff would know that if Bobby really could and would kill him, he would just kill him. Bobby had nothing to threaten with. Bobby couldn't be meaner than Skiff. Bobby couldn't be smarter than Skiff. But Bobby could be more Random than Skiff.

Bobby rolled Puppy Paws, ten the hard way, two fives. He headed down to the business center of the Golden Nugget. He got online and started researching like a freak. He was searching, taking notes, and rolling: Little Joe from Kokomo, Big Red, Ballerina, Benny Blue. The center closed. He went to the Golden Nugget Bucky's with the patio on the Fremont Street Experience with his Golden Nugget scratch pad and Golden Nugget–branded ballpoint pen. He got himself a Six Five No Jive, eleven, Venti Matcha Crème Frappuccino Blended Beverage and kept rolling and writing: Six One You're Done, Yo Eleven, Boxcars. He rolled the Fever, five, and that told him it was time to go.

It was a bit after nine thirty, Skiff would be at Andiamo by now. Bobby walked back into the casino to go to the restroom. He pissed and then washed his hands really well. He sang "Happy Birthday" to the germs twice, though slowly, while he scrubbed and scrubbed. He was playing it safe. He looked in the mirror. He was full-on Lee Harvey Oswald. His weight, his hair, his T-shirt, and his five o'clock shadow were perfect. He had his notes in his back pocket. He pulled out a picture that he'd printed on the Golden Nugget business center printer. It was a black-and-white picture. He stood there matching the face, matching the body. It took him awhile, but he matched the picture perfectly. He shook it off and went back to his normal look and then closed his eyes and made the face and the pose again to make sure he could do it without the mirror. When he opened his eyes, his image in the mirror matched the picture. He was ready.

L. Harvey Oswald walked into the Fremont Street Experience. It was a little less crowded than usual for a Thursday night. He got to the D and walked in.

"Do you have a reservation?" Wasn't there a lawsuit saying casinos weren't allowed to hire people based on looks? Maybe that was just the fake-model, topless-pool-party, dayclub women pretending to listen to Tiësto. Nope, it couldn't be them, they were picked only on looks, right? Maybe it was flight attendants or something. But this host was picked on her looks, goddamnit. Bobby was on his way to be killed and she still stopped his heart.

"Nope, I'm meeting someone. I'm just going to look around," Bobby said and winked. He winked. What a fool.

He had never seen Skiff or even had him described. But even in a restaurant with its fair share of assholes, Bobby knew he'd recognize a prolapsed one like Skiff. The restaurant had only been open seven years, yet it was the vibe of old Vegas. In case enough cows weren't tortured and killed for the heart-attack meals, the booths were made of leather too. You dined inside a slaughterhouse with mood lighting. It was even easier to find Skiff than expected. He was sitting in the biggest, fanciest booth. He had a couple toadies around him. There were no women, of course. Skiff was trying so hard to look the part of a bad guy, while building that look on top of his Stanford frame. It was what they were trying for in *Breaking Bad*. Skiff's head wasn't shaved but he had the stupid goatee and the glasses. Bad guys now looked like *Breaking Bad*. Life imitates art. It's like *The Godfather*. "Godfather" wasn't even a Mafia term before the movie (losers didn't read the book), but now it is. Gangbangers started shooting their guns sideways because they saw gangbangers in movies shooting prop guns sideways. Movies make this shit up and then assholes live it. At least Lee Harvey Oswald was a real person, he wasn't trying to be Sinatra in *The Manchurian Candidate*. Lee Harvey was his own man, and now Bobby was him too. He stood in front of the booth in his white T-shirt and looked at the Walter White cosplay dude with a huge steak in front of him.

"Excuse me, are you Skiff?"

The person on Skiff's right wasn't in the same cosplay fantasy. He was acting like Jilly to Skiff's Sinatra, but Skiff had moved from the Chairman of the Board to Walter White. These tough-guy circle jerks moved fast. In a flat, threatening New York monotone, Jilly asked, "Who wants to know?"

"Almost no one."

The third person in the booth was dressed in the part of the fat guy, taking up two seats and wearing an ill-fitting suit, or maybe any suit would be ill-fitting on that frame. Fat guy asked, "Who the fuck are you?"

Bobby didn't want them to think he was going for a gun. He very carefully with just his index finger and thumb reached into the little watch pocket of his jeans and slowly pulled out his Dice. He showed his hand empty except for the Dice. He smiled and rolled them right on Skiff's table. It wasn't a traditional sign of disrespect, but everyone understood it as a minor *fuck you*. Four the Hard Way. Bobby answered, "Skiff, you know me as Bobby Ingersoll. I know you ran that ever-so-clever casino scam; Stanford and your rape victim must be so proud. I was on the phone when you slit my friend Bill's throat. You might remember saying to me on Bill's phone that you were going to kill me. I was just finishing up a fluffernutter at the time. So yeah, I'm Bobby, but now you can call me L. Harvey Oswald."

Jilly and Fat Tony laughed a little. Skiff started to laugh and then coughed. He didn't cover his mouth.

Bobby reached across the table and picked up the Dice and held them in his hand. "You're taking your little Walter White dress-up a little far, aren't you, doing the empty-dry-lung-cancer cough?"

Skiff coughed again and said, "I am going to kill you, Ingersoll. The only reason you're still alive now is I've been out of town. I left right after I sliced the pussy cowboy's throat, and the people I entrusted to snuff your punk ass let me down." He gave Fat Tony and Jilly the haggard disappointed look of an eighth-grade substitute social studies teacher. Normally Skiff would have laid into them, but he just didn't have the energy, though he continued with Bobby, "Are you here to beg for your life? You gonna promise me you won't go to the police? Go ahead, beg, Lee Harvey Oswald." Skiff felt like shit. He was almost too tired to play the bad-guy role. Right now, even if they were somewhere secluded, he was too tired to kill Bobby. He'd barely touched his Flintstones-sized hunk of bone-in meat with the meat sauce and the side of meaty meat. Skiff felt light-headed and confused. He had a fever. He coughed again. He'd been back in Vegas less than eighteen hours after a twenty-four-hour flight that included a two-hour layover in Frisco. He was still on a time zone that was fifteen hours ahead of Vegas. He had the future sickness. He coughed again. He didn't look mean. He looked like a sick senior citizen.

"I have no intention of begging, Skiff. I sure would if I thought it would work, no doubt about it, I'm not proud about how I act around assholes. I don't mind submission, humiliation, not in front of a needle-dick like you. I would present my neck to you. I'd present my neck to anyone who craves that alpha-jive high. I've never understood why someone would fight an asshole for honor." Bobby had expected that maybe Skiff would come at him right there at the restaurant. He was ready for it. He had his body and face ready to be shot in the stomach right then, but Skiff just sat there, so Bobby continued with the plan: "You ever read the Bible, Skiff?"

"No."

"Yeah, that isn't the way it goes. You're supposed to say yes."

"Fuck you," Skiff coughed.

"There's a passage that I got memorized, seems appropriate for this situation." Bobby carefully reached into his back pockets, again being careful to emphasize that he didn't have a gun. He pulled out his notes on the Golden Nugget business center notepaper. "Except I don't have it memorized. I need my notes. I don't read the Bible either."

"What the fuck is he doing?" Fat Tony being rhetorical.

"Second Chronicles, chapter eighteen, verse thirty-three, I'm using the twenty-first-century King James Version of the Bible: *And a certain man drew a bow at Random and smote the king of Israel between the joints of the armor* . . . blah blah blah . . . *And about the time of the sun going down he died.*"

"Shut the fuck up." It doesn't matter which one of them said it.

Bobby kept going, "I got another one. This one is even better. Proverbs, chapter twenty-six, verses nine to eleven. For this one, I like the New International Version of the Bible:

Like a thorn bush in a drunkard's hand is a proverb in the mouth of a fool. Like an archer who wounds at Random is one who hires a fool or any passerby. As a dog returns to its vomit, so fools repeat their folly."

Fat Tony was the first to speak: "You talking dog vomit while the boss is eating?"

Skiff coughed all over Jilly and Fat Tony and finally looked directly at Bobby for the first time. He said simply, "You are going to be very sorry you ever poked around in my business."

"Say my name."

"You're going to be very sorry, fuckhead!"

"Thanks. I want you to see something. I want you to see, right now, the way I'll look if you shoot me in the stomach. I've practiced. Bobby brought his left hand up against his chest and put his right hand on his left elbow. He squinted his eyes and opened his mouth in a painful *O*. He squeezed his shoulders in. He froze in that pose. For way too long. "Did I get it? All I ask is that you let me have time to hit that pose."

Jilly seemed to be the only one who recognized Bobby nailing the exact face and posture of Lee Harvey Oswald being shot by Jack Ruby. "Hey Skiff, this guy ain't right."

Skiff coughed out, "I have plans for you, Bobby Ingersoll."

"Skiff plans, the Dice laugh. I'm staying at the Golden Nugget. C'mon by. Cosplay in a cute room-service outfit and knock on my door. I'll say, *Hey, wait a minute, I didn't order room service,* and you push your way into the room, all butch and shit, and kill me, shoot me right in the fucking stomach. Just let me make that face as you're doing it, okay? I really want to hit that pose."

Skiff looked at Jilly and Fat Tony and indicated Bobby with a slight movement of his chin. The Dice were still on the table, but Bobby grabbed them fast, barely shook them, and threw an Easy Eight. He grabbed a wineglass from the table and smashed it on the floor. "Attention, patrons of Andiamo. I hope you're enjoying your overpriced and cruel carnivorous feasts on this Thursday, March 12." Bobby was campaign shouting like a Southern diplomat. While he spoke, he pulled his T-shit over his head and threw it on the floor. "I'm dressed like Lee Harvey Oswald, but my name is Robert Ingersoll. Robert Ingersoll. Remember that when you see it in the news." He took off Oswald's belt, unbuckled his pants, and started pulling them down. His pants held down his cock until they hit the thigh, when it sprung free. Bobby was rock hard, a nice surprise as he continued, "The man sitting there is named Skiff." Bobby pointed and then went back to sliding his pants down. "Skiff, like a little dinghy. Speaking of which, take a look at my little dinghy. Skiff is going to kill me. Skiff like a dinghy, Skiff like a dinghy, Robert Ingersoll naked like a jaybird, hard as a rock, soon to be dead like a doornail. Remember Skiff like a dinghy. I'm Robert Ingersoll." He was getting those mnemonics out there. He was trying to talk clearly. He didn't want them just to remember a crazy guy stripping. They needed the names too.

The stripping didn't go as well as he'd hoped. He was wearing Lee Harvey Oswald loafers so they should have just slipped off, but they were newer than Lee's and a little stiff, like his cock. He'd bunched his pants around them and now one foot couldn't get a purchase on the other foot's heel to slip off the shoes. Damn, he thought the loafers would slide right off and he could step out of his pants and throw them at Skiff, but everything was bunched at his feet. His mind was wrapped up in trying to get the loafers off, so his cock was getting soft. The idea of getting killed seemed to turn him on. The idea of not being able to slip off loafers was a hard-off.

He was learning a lot about himself. He picked up another wineglass off the table. "I wonder if my cock and balls will fit in here. Let's try." He attempted to force both his balls and his semi-hard cock into Jilly's wineglass. It wasn't graceful and he was close to falling over with his pants at his ankles while he kept wrestling with his loafers. Now yelling, "Just remember, when Bobby Ingersoll is dead, think back on this night! Skiff! Skiff! Skiff! Skiff! Skiff! Oh, and Skiff masterminded the baccarat scam. Tell the casinos that. And he killed Bill Wills, slit his throat. Skiff! Bill Wills! Someone remember! Skiff slit Bill Wills's throat while I was eating a fluffernutter. You don't need to remember the fluffernutter part. Mostly remember Skiff. Fucking loafers."

By this time the casino security was all over Bobby. He looked over at the sexy host and addressed her: "I'm so sorry. I didn't want you to see me like this. Well, to be honest, I really wanted you to see me like this, just not in this context. I'd look less pathetic if I had just kicked my loafers off first. Remember that, if you ever decide to strip out of Lee Harvey Oswald drag in a public place."

Security got some zip ties on his hands. They were having trouble pulling his pants up over his ass, but they did it. They were not tucking his cock in properly. "Gentlemen, I dress left, you're right . . . Please just push it over that way a little . . . damn."

"Shut up." Every security guy said it a few times.

Casinos don't want to call Metro. They can't have real police coming to the D too often. They don't want things officially written up. They took Bobby directly to their little backstage holding area and told him he was in big trouble. Bobby asked if he was being detained. "May I leave?"

They didn't want to answer yes, but they had to, or they

would be looking at a kidnapping beef. Security told him that it was indecent exposure and disturbing the peace, though they didn't want to call Metro, so he could go. If he ever came within a hundred yards of their private property he'd be charged with trespassing.

"Got it. Now which one of you outstanding private police has my Lee Harvey Oswald white T-shirt?"

Bobby hit the Fremont Street Experience to walk back to the Golden Nugget. He reached into his pants and flipped his dick nicely to the left. He did it with his right hand, which was clutching the Dice, and since he was right there, he rubbed the Dice all over his balls. He brought the Dice and his fingers up to his nose. The funky aroma mixed with the funky carnival smell of french fries in the air. He didn't know for how long, but Bobby was still way alive.

39

CALVIN TRILLIN WRITES FOR THE *NEW YORKER*. Calvin's wife, Alice, died in New York City on September 11, 2001. She died that day of heart failure brought on by radiation damage from her lung cancer treatment. Her death was not related to any terrorist activity. Congressman Gary Condit was in deep shit about the disappearance of Chandra Levy, an intern who he might have been banging. Gary turned out to be innocent (of the murder; we don't know about the banging), but there was planned to be more of his scandal in the papers on September 11, 2001, yet it ended up not getting that much coverage in that Tuesday's papers.

There must have been someone on a stepladder at eight fifteen a.m. Japanese time on August 6, 1945. Someone who was recklessly on the top step of a stepladder who should have heeded the sign that read, 危険！上段に立たないでください *(Danger! Do Not Stand on Top Step)*. Maybe they were trying to change a light bulb or annoy a spider. It seems statistically likely that someone was doing something wicked stupid in Hiroshima a few seconds after the *Enola Gay* opened its bomb-bay doors. That person, on the top step, or getting out of a slippery bathtub, or tripping down the stairs over their little Shiba Inu, got fatal head trauma the instant before the instant the atomic bomb killed all those innocent people and changed our world forever. Some unrelated newly dead bodies must have vaporized along with everyone else.

The Dark Knight has his psychological demons and those demons give Batman his power. Random made Bobby crazier than a shithouse rat, but it also gave him power. Chance gave Bobby more chances to get lucky. Sometimes just waiting solves your problems. Gives Chance a chance to work. The world planned; Bobby rolled. A person carefully planning would rarely choose to strip naked in a steak house in front of his murderer. Bobby had no idea what his next move was so Skiff couldn't know either. Skiff was trying to kill a black box, and flight recorders are immortal.

Bobby sat in his hotel room. He'd had a pretty good night's sleep and now he was sitting.

He wasn't waiting for anything. He didn't have the slightest plan in his head. He didn't even have a decision to roll on. It was so weird. He felt like masturbating. The Weather Channel was on the hotel TV and Bobby started masturbating. Not a plan in his head. Not even really a fantasy in his head to help with the jerking. He was certainly going to die, and he was jacking off.

Meanwhile, southwest of Bobby, Skiff was in his tasteless palatial house, sweating. He was feverishly figuring and planning. Bobby had stood naked in front of Skiff and yelled Skiff's name and some of his atrocities. The other patrons and staff in the restaurant didn't witness any major crimes. They just saw a not-too-hairy naked ass and an average erection. Something to email home about, yes. Certainly, something to post on social media about (was there video?), but nothing to go to the police about. Skiff was trying to figure Bobby's next move. Trying to get a couple moves ahead. What was Bobby's play? Bobby had invited Skiff to kill him at the Golden

Nugget. Was that a trap? Bobby had already had a few weeks to go to the police, but he hadn't done that. What was the play? Skiff was going to kill Bobby, though he had to do it right. What did Bobby think Skiff was going to do? And what was Bobby going to do to counter that? There's a concept in poker that you can't put a player on a hand if the player doesn't know what hand they have. You can't outthink someone who's not thinking. Skiff should have just walked away, except Skiff didn't ever walk away from anything. He was smart. He out-smarted. He figured. He got things done. That's why he was rich. That's why he was powerful. That's why he was misera-ble. Skiff couldn't figure what he should do. He was paralyzed with hate and rage, yet mostly he was paralyzed by not being able to figure out what Bobby was planning when he stripped in the restaurant.

Business books preach that in negotiations it's very im-portant to know something that your opponent doesn't know. If it's real estate, maybe you know they are about to build a Native American casino. If you're cheating a Native American casino, maybe you know when the shaved dice are going to be rung in across the floor to set off a stranger at a craps ta-ble. Bobby knew something that Skiff couldn't possibly know. Bobby knew that Bobby didn't have a plan. He didn't have a thought in his head. He was just masturbating. He had no other plan. *Your move, Skiff!*

Skiff did not have Ruphart's problem. He did not have to conceal that he was the one killing Bobby from the bad-guy and fuckup communities. He had to conceal it from the po-lice, but that was all and that was easy. Bobby had screamed both their names while naked, and what did that accomplish? Not very much. Even if someone who was there went to the police and said, *That dead guy was naked and screaming that a guy named Skiff was going to kill him*, it didn't matter. Skiff would have an airtight alibi. He had people who would swear he was somewhere else. But he best not be seen going into the Golden Nugget right before Bobby died.

Skiff was dry-coughing his guts out. He was sweating bad. Bobby was up his ass and he hated it. He called up the goon who looked like Jilly. "Listen, I want you to go over to the Nugget."

"And kill that naked Lee Harvey Oswald asshole."

"No, *I* want to kill him."

"I'll go with you."

"No. I'm not going. You just go over and watch the lobby. When he comes down, just follow him. I want to kill him someplace other than his hotel. Find out where he goes, what he does."

"Boss, doesn't he go anywhere and do anything? The guy's a fucking nut. He pulled out his little wang in a steak house." Jilly wasn't smart enough to try to impose a pattern on Random. Skiff wasn't smart enough to see no pattern on Random.

Bobby came.

(Above is the shortest verse in this book. You know, like *Jesus wept*.)

Jilly was on his way over to the Nugget as Bobby cleaned up with a nice warm washcloth. Bobby dressed in his Lee Harvey Oswald drag and rolled the Dice. Easy Eight—Bobby was about to head over to Trump International and fuck with Ruphart. He'd stirred up Skiff and now it was time to piss on the other deadly spark plug. When a bad pool player doesn't have an easy shot on the table, they just scatter the balls and try to find fun that way. Bobby was going to smash everyone's balls.

Bobby got on his scooter and headed to Trump International. He took Las Vegas Boulevard from downtown until it turned into the Strip. It was four in the morning, Friday, the thirteenth of March, and there were still a lot of cars. He didn't have his helmet on. The scooter created a breeze through his hair out of the still-hot Mojave air and billowed his Oswald T-shirt. It was all just lights, videos. Everything he could see was man-made, even the wind in his face was man-made, but the air he was breathing was hot nature full of surprises. Bobby was alive. He had nothing in his pockets but his Dice. He was free and very dangerous.

As he rode south on LVB, a black Escalade headed north. Bobby and Jilly went right by each other. Both Skiff and Ruphart lived at Trump International. They both wanted Bobby dead and Bobby was heading over for a visit. Bobby started singing to himself, *"Doo doo da doop da doop dah dah doop doop,"* just thinking out loud.

40

HE Trump International valet was slow at this time of morning and wouldn't handle his scooter anyway. He didn't look for a place to plug it in, he didn't even lock it, odds said he wouldn't be coming out anyway. The building was jive, so Bobby, getting off a scooter dressed as Lee Harvey Oswald before dawn, walked in and asked, "Where are the elevators to the penthouse? I'm going to 6303, Ruphart." He remembered it from when he made the delivery of a Hawaiian pizza with a side of a couple million dollars. The security guy just pointed to the special high-speed elevators to the penthouse. No checks at all. That was the world-class security and concierge. He didn't even have white gloves on.

"Thanks."

"I'll need to announce you." It was an afterthought.

"They know I'm coming up. My name is Bobby Ingersoll."

The world-class security went to the phone as Bobby hit the button and the door closed behind him. He checked himself to see what he was feeling. He was feeling very alive and tingly and fairly blank. The Dice had gotten him into this elevator, and they would take him through the rest.

Last time he was here, he was holding a pizza and had bodyguards; now he was alone playing with the Dice in his pocket. What an ugly elevator. Shiny opulence, like it was designed by a giant tasteless parakeet. This wasn't supposed to be Ruphart's primary residence—he had had some bullshit house in Summerlin and this was his place near the Strip. Ruphart had sold the Summerlin place a week ago and everyone figured he was just going to buy a bigger, uglier place. Maybe one with a disco in it. Skiff had a place two floors down at the Trump International and also an embarrassing place in Summerlin. There were big double doors so you could move a piano in and out any time you wanted. The doorbell was lit and had shiny brass all around it, though Bobby never got a chance to use the doorbell or knock on the door. The elevator opened to a gun pointed directly in his face. The thug holding the weapon might have been well-dressed forty-eight hours ago, but fatigue had taken all the crispness away. His tie was undone and things were very wrinkled. Even his anachronistic eurotrash ponytail had a few errant wisps. "What the fuck do you want?"

"Have you heard the good news about Jesus Christ, Our Lord?"

"Fuck you."

"Even though I'm dressed like Lee Harvey Oswald, my name is Bobby Ingersoll and I'm here to talk to Fraser Ruphart."

"It's pronounced "RuPe-HART.""

"I know."

"You upset the boss by delivering a pizza. I'm going to blow your brains out right here."

"No you're not. You can't have a gun go off in this building and then try to get rid of my body and clean up all the blood. It's too risky for *the boss*."

"Maybe I'll take that chance." He cocked the gun, which didn't need cocking.

"What chance? There's no chance. I know Chance and there's not much of a chance in that. Too risky to fire the gun.

But you could beat me to death. Or choke me, or something. There are lots of ways a big boy like you knows to kill. You could take a chance with that. They know my name at the desk, but this is a shitty building—they might not even report me not leaving and you could move my body out of the building somehow or cut me up and eat me. I don't know what you bad guys do."

Another thug came out of 6303. "Listen, Bernard, don't fire the gun. We don't want gunfire in the boss's building."

"Yeah, I was just telling . . . Bernard . . . *really?* . . . I was just telling . . . You don't go by *Bernie?* I guess Bernie is even worse. I was just telling Bernard here that he didn't really want to shoot me."

"Shut up."

"I take that back. You do *want* to shoot me, but the big boss doesn't want you to, and you are just an employee. Me, I'm self-employed. I could shoot you if I wanted, but I don't want and I don't have a gun."

"Shut up."

"Nope. I'm going to reach into my pants pocket and pull out my Dice. I have a lot of decisions to make, and the Dice help me with that. So don't get nervous if you see me start to pull out a gun, just blow my fucking brains out and tell security and the neighbors that the boss's nephews were visiting and setting off firecrackers in the elevator while they were having close-range red paintball fights with little pieces of brain. Watch my fingers, I'm just going for my Dice."

"Don't fucking move."

Bobby didn't care; he carefully reached in his pocket and got the Dice.

Another thug came out, his gun drawn and pointed at Bobby.

Bobby addressed all three of them: "Are you going to invite me in, or at least off the elevator? Someone might need to deliver a Hawaiian pizza right now to some other asshole in the building. We need to be considerate of other assholes' needs."

"Get off the elevator."

"Did you just command me to do what I asked to do?"

Bernard drew his hand back.

Thug Two said, "I don't think we should fuck him up until we know what the boss wants."

Thug Three agreed: "Don't let him get to you, Bernard."

"Oh, I'm going to get to you. But here's the problem, you see. I paid my asshole father's whole $2,500,000 debt—remember that, a few months back? I think people might still remember that. So if you kill me, it might be bad for Ruphart's business."

"It's pronounced RuPe-HART," Thug Two corrected.

"I know." Bobby shook the Dice in his hand and looked down at the seven—six and one. "Let's go in and sit together, with guns pointed at me, of course, and wait for Ruphart to wake up, and ask him about killing me." Bobby looked at his watch. "I hope he's an early riser."

Thug Three seemed to be in charge: "Bring the asshole inside."

"Good thinking."

Last time Bobby was in this room he had been a different person. He was enough of who he was now to bring the pizza, but last time he was scared, he was still in shock. He had really just confronted his death forty-eight hours before, and then confronted life continuing about five hours before. This time he was crystal clear and, holy shit, was that wallpaper flocked? It was flocked. It was a fucking whorehouse without the good parts. He flopped down comfortably, sprawled on the ugly white couch. He had three guns pointed at him and his Dice in his hand. The door to Ruphart's bedroom was open. The guy wasn't in there.

Bernard started the discussion: "We need to just fucking kill him. The boss wants him dead; we know that. We just kill him some quiet way and then bring the body out with the trash."

Thug Two threw his thinking into the brain trust: "We can't make that decision. Not in the boss's place."

Bobby had a question: "So, big daddy boss man isn't sleeping? He's not in the bedroom?"

"Shut up," demanded Thug Three, with no hope his commanded would be followed.

So that meant that Ruphart was in the office? Where Bobby had given him the money just a few months ago? That door was closed. And why did the thugs look like they'd been here for a couple days? Something wasn't right.

Bernard: "I just want to fucking kill him. We'll be forgiven. I hate everything about this guy."

"Jeez, I'm sitting right here."

"Shut up." That was Thug Three weighing in.

Bobby shook the Dice in his hand. He weighed his options carefully:

Two (2.78%)—Offer the goons a hundred grand each to quit right now and pose for pictures on Fremont Street wearing Buckingham Palace fur hats (with me dressed as the queen).

Three (5.56%)—Stand up slowly and walk into the bedroom and take a nap.

Four (8.33%)—See if there is soda in the fridge.

Five (11.11%)—Turn on the TV.

Six (13.89%)—Knock on Ruphart's office door.

Seven (16.67%)—Start yelling Ruphart's name.

Eight (13.89%)—Open the cupboard and see if there are any snacks.

Nine (11.11%)—Ask to go to the bathroom and, when in there, take a bath.

Ten (8.33%)—Run into Ruphart's office, screaming.

Eleven (5.56%)—Ask which one of these assholes felt up my sister.

Twelve (2.78%)—Try to grab one of the guns, like they do on TV.

41

BOBBY RAN RECKLESSLY INTO AN EMPTY ROOM. FRASER Ruphart was long gone. He'd been traveling for two full days. Gone from the office. Gone from Trump International. Gone from Paradise. Gone from Nevada. Gone from the United States. And soon gone from the hemisphere.

Ruphart had been cheating, stealing, robbing, threatening, and exploiting since he was a child. He had money coming out his ass, and he used it. His exodus cost him nearly all of it. He started spending a week earlier, when he bought a beautiful estate right on the ocean in the Solomon Islands. He bought it sight unseen with Bitcoins. Bitcoins had taken a pretty bad hit, but he still had some money there and in other cryptocurrencies. He did a "going out of business" sale on his drugs. He turned all his drug inventory into cash. He owed a bunch of money to people he'd been in business with over the decades and no longer had any reason to pay them, so that was more cash. His crew knew nothing. They were in the dark. He was just selling drugs as usual, and then he was gone. They didn't know where he went or when he'd be back. He'd sold his house in Summerlin for a big loss, but he didn't care, it was more cash. He couldn't flip the condo, no one would buy a fucking Trump property, so he just let his lackies fight over it, severance, if they could figure it out. He had *Scarface* amounts of cash in suitcases, duffel bags, backpacks, some of it in trash bags with the amount written on the side in black Sharpie. He'd used most of his Bitcoins and chartered a 747 to fly him from Mexico to Brisbane. Normally that would have been about seven million dollars. Now that some intercontinental air travel was either frowned on or outright illegal—the status was changing as he was planning—it was almost double that cost. He got a "cheap" charter flight to Mexico. Money could make people see even his flight from Mexico to Down Under as necessary. Brisbane to Honiara Airport in Guadalcanal was going to be tough. With advisories and quarantines, it would take bags of money. He had bags of money; he would get to his new home. He wouldn't need any of his fancy suits or jewelry, though he threw some art and collector's shit into a few huge suitcases and had them put in the Escalade. Some of the trunks wouldn't make it, but he didn't really care. He drove himself to McCarran and just left the car there with the keys in it. He arrived with one full suitcase of respirators (what an asshole) and a fresh one on his face. Bye bye, Las Vegas.

42

B Y THE TIME BOBBY BURST INTO RUPHART'S OFFICE, Ruphart was on the other side of the world talking through his N95 in Brisbane, making deals for an illegal charter. Bobby had the three thugs following him in. Bernard tackled him a few steps into the room. The office was trashed. Ruphart had taken everything he wanted and just split. He'd told his "staff" nothing. He was just gone. The assholes had been there for two days waiting for orders and guarding an empty room. Had they known the room was empty? They must have.

Bernard had knocked Bobby down hard, but he was okay. "You're protecting an empty room? I came here to see Ruphart and he's not here. So I'm just going to leave, okay?"

"No, that's not okay."

"What would you rather I do? You want to stay here with guns on me? Your arms are going to get tired. You want to torture me? Just for entertainment? I have nothing you want. You have no orders to do anything with me. Ruphart never considered I'd come here. I barely considered it, I just rolled the Dice and here I am. Now, I'm leaving."

The thugs all looked at each other. "We can't let him leave."

"Why?" Bobby was trying to be helpful. He was still on the floor with Bernard on top of him.

The thugs just stared at each other. Bernard hit Bobby in

the head, but his heart wasn't in it. It was kind of a really bad noogie.

Bobby went down the ugly elevator, got on his scooter, and rode back to his room at the Golden Nugget. It was dawn and he looked out over Fremont. He'd been trying to stay oblivious but that was no longer an option—most people figured they'd be closing all the hotels in a couple days. He rolled an Easy Six and called his mom. It had been awhile; he hadn't even told her he'd been in Dallas. With everything going on, he wanted to make sure she was being smart.

"Hey, Mom. You doing okay?"

"I'm doing fine, Bobby, how are you? Are you okay? I've missed you, Bobby."

"I've missed you too. Are you hunkered down?"

"Safe and sound in my beautiful home. Thank you, Bobby. I have plenty of food, my audiobooks, my podcasts, and my MSNBC. Trump is in way over his head."

"He was in way over his head at the Miss USA pageant. He hasn't got a chance on this. It's up to everyone else. Please stay safe. How is Sis?"

"There are rumors they're going to take her out of school and put her to work caring for the sick people."

"Jesus."

"And you're okay, Bobby?"

"Yeah."

"Bobby, is this the end of the world?"

"I don't know, Mom, we've made it through bad things before."

"Nothing this bad in my lifetime."

"Maybe 1968? I don't know. Yeah, I guess. I love you, Mom."

"Hey, Bobby, call your father."

"What?"

"It must be important. We haven't talked in years, and he's called me four times today trying to find you. Call him, Bobby."

"I'm not going to promise, Mom."

"You know, Bobby, I've never known you to break a promise."

"Thanks, Mom."

"That wasn't a compliment. The reason you've never broken a promise is that you don't make them enough. Even with the Dice you've got to promise. You have to let your heart make a guess. You should promise more, Bobby. Life is short. Make more, break some."

"I promise I'll call your asshole ex-husband right after we hang up."

"Good for you."

"Mom, do you need anything? *Anything?* I could come over and bring you stuff."

"You could come over and maybe bring me the virus. I'm fine, Bobby. Take care of yourself, that's all I want. Now say goodbye, hang up, and call your father. Be nice to him. These are hard times. I love you, Bobby."

"I promise. I love you, Mom. Bye bye."

Bobby picked up the Dice . . . and put them in his pocket. He called his dad. "Hey, Dad. Are you safe?"

"Yes, and so are you, Bobby, so are you!"

"Well, I'm in a hotel, that's not the safest place to be, but I'm—"

"Yeah, get out of the fucking hotel now, but that's not what I meant. All your problems have gone away. Fraser Ru-FUCK left town. Word is he left town forever. FOREVER,

Bobby! He's gone. And Skiff is going to die. Soon! He's got the bug and he's in the hospital wicked fucked up. He was a smoker, Bobby, a fat smoker, and he's fucked. Smart money has him as Vegas's first casualty."

"Okay, Dad, let's unpack this. First of all, his name can be pronounced RuFART. If a guy you don't like has the word 'fart' right in his name, you don't have to change his name to insult him. Just call him RuFART. You don't need RuFUCK. The taunting work was done generations ago. Second, I guess I knew that about RuFART. I was just over at his place at Trump."

"What? If he'd been there, he would have killed you. He's tried a few times to kill you. One time I tried to warn you, but I couldn't get through."

"One time?" Bobby said.

"Yeah, I couldn't get through. He hated you. Hated the whole family, but—"

"He didn't hate Mom and Sis except for hating you so much it spread."

"Right, but he hated *you* on your own."

"Okay, so he's gone. Third issue: are there really people betting on Skiff dying from the virus?"

"Yup, I took the under on 'Dead by mid-March' two days ago when it was a long shot, and now it's better than even. Skiff will be stiff, and I get a payday."

"It's mid-March now, isn't it? You promised me you'd stopped gambling."

"Yes, I did."

"Dad . . . ?"

"Yeah?"

"Dad, are you safe? Sheltered in place? Are you doing everything right? You're an old man, a smoker."

"Yeah, I got a card-playing buddy and we're holed up together at his place. We got food. We're safe. We can play poker heads-up for Frosted Flakes. I'm safe, Bobby, and so are you, it's over. You got lucky."

"Yeah, *lucky*. Jesus, Dad."

"You got nothing to worry about except the virus. You finally have the same worries as the other seven billion of us poor assholes. Take care of yourself, Bobby, be safe."

"I'll be safe, Dad, I promise. Bye."

"Bye, son."

Deus ex virus.

43

SKIFF WAS ON A VENTILATOR AT THE UMC TRAUMA Center, gasping for breath. Skiff was such a bad guy that he killed people and ruined their lives even when it wasn't his intention. He'd coughed all over Frisco and might end up being the index case in Nevada. He was barely conscious when his nurse came in.

"Mr. Reynolds?"

Skiff heard her and mumbled a "Yeah?"

"You need to know this right now. We just found out that there's a cure for this virus. A complete cure. It will stop the virus and reverse all the damage that's been done. We'll have it to you by the early afternoon. You should be all better this evening. Fully healthy. You might even sleep in your own bed tonight, Mr. Reynolds."

Even through the haze, Skiff understood and smiled. The relief he felt was complete. His whole body relaxed. The weight on his chest seemed less. He got a few good breaths. He had never been happier. He looked in the nurse's eyes as she leaned over him and he rasped, "Wow. Amazing. Are you kidding?"

"Yes, Mr. Reynolds, I am kidding. No one has any idea what this thing is or how to fight it, and the damage it's done to your body already is irreversible and lethal." She brought her lips tightly together in a sad smile and shrugged.

Skiff was given extra-special care for his last seventeen hours. Although the hospital was fairly full (not as bad as NYC), he was well cared for and then he died. The nurse had ten grand extra in cash, and all the nurses on the floor were given a little something for their assurance that everything possible would be done for Skiff—if not to get him better, then to at least make his final hours as comfortable as possible. The UMC medical facility got a huge donation to buy more ventilators and masks to protect the health workers. Well, that's what they used it for—they weren't actually told how they had to spend it. Only the nurses on Skiff's floor were given specific instructions.

Melvin hadn't stolen a penny from Bobby; all his money was now available to him. He was no longer L. Harvey Oswald. He threw his white T-shirt away and decided to let his hair grow out. Finally, no one was trying to kill him specifically. The virus that was trying to kill him was just Random. He was just another potential host. His fate was Random . . . like everyone's.

44

⚃ ⚁

Two (2.78%)—Shelter in place for as long as they say I should, then fly to Newfoundland and move in with Terri.

Three (5.56%)—Get the next flight to Newfoundland before they close the border. Self-quarantine there for fourteen days, and then move in with Terri. While in self-quarantine, finally memorize "Howl" by Allen Ginsberg.

Four (8.33%)—Get the next flight to Newfoundland before they close the border. Self-quarantine there for fourteen days, and then move in with Terri. While in self-quarantine, reread all of Nicholson Baker.

Five (11.11%)—Get the next flight to Newfoundland before they close the border. Self-quarantine there for fourteen days and then move in with Terri. While in self-quarantine, watch nothing but The Three Stooges.

Six (13.89%)—Get the next flight to Newfoundland before they close the border. Shelter in place with Terri, doing whatever she wants.

Seven (16.67%)—Get the next flight to Newfoundland before they close the border. Shelter in place with Terri, doing whatever she wants.

Eight (13.89%)—Get the next flight to Newfoundland

before they close the border. Shelter in place with Terri, doing whatever she wants.

Nine (11.11%)—Get the next flight to Newfoundland before they close the border. Self-quarantine there for fourteen days and then move in with Terri. While in self-quarantine, watch nothing but The Three Stooges *with Shemp.*

Ten (8.33%)—Get the next flight to Newfoundland before they close the border. Self-quarantine there for fourteen days, and then move in with Terri. While in self-quarantine, reread Moby-Dick.

Eleven (5.56%)—Get the next flight to Newfoundland before they close the border. Self-quarantine there for fourteen days, and then move in with Terri. While in self-quarantine, listen to nothing but Bob Dylan and dance beneath the diamond sky with one hand waving free.

Twelve (2.78%)—Shelter in place for as long as they say I should, then fly to Newfoundland and move in with Terri.

Acknowledgments

This book is complete fiction—I mean, what kind of nut would ever think that way, right? But there are people in the real world that got me thinking. In some cases, it was just an image or a story they told me, and then in some cases I even ripped off their fucking names. Trust me, if you see yourself in this book, it was the good parts that I took from you. All the bad parts I made up.

I took some great stories from Norman Beck, and believe me, he still has a zillion more all as good as the ones I copped. I'll bet anyone any amount of money that Norman is a trip and he'll cover the action.

Piff the Magic Dragon and Jade Simone are my friends and I had to have these fictitious characters meet them.

I mentioned Johnny and Pam on the dedication page, but I'll mention them again here and will keep mentioning them for the rest of my life. I will love them forever.

Carrot Top lets me make fun of him, because as long as it's funny, he's happy with anything anyone says. I don't think there's a higher compliment I can pay him.

Sandra Boyd, Perry Friedman, Gene X Kelly, Penny Lane, Tony Fitzpatrick, and Erika Larsen got various good parts of themselves in this book. Perry even did a lot of the hard arithmetic for me.

Gary Lennon and I tried to take the first seeds of this idea and make a TV show out of it, and a TV network even bought it, but then . . . showbiz happened, and it all fell apart. I loved the little bit of work I did with Gary, and I hope our paths cross again.

Handsome Jack, Martin Mull, Lawrence Krauss, and Kramer were reading early drafts and cheering for me, and you know, a fellow needs that.

I need to thank Glenn Alai for running everything. He is the boss of me and the genius of himself. Laura Foley makes the stuff Glenn decides should happen for me, happen.

Everything I do has the vibe of Teller all over it. After forty-six years, he just lives in my head and makes things better.

I have no idea how Steven Fisher found Johnny Temple and the cats and kitties at Akashic Books, but I guess that's an agent's job and he does it well. I mean, Johnny is my publisher and I'm happy when he calls. How is that even possible? Johnny is a bass player and a great one. You've just read a book that has two bass players, like his band.

Robbie Libbon has been my friend for longer than I've been working with Teller. When I think I've finished a book, I give it to Robbie and the real work starts. He cleaned up all the spelling, grammar, and logic, so when Mr. Temple first saw it, it looked like a grown-up wrote it. Robbie also asked really hard questions that, when I answered them, made the book better. And when I couldn't answer them, he helped me there too. I hope to hell you never see a version of the book before Robbie got ahold of it.

And there's Emily Jillette, Moxie CrimeFighter Jillette, and Zolten Penn Jillette, because without them, why bother?